THREE
STORIES
ABOUT
GHOSTS

MARTIN HALL
MATTHEW MARCHITTO
ALI NOURAEI

An Abaddon Books™ Publication
www.abaddonbooks.com
abaddon@rebellion.co.uk

Published in 2019 by Abaddon Books™,
Rebellion Publishing Ltd,
Riverside House, Osney Mead, Oxford,
OX2 0ES, UK.

10 9 8 7 6 5 4 3 2 1

Creative Director and CEO: Jason Kingsley
Chief Technical Officer: Chris Kingsley
Head of Books and Comics Publishing: Ben Smith
Editors: David Thomas Moore,
Michael Rowley and Kate Coe
Marketing and PR: Remy Njambi
Design: Sam Gretton, Oz Osborne and Gemma Sheldrake

ISBN: 978-1-78108-582-0

Printed in Denmark.

THREE STORIES ABOUT GHOSTS

MARTIN HALL
MATTHEW MARCHITTO
ALI NOURAEI

Introduction

IT CAN'T BE especially controversial to suggest that ghost stories
are the oldest genre there is. Homer's *Odyssey* has Odysseus
descending into the underworld to confront the dead; the Old
Testament *First Book of Samuel* has Saul calling on the Witch
of Endor to raise the spirit of the prophet. Go further back
than that: archaeologists are forever identifying the oldest
artifacts of civilisation as sites of burial, of ritual propitiation
and communion, and if our earliest ancestors built places to
deal with spirits, it's certain they told stories about spirits.

Ghost stories can do so *much*. Ghosts remind us of our
own mortality; they tie us to our history; they show us a
bleak reflection of ourselves. M. R. James' ghosts chilled us;
Charles Dickens' ghosts warned us of our own moral failings
(and the sure punishment that awaited us if we did not correct
them). Poe's Red Death visited righteous punishment on the
unworthy, while Irving's headless Hessian proves to be nothing
more supernatural than a ruse by a lover, seeking to better his
rival. The ghost is the ultimate McGuffin, a device that can

serve whatever purpose—instructive, moralising, surprising, horrifying, reflective, nostalgic or anything else—the writer needs them to.

In Matthew Marchitto's *The Boneman*, ghosts stand for loss and longing; the dead linger because of their bonds to the living, and the living linger over their love of the dead. The horrifying in-betweener is a vivid lesson of the inadvisibility of clinging too hard, dragging the dead across the line, to tragic ends.

For Martin Hall, ghosts are the burden of history. The noble families in his *Unmasked* are held back by centuries-old feuds, by the crushing weight of tradition, and by ghosts who literally possess the bodies of their descendents, forcing them to relive old glories. It is only by rejecting the past that the young can live their own lives.

And in Ali Nouraei's *Magistra Trevelyan*, the titular ghost is a reminder of promises made, and ultimately a symbol of hope for the future. What starts as an investigation into a murder leads to the verge of war, and to revelations that will alter the hidden world of magic forever.

Three stories about ghosts, in different ways and to different ends. Take comfort in them.

David Thomas Moore
Oxford
July 2019

THE BONEMAN

By Matthew Marchitto

Chapter One

The Deal

MARTY'S SPINE CRACKED as his back arched and his ribs distended like splaying fingers.

You promised. The voice, lecherous and grainy, spoke through a film of congealed sweat. *Get him for me.*

In the corner of Marty's room stood a figure of flayed flesh. A skeletal jaw contorted into a permanent grin, lidless eyes glared with bloodshot fury. Bones hanging from its neck rattled from an unseen wind.

Marty's eyes bolted open and he clutched his bedsheets, writhing in a damp pool of sweat. In the corner of his room, where the streetlight touched, was nothing.

He let out a breath, trying to calm the hammering in his chest.

He grabbed his phone: 4:45 A.M., way too early. Marty rolled over, shifting his blankets around to find a dry spot, and closed his eyes. But sleep wouldn't come. As hard as he tried he couldn't drive out the image of the Boneman.

* * *

FOUR DAYS EARLIER—noon, he'd been on his way to Chester's, a mom-and-pop restaurant where he washed dishes. Walking down St. Catherine like he always did, watching university students saunter along. He stopped to get a latte at Second Cup; he didn't really have a reason why he avoided Starbucks and Tim Hortons—maybe a little part of him wanted to stick it to *The Man* or whatever. It was there, at the point where the three franchise coffee shops stared each other down, that he saw Abbi. She looked uncomfortable, one arm held around herself in a tight hug, skin a pallid transparent gray, wheeling her innards around on a rusty cart.

Abbi looked at Marty, and from across the street he could see something was wrong. He walked to her, ignoring the car honking at him for crossing in the middle of the street.

"Abbi?"

"Shit, Marty. Just, shit, man."

"Did something happen?" Marty tried to bury his worry. It couldn't be that bad: Abbi was already dead. How much worse could it get?

"Someone's looking for you, Marty."

Marty tilted his head, the cogs of his brain whirring. No one looked for him. He went to his job, went home, and sometimes hung out with Abbi and Carla. No one looked for him.

"It's—" Abbi swallowed, whatever word she had been about to say left a bad taste in her mouth. "You're one of the few. So, I guess, I mean"—she ran her hand over her forehead to wipe away sweat that wasn't there—"it had to happen eventually."

"I'm lost, Abbi."

"You can see and touch us. It makes sense that eventually somebody would come looking for you. I just"—she let out a long and slow sigh—"I just didn't think it would be someone so deep."

Marty sipped his coffee. He tried to ignore the people walking around him, giving him the side-eye for talking to himself.

"You say he's 'deep,' what's that mean?"

"Like, *deep*, man. Me and the others"—she gestured to the other ghosts meandering through the streets—"we're shallow. Get it? Him, though, he's deep. From a darker, meaner place. Somewhere none of us want to get near."

Marty ran his hand through his hair, fingers combing through his short curls. Marty had gotten used to seeing ghosts, but a long-buried fear was creeping up on him.

"Okay, alright, well, what's this guy want?"

"Don't know, Marty. But trust me, it can't be anything good."

MARTY ROLLED OVER in his bed, kicking away the damp sheets. Abbi had been right, and he was a dumbass for not listening to her.

Marty should never have made a deal with the Boneman.

SOAP UP, SWISH-SWISH, rinse.

Six hours of mind-numbing repetition.

Rush hour was the worst. The dishes piled up beside Marty's sink, and his eye would catch onto a bit of gruel dripping down the side of a glass, or a plate with crusted sauce that he knew he'd have to scrape away.

Joe—the busboy—thrust another stack of dishes onto Marty's station. They chimed and clinked and a few threatened to break.

Soap up, swish-swish, rinse.

Marty hated being a dishwasher, and he hated hating it. Everyone in the kitchen was nice enough. Marty told himself he should be happy to have a decent job, even if he spent all day scrubbing at other people's spit stains. But there was always that niggling voice in the back of his head: You going to do this dead-end crap for the rest of your life?

Soap up. Marty was pushing six years working the dishes. *Swish-swish*. A university dropout with no measurable talent, he was going nowhere fast. *Rinse, repeat*. Yeah, dead end alright.

Steph—one of the waiters—sauntered in and exchanged a long string of French with Alhad, the chef. Another reason Marty was the perpetual dishwasher; his French had become so weak he could barely understand anything faster than baby talk.

"Hey Marty," Steph said, in English with a thick Québécois accent.

"Hey."

"You look perturbed."

Marty shrugged.

She bumped her shoulder into his. "C'mon man, what's up?"

Hell spawn is on my ass, and if I don't do what it wants I might end up in eternal torment. Oh, you too? "Nothing, just tired."

"Sure, sure." Steph ran her hand through her golden blonde hair, exposing black roots. "You up to see a movie? Everyone else is coming."

"Think I'll pass."

* * *

FOUR DAYS EARLIER—evening, Marty was on his way home. He took a shortcut through the small concrete plot to his tiny Ville-Émard apartment. His apartment was one of four in a squat building wedged between duplexes. On one side, just under the landlady, was a boarded-up store with a crusty *dépanneur* sign.

He put his key into the lock and held the knob in place to keep it from wiggling around in its loose casing. The door unlocked with a grinding *chunk* and opened on hissing hinges. Marty clomped up to the second floor, the stairs groaning with each step.

Standing in front of Mrs. Hubbard's door was Wallace. Wallace huffed, raised his hand to knock—paused—lowered his hand and shook his head.

"Hey, Wallace."

The old ghost turned his crinkled features to Marty. "Hiya, kid."

"How's Mrs. Hubbard?"

"Fine, fine. Don't want to disturb her is all." Wallace ran his hand over his balding pate. "Listen, Marty, maybe you should head out for a bit. See the city a little."

"Maybe later."

"But"—Wallace tensed, his eyes darting to Marty's door and then away—"you've been staying in a lot. It'd do you good."

Marty slid his key into the lock. "I'll think about it."

Wallace's hands balled up into fists.

"Everything alright, Wallace?"

"Yeah. Fine." Wallace marched away.

Weird. He's usually not so uptight.

Marty walked into his dim hallway, popped off his shoes,

dropped his bag in the corner, and trudged into one of his apartment's two rooms.

He froze, heart pounding. A silhouetted figure stood in his living room, eyes burning coals. Marty's hand thrust out and flicked the light switch on, and he swallowed a dollop of bile. A man of flayed flesh, bones hanging from his body, stared at Marty.

"Hello, Marty," the Boneman said.

Marty was too terrified to move, eyes pinned to the Boneman's fire-red eyes.

"You see us," the Boneman said. "One of a few who can. I've chosen you, Marty. You have a task, and you will complete it.

"There is a ghost who is not a ghost. Trapped in-between, refusing to die, yet not alive. And they can do something horrible, Marty. They can hurt your friends in a way you can't understand." The Boneman extended one hand, long skeletal fingers creaking as they uncurled.

Marty's eyes followed the motion, and there was a length of parchment on his coffee table that hadn't been there before.

"A contract," the Boneman said. "Signed with a drop of blood, and then you will be able to help me put away this danger. That will be a favour paid."

"I..." Marty's mouth felt dry, his throat hoarse. The contract's words were unreadable, written in symbols he didn't recognize. The paper—was it leather? He didn't want to know what animal it'd come from.

When he looked back up, the Boneman was gone.

"Fuck me."

* * *

MARTY STARED AT the blinking cursor in the browser's search bar. How am I supposed to find this in-between person? Abbi's cart squealed as she paced in a circle around his coffee table.

"I don't think typing in 'ghost monster' is going to work," Marty said.

"No, probably not." Abbi's eyebrows knitted together in agitation. "You should've burned the contract, or something."

She was probably right. "That'd only piss him off."

"Better that than this."

The blinking cursor seared itself into Marty's retina. He exhaled, and typed in *disturbing sightings*. It was a start.

THREE DAYS EARLIER—evening, Marty sat on the second floor of the Second Cup near Peel. He was pressed into the corner, pretending to talk into a headset. Abbi sat beside him, one foot mindlessly rocking her gut-cart, and Carla sat across from him.

"He said what?" Carla's too-loud tone made Marty's ears ring. "The nerve!" Carla puffed up her cheeks and huffed angrily, her bundle of white hair shaking from the motion. She hunched lower, speaking in a still-too-loud conspiratorial tone. "You should ask for some kind of deal of your own. If he's going to pester you, you might as well get something out of it."

"Carla!" Abbi said. "He shouldn't make any deals with anyone. I say you burn the contract and be done with it."

Marty sipped his latte while watching people walk by on the street below. Among them were ghosts, pallid like Abbi and Carla, acting like their lives had barely been interrupted by death.

"He said this in-between person can hurt you," Marty said. "I don't know how, but if I can help stop him, then shouldn't I?"

"Marty, it's not your job to stop anything," Abbi said. "There are other people who deal with this kind of scary shit. That's what this is, *scary*. Walk away, trust me."

"You said this person can hurt us?" Carla asked. "I heard some of the other old ladies nattering about something. I assumed they were blowing hot air, but maybe they weren't." Carla sipped her tea, which she'd gotten from the barista with a charred face working beside the warm bodies.

"What did they say?" Marty asked.

"It sounded ugly, but if it might be real…" Carla sighed. "Well, apparently old Jean saw this weird-looking guy, all shambly and muttering and so on, and there was another lady—a ghost— walking toward the shambler. And then, he just touched her, and she started to turn into *something*. Like a sack of meat that made slopping and burbling noises. Jean ran away after that. Supposedly; you know Jean used to travel all over looking for Bigfoot? Every year, from Nova Scotia all the way to B.C., and he's convinced that if he had a few more years he would've found the feller. He's lucky he made it to ninety-four. I take his opinions with a grain of salt."

"Wait, this shambling guy, was he a ghost?" Marty asked.

"I assum so."

Marty rubbed his chin, his stubble coarse against his palm. If all this in-betweener had to do was touch a ghost to hurt them— or transform them?—then he was more dangerous than Marty had thought. It didn't help that this guy sounded unstable.

"Marty, I don't like that pensive shit." Abbi jabbed him in the shoulder with a finger.

*   *   *

MARTY'S EYES WERE starting to hurt from staring at his laptop screen. There were no stories about ghostly monstrosities. He supposed that would've been too convenient.

"Have you tried social media?" Abbi said from the couch. She was lying on her back, twirling a length of intestine between her fingers.

"What am I going to find on social media?"

"I don't know, do a search for 'weird shit' or something. What would people use if they saw something ghostly but didn't know?"

That wasn't a bad idea. Marty typed in *weird shit* and groaned at the page of results. It was going to take a while for him to search through.

TWO DAYS EARLIER—midnight, Marty couldn't sleep. He'd tried ignoring the contract, but it kept pulling his eyes like a spider on the wall. He started to pace, moving in an agitated circle around his coffee table.

Why shouldn't he sign? He could help his friends, put this in-between guy away to keep them safe. Whatever Carla's friend Jean had seen, it sounded nasty. What if he ignored this and then it happened to his friends?

He sat on his couch, the contract staring him down. Marty wasn't getting much out of this deal, but the Boneman didn't seem like the kind of person that negotiated. And what would happen if Marty refused? Ghosts could touch him, which meant the Boneman could touch him.

Marty shivered.

But what did this contract say? Marty couldn't read the symbols. Was he selling his soul to a nightmare creature?

Marty picked up the parchment: it felt like smooth leather. At the bottom was a dotted line, and beside it a needle-like pin pointed up from the scroll. Signed with a single drop of blood.

"Fuck it." Marty pricked his finger.

A bead of blood balanced on the tip of the pin, teetering before sliding down the smooth metal and onto the parchment. The bead of blood traced a path along the dotted line, swirling and curving, until Marty's name was spelled out in bright red.

"Holy shit."

"Thank you, Marty."

Marty jumped, his head whipping around to stare at the Boneman standing in his living room. The contract was already in the Boneman's hand. His skeletal grin seemed to smile wider.

"Do you understand the task?" The Boneman's voice, grainy and lecherous, made Marty's skin gooseflesh.

"Yeah, uh, catch the in-between guy."

"No, not catch. *Find*. Find him for me. And when you do, stab him." The Boneman held out a jagged shark tooth the size of a cleaver. "Once he is marked, I will send him away."

With a trembling hand Marty took the tooth. "Why can't you do this?" God, Marty, keep your mouth shut.

"What he touches turns to torture, screaming to be in one world or the other, caught in the middle. I will not touch him, but you can. And will. A favour is owed."

Marty turned the shark tooth in his hand; it was nicked, and the base was wrapped in dirty cord. He looked up, and the Boneman was gone.

* * *

SCROLL, SCROLL, SCROLL. The social media idea wasn't working out. Everybody was talking about video game monsters, and scary movies, and all kinds of other shit that wasn't helping Marty find anybody.

His eyelids started to droop, his chin drifting toward his chest. How long had he been searching? Shit, he had to go to work tomorrow. Just a few more minutes...

Marty fell asleep, slumped on his couch with his laptop painting him in electronic light.

Faster, Marty.

ONE DAY EARLIER—afternoon, Abbi stomped in a circle, shaking the knickknacks on Marty's bookshelves.

"You did *what?*"

"I signed it, okay. I just did it."

"Why? What's the matter with you? Does your brain work? The Boneman's not like us, not like me. Do you not get that?"

Marty threw his arms into the air. "It's done. Okay. That's it. Signed. Done."

Abbi growled—full on *growled* at Marty.

"Abbi?"

"You're an idiot."

"Okay."

Marty waited for phantom steam to hiss out of Abbi's ears, but instead she let out a long sigh.

"I don't believe you're getting us into this."

"Us?"

"I'm not going to let you do this alone. Jesus, Marty, I don't think you understand how bad this can get."

"Like, weird nightmares bad?"

"He's in your dreams?"

"Is that... not normal...?"

Abbi pinched the bridge of her nose. "You didn't read the contract."

"The letters were all weird and shit."

She groaned. "I bet they were."

"You seem to know a lot about this stuff?"

"All of us—the dead, ghosts, whatever—know about deals of the deep. Some of us learn the hard way, some get warned. Every ghost finds out eventually." Abbi pushed her cart back and forth, its hinges squeaking. "They offer things in exchange for favours."

"The Boneman didn't offer me anything."

"Sure he did, he got inside your head and convinced you that signing would help people. Made it seem like you'd be a hero. That's what they do, they get in our heads." Abbi hugged herself.

"Did they ever offer you anything?"

Abbi looked away. "We need to figure out how to find this rogue ghost."

Chapter Two

A Lead

AN OBNOXIOUS RAY of sunlight poked Marty's eye. He woke with a sore neck and stiff back; he'd slept the whole night slumped on the couch. His alarm clock blared, tempting him to throw it out the window.

Abbi was gone, back to wherever she called home. He'd never had the nerve to ask.

He got up and started getting ready to go to Chester's. He thought working for hellspawn would've let him quit dishwashing, but only the latter paid him.

WALLACE WRUNG HIS hands in front of Mrs. Hubbard's door. "You think it's too early?"

"I don't know. I'm sure she'd be happy to see you, though."

"No, no." Wallace shook his head. "It's too early. I don't want to disturb her."

"Sure. So, uh, did you see my friend Abbi come through last night?"

"Oh, yeah. She left around three in the morning. She looked a little agitated, anything you want to talk about?"

"Not right now." Marty started down the noisy stairs.

"You sure? I really don't mind," Wallace called after him.

Marty was already out the door.

MARTY SCRUBBED AT a dollop of gruel. *If I were a shambling, unstable half-ghost, where would I go?* He had no idea.

But if ghosts were being turned into real, physical *things*, then why wasn't it all over the news? Shit gone viral, think pieces and debunking theories. But there was nothing. Maybe they just dissipate after a while? Like dead bodies in video games.

Stephanie nudged his shoulder, startling him.

"Woah, you okay?" she asked.

"Yeah. Just tired."

"Are you sure? You look like you barely slept."

It's been one day and I'm already a mess. P.I. Marty, on the case. "Fell asleep at the computer."

"Ah, I got it. Tough." She reached into her jeans and pulled out her phone. "You hear about this mad dog story?"

"What? No."

She tip-tapped on her phone and then held it up to his face. *Diseased dog goes rabid, has to be put down. Investigation ongoing.*

"Oh, that sucks. Poor dog," Marty said.

"Right, right, but listen to what some of the witnesses said." She scrolled through the article to find the quotes and read them aloud. "'It was like gurgling, man, all coughing and gurgling and shit was scary.' And here's another: 'It looked fat and gooey, like it was melting on the inside.'" Stephanie pushed hair out of her eyes. "Creepy, right? The police say whatever it had isn't contagious."

Marty's mind reeled. That had to be one of the monsters made by the in-betweener. Gurgling and melting? "Can you send me a link to that story?"

"Sure."

Marty's phone vibrated in his pocket, and a surge of excitement shot through him. It was his first lead.

But the dishes needed to get done.

Scrub, scrub.

MARTY HUNCHED OVER his phone in the corner of the kitchen, wolfing down a chicken sandwich while he read through the article for the twelfth time. It had happened in his neighbourhood, Ville-Émard. But there were no street addresses in the article.

He swiped over to Twitter and found the account of the reporter who'd showed up after the police. There was a picture of a couple cop cars and police officers standing near the lip of a lane. The post read: *Animal Disturbance Near Mazarin And Jolicoeur, Ongoing.* Marty refreshed the page to see if the reporter had said anything else and—the post disappeared.

Deleted? Weird.

Marty had a location. He didn't know what he'd find, if anything. But it was a start.

Alhad sat across from him, hairy arms folded on the table. "Like the sandwich?"

Marty nodded with a mouthful. It was made from fancy-ass

bread and a bunch of toppings Marty didn't recognize. It was damn good, though.

"I can give you some to take home, there's always leftovers," Alhad said.

Ah, right. Alhad always offered to give Marty food, because he knew Marty didn't work full-time and lived on his own. Montréal was an affordable city to live in, as far as metropolises went, but it wasn't *that* affordable. What Alhad didn't know was that Marty only paid $400 a month in rent.

The landlady thought her apartment was haunted. So Marty, being a young entrepreneur, had offered to perform a séance. "I've done it before, trust me." She didn't, but offered an obscenely reduced rent if he could actually perform one.

Marty, the landlady, and her daughter all sat around a table holding hands. Marty had lit some candles because that seemed right. Marty did a lot of *ohming* and rocking back and forth. The landlady was unimpressed.

Enter Abbi and Carla.

Carla shuffled in with her walker, a coy smile on her face. With some groans and curses, she climbed onto the table, hauling her walker up with her, and started stomping around. The table shook. Now the landlady was paying attention.

And then Abbi started jabbing the light switch, making the lights flicker.

Now the landlady was really impressed.

All the while, Jeff—the ghost that actually lived in the landlady's apartment—was chuckling hysterically. Jeff had OCD, and couldn't help his impulses to open and close cupboard doors and turn faucets on and off. He didn't mean any harm.

It was ridiculous, but it had both impressed and freaked out the landlady. And he'd needed the reduced rent.

Alhad brushed his beard. "It's no problem, Marty. I'd like you to have it."

"Why not give it to a shelter?"

"There will always be more to give away tomorrow."

"Well, if you insist."

Alhad grinned wide, and within minutes there was a stack of foam containers in a plastic bag waiting for Marty to take home.

Marty was glad to have the leftovers, even though a part of him felt bad, like he shouldn't take it unless he *really* needed it.

MARTY WAS PULLING on his hoodie and backpack when he saw Abbi waiting by the door. Her cart was just outside, and a length of intestine was keeping the door from closing all the way. Joe kept cursing as he tried to pull it shut, opened it to look at the hinges, and then failed to close it again.

Marty shooed Abbi outside, and when the door closed behind him he heard a muffled "What the fuck?"

"Something's definitely wrong," Abbi said.

"What do you mean?"

"Remember what Carla said about that shambler guy? More people are talking about him. And it all boils down to *avoid him*. No one's said why, exactly, but I think he's more dangerous than we thought."

"Okay, that helps. But we still have to find him." Marty took out his phone and loaded up the news article. "I have a lead."

* * *

THE CORNER OF Mazarin and Jolicoeur was entirely uninteresting and quiet. No police cars or hellfire demons.

"So, uh, what should we look for?" Marty asked.

"You're asking me?"

"I don't know. Can you, like, sense ghost stuff?"

"No."

"Okay, alright. Let's look around."

Marty and Abbi made a round of the nearby streets, walking through the lanes. There was a lot of nothing.

Until they found a wide swatch of darkened concrete that looked like it'd been hosed down.

"You think this is where they found it?" Marty asked.

"I guess they washed away whatever was left."

"This story online happened today, at like 3:00 A.M. They dealt with it really fast."

"Is that unusual?"

"I don't know."

Marty circled around the wet patch of cement. Quick clean-up. Is that normal? He guessed they wouldn't want a dead dog's blood lying around. Of course, if this wasn't a dog, then they wouldn't want people finding out about it. "The reporter who was on the scene deleted her post about the story."

"Maybe she got something wrong and didn't want it staying up?"

Marty refreshed the reporter's profile: a few new posts about unrelated stories, nothing about the 'diseased dog.'

"I think they're covering it up," Marty said.

"The police? Shit, that makes sense. They don't want people knowing about this stuff, that's if they even understand what's happening."

"And they washed away any clues."

"I don't think you were going to find much, Marty." Abbi glanced at the wet patch. "It's probably better that way."

IF ABBI HAD to keep watching Marty refresh news sites and social media searches, she was going to lose her mind, which impressed Marty given she was dead. They decided to hit the streets and do 'verbal reconnaissance' (talk to people).

Jean wasn't much help. All he knew was what Carla had already told them, and then he started going on and on about Bigfoot. Marty had never thought an urban myth could be so boring. Jean was convinced Bigfoot was out there, and that the Sasquatch was Bigfoot's cousin. Apparently, he'd been working on a book titled *Yeti*, and damn wasn't it a shame he hadn't finished it. Well, bye. Nice talking to you.

Next was Granny Greta, a lovely old woman who spent her time in a rocking chair near a seldom-used park (probably seldom-used because the chair kept rocking with no one in it). She didn't know much either, other than that Carla was trying to nick her carrot cake recipe, and O lord have mercy that wasn't going to happen. Okay, thanks, bye.

Bernard was more forthcoming. A grumpy middle-aged guy with an ashy face and sandpaper stubble, he told them that folks were walking carefully in the whole area between Verdun and Lasalle. He'd heard more than a few warnings to avoid any ghosts that looked unstable. Also, he'd heard a rumour from Kyle that the Boneman was on the prowl. When Marty asked what that meant, Bernard just shrugged, adjusted his toque and sauntered away.

They had a general area, then, but it was still a big swath of land for the two of them to canvas.

It was afternoon when they decided to take a break, grabbing some coffee. Marty pressed himself into the café's corner as usual, headset on, as Abbi sat across from him. He would be perpetually perplexed by how people just walked around her cart, without even noticing.

That was why it'd taken him so long to realize what was going on. He'd mentioned it to his parents early on, not thinking it was abnormal. A few psychiatry visits and a brain scan later, and Marty learned to keep his mouth shut. There was a time when he would lose his temper; he'd go red-faced screaming that this was all real. He couldn't remember what the pills were, but he hadn't liked them. They never made the ghosts go away anyway.

"Well, we have a chunk of potentially searchable land," Marty said.

"Yeah, but what are we going to do with it?"

Marty sipped his latte, watching the cream swirl inside. "Maybe we could narrow our searches for news articles in the area."

Abbi nodded. "Yeah, okay. Maybe do the same with a bunch of social media, look for people posting in and about certain locations."

"It's worth a try."

Out the window, the living walked among the dead, their rosy cheeks a sharp contrast to the pallid complexion of the ghosts.

Sometimes Marty wished ghosts were more like they were in cartoons. Transparent and wispy, passing through walls with big, dopey eyes. These, what he saw; they were too real.

He'd only been to one funeral: his father insisted that he see the open casket, even though he was only eight years old. Ghosts look how grandpa's body did: cold, pale, unsettling.

On the corner stood a solitary figure, half obscured by shadow. Flayed flesh, burning eyes, and a skeletal grin.

Marty gasped. "Look."

But he was gone.

"What was it?"

Marty's blood went cold and he felt jittery, on edge. Too much coffee, I've got to lay off it.

"Marty?"

"Nothing. I'm just tired."

Chapter Three

Running Around Corners

MARTY HAD SO many tabs open they were like pinpricks in his browser. He kept switching through them, hitting refresh on each one, and repeating the process.

Abbi had left because she couldn't stand watching him tab through them anymore. His computer was making an alarming churning noise, too.

But he kept tabbing anyway. It was all he could think to do. He had a mix of local news sites and social media search queries open, hoping to catch any hint of the in-betweener's movements.

A Twitter post popped up linking to a news article about a raging homeless man. Weird, when Marty went to the site he couldn't find it on the home page or in recent entries. Whatever, the link still worked.

A homeless man became unstable last night, threatening passers-by. He seemed unable to move when police arrived on the scene to arrest him. One witness claims the man made an unusual wailing noise as he was pushed into the back of a police car. When asked to describe him, the witness said he looked 'like his bones weren't right. Like, they were all in the wrong place.' Police say there is nothing to worry about and the man will be referred to psychiatric support.

Woah. Marty did a search for 'homeless' posts timestamped the night before. After a few minutes he found one that looked right. The caption read *Creepy Homeless Guy Was Freaking Us Out*, with a picture of police pulling a figure with a blanket over his head into a police car. But the homeless guy's silhouette was off, bulky and inhuman. If he hadn't read the article, Marty wouldn't have thought it was a person. The more he looked, the more it unsettled him.

That had to be one of the transformed ghosts from the in-betweener. Was there a pattern in who he chose, or was he just doing it to anyone that got near him? *I've got to hurry, or he's going to hurt more people.*

Marty wondered what it felt like to be a ghost and then turned into one of those monstrosities. He didn't think being alive again, if it could even be called that, was worth how tortuous the transformation seemed. He didn't want that to happen to any of his friends.

He kept tabbing through his browser, refreshing each page.

MARTY WOKE UP drooling onto his keyboard while Abbi poked his face.

"Whauhguh."

"You're late and Alhad's been texting you like crazy." Abbi pointed to Marty's buzzing phone.

The screen lit up with *Where are you?* and *I can only cover you for so long.*

"I ugh, pfft, kay."

Abbi hauled Marty off the couch and shoved him toward the bathroom.

Work, right. He still had to go. He should've gotten the Boneman to include a stipend. He chuckled through a mouthful of toothpaste.

"Holy shit. Marty, look at this."

Marty stumbled out of the bathroom, and one of his keyword searches had just refreshed with a post that was only a few seconds old. There was a pic of a shadowed creature with the caption *wtf is this?* Marty recognized the street: it was nearby.

Marty threw on his clothes and dashed out the door, Abbi's calls muffled by the door closing behind him.

MARTY ROUNDED THE corner and knew something wasn't right. There were no police cars, but two large black vans blocked the street and a gaggle of meatheads in black suits stood blocking the sidewalk.

Marty wasn't getting in that way, but he wasn't letting this chance go either. Instead he entered the laneway, walking a good distance to get past the vans, and then he climbed the fence into somebody's backyard.

He heaved himself over the top, sweat beading his forehead, and then tumbled onto the lawn with a groan. *I need to go to the gym.* He groaned his way over another fence, confident he had pulled a muscle, and then he was standing on the closed-off street.

Marty recognized the house he'd seen in the picture's background. A black car was parked in the middle of the street, and just beyond it was where the creature should be. Marty sidled up to the car, peering into the space between two houses.

Obscured by shadows was a writing mound of flesh. It gurgled and undulated, its skin stretching and twitching like a sack filled with twigs. Marty turned away, willing himself not to vomit.

But standing around the creature were three people: a blonde woman with a buzz cut, a doughy guy, and an unnaturally thin bald man with pallid skin—a ghost. The ghost was talking to the two people.

Talking to them.

They can see him.

Holy shit. I thought I was the only one.

The bald ghost hesitated, and then looked right at Marty. The woman pulled back her jacket, revealing a gun.

Marty bolted, fear pumping blood to his legs. The doughy guy charged after him.

Marty wasn't doing the fences again, so he ran right for the black vans. The meatheads looked perplexed, unsure how to react to this huffing, out-of-shape dude pounding towards them. Behind him, the doughy guy was shouting, his face red. Marty couldn't hear him: he just needed to get out of there.

He reached the vans and vaulted over them—about part way before his face smacked into the hood and he rolled off onto the street, taking one of the side mirrors with him.

The meatheads scrambled forward, but Marty was up

and running before they could reach him. Looking over his shoulder, he saw four meatheads and dough guy chasing him through the street. Panicked, he ran for a house, darting down the side path into the back yard.

He jumped at the gate, smashed his knee, and groaned his way over the top. A dog inside the house barked. Marty stumbled over a kids' play set and sidestepped a swing that threatened to break his nose. By the time he got to the other fence, the meatheads were falling over each other to get into the backyard.

Marty got over the fence, mercifully waist high, and ran down the lane. If he could just get around the corner, he'd be able to lose the meatheads.

Dough guy stood at the end of the lane. *Shit*. Marty turned on a heel, and the meathead gaggle were bearing down on him.

Marty jumped over a wooden fence, his out-of-shape arms shaking as he pulled himself up and over and—splash—he fell right into a pool. Fuck me.

He dog-paddled to the edge, disgruntled grunts coming from the other side of the fence. Sopping wet, he ran from the backyard and into the street.

He was alone: turn a corner or two, and that'd be it. Marty started jogging away, but fuck was he tired. His legs felt heavy, and he had to stop, hands on his knees, to get his breath.

And then the doughy guy rounded the corner. Marty bolted, which wasn't very fast. Doughy guy wasn't doing so great either, his face was flushed, sweat dripping down his forehead. Marty tried to out-jog him, and they kept pace like a pair of retirees.

Marty turned into a mom-and-pop store that sold kitchen

utensils. Pots and pans jangled as Marty's shoulder's brushed against them. Marty ignored the owner's hollering as he ran for the back door—only to realize the back door was locked.

Fuck fuck fuckfuckfuck.

Dough guy limped into the store, hand on his side.

"Alright, you little shit," he said with a thick French-Canadian accent. "You're coming with—"

Marty chucked a pan at his head.

Dough guy raised his arms and the pan *thwonged* against him. Marty hobbled around the isles and to the door.

He was exhausted, breathing heavy, feeling faint. He charged at the door and…

Whoever owned the mom-and-pop shop must have been meticulous about keeping it clean, because Marty would have sworn that the door was wide open.

…Marty crashed through the glass with a yelp. Shards cascading around him like flecks of snow.

He kept running, looking over his shoulder once to see the doughy guy—face flushed and breathing heavy—trying to placate the screaming owner.

Chapter Four

BOA

Marty leaned against his sink, topless. Abbi looked over his shoulders, back, arms, everything.

"You got lucky. Like, really lucky," Abbi said. "That hoodie is garbage now, by the way."

Marty had managed to avoid getting any glass shards stuck in him, but his pool-drenched hoodie wasn't so lucky. With a grimace, he stuffed his clothes into a garbage bag.

Pajamas equipped, he slumped onto the couch, feeling like his entire body was made of jelly.

"Who were those guys, cops?" Marty asked.

"Maybe, maybe not." Abbi sat cross-legged on the couch, her cart creaking as her intestines pulled it nearer.

"Don't tell me they're, like, the FBI or something?"

Abbi chewed her lower lip. "Okay. I'm not supposed to tell you this, okay? But—ah, shit. Just"—she palmed her eyes— "they were probably the BOA."

"And that's…?"

"It's the Bureau of Otherworldly Affairs."

Marty scrunched up his face. The cogs in his brain were whirring and churning; he was so damn tired. "Wait, I've heard of them. They're the ones that record people's ghost stories and go into the woods looking for yetis. They're a joke. Not the kind of people that wear black suits and have black vans and shit like that."

"That's a front, Marty. They do some serious shit."

"You're kidding? You have to be. The BOA have that dinky little shithole wedged into the corner of Place des Arts, the place that sells those cute Casper-wannabe hats in a gift shop. They don't walk around with guns."

"Marty, trust me. The BOA is serious."

"Remember that story from a couple years ago? They spent two weeks in a woman's house recording this mysterious white noise, and it turned out to be an old radio the woman forgot to turn off."

"It's. A. Front."

"I'm pretty sure the BOA museum has a bake sale once a year."

"Marty…"

"They're like that *Ancient Aliens* guy."

"*No they're not!*" Abbi threw her hands into the air. "This shit is serious, Marty. And if the BOA is involved, then you should be scared."

Marty crossed his arms. "Okay, jeez, I get it."

They were silent for a time. Marty mindlessly refreshed the browser tabs on his computer.

"Could they help?" Marty asked.

"That's probably a bad idea." Abbi sighed. "And I think they and the Boneman are sort of not on the same team."

"I'm working for the bad guy?"

"I wouldn't call either one of them good guys, but basically, yeah."

Marty groaned, letting himself sink into the sofa. His phone vibrated. Eighteen texts and six voicemails. He set his phone to night mode and put it face down on his coffee table.

"Your friends are going to be angry," Abbi said.

"It feels like that's not really important now."

"It could be, or should be. The world's not stopping."

"It'll stop if I piss off the Bonedude."

Abbi smirked. "Heh, *Bonedude*."

They both laughed. Tension bled out of him, rising off his body like mist. As he wiped away the tears from his watering eyes, he couldn't help but notice that even while laughing, Abbi was still that same sickly pale tone.

"What's it mean if the BOA is involved?" Marty asked eventually.

"I'm not sure, but it's not good. I don't know if they have the full picture, they might just be tracking down the monsters and not know what's happening to them."

"But if they're with the government, then maybe I can talk to them? Get them to understand that I need help."

"That's probably not a good idea."

"I can show them this, maybe they can even do it for me." Marty reached into his backpack and brandished the Boneman's shark tooth dagger.

Abbi scuttled back, trying to get as far away as possible, her feet digging furrows in the couch's cushions. "Jesus fuck, Marty, get that thing away from me."

Marty brought it close to his chest. "What?"

"Don't touch me with it. Don't come *near* me with it. Get it out of here."

"I don't understand." Marty stashed the shark tooth back in his bag. "I wasn't going to touch you with it."

Abbi closed her eyes, slowing her breathing. After a few moments she said, "The Boneman gave that to you?"

"Yeah."

"And you just took it?"

"Well, uh, I mean, yeah."

"Okay," Abbi sighed. "Okay, first of all you should be scared shitless of anything a ghost from the deep gives you. Especially because it's one of the few ways ghost objects become material objects, and any ghost that wants that should be treated with a giant wad of scepticism. Second, what are you supposed to do with it?"

"I'm supposed to use it on the in-betweener—I guess to stab him?—and then the Boneman can make him pass on."

"'Pass on' is a polite way to put it."

"You know, I don't get it. These deep ghosts are supposed to be all scary and evil and shit, but then why is he trying to get the in-betweener to pass on? That seems like a pretty good thing to want, so why's the Boneman all messed-up and scary and shit?"

"I don't know. I don't really know why *anything* is the way it is. What I do know is that ghosts like the Boneman have a job, a purpose. They help keep some semblance of order between ghostness and humanness. I don't know why they have to be fucked-up to do it."

Marty paced around his coffee table. "But if they keep order and stuff, does that mean they have bosses who tell them what to do?"

"It's better not to think about it."

"So there's, like, an all-knowing Cthulhu that's running the show?"

"I don't know. I honestly don't. But whatever kind of things are the Boneman's boss, you don't want to even think about them, because the second they start thinking about you—" Abbi looked away. "Let's not talk about this anymore, okay?" She nudged his laptop with her foot. "You're due for a refresh marathon."

Refresh, refresh, refresh. Marty had expected hunting down a ghost monster to be more thrilling than this. Refresh. *Maybe I should try new keywords?* Refresh. *Maybe I need to try something entirely different...*

One of the news sites' Facebook accounts updated with a new story. *Picture of sick animal sparks Twitter outrage.* The story went on:

> *Early this morning a woman shared this photo of a sick animal in her backyard. Users immediately started chiding her and the city for letting a creature devolve to this state. Authorities say that the animal was terminally ill and has been cared for in a humane fashion. Users are demanding answers, saying that no animal should've been allowed to degrade to such a point. The animal is assumed to be a dog, but police would not confirm or deny whether it was or wasn't a dog.*

The picture was blurry, and the creature was half under shrubbery, obscured by shadows. Marty read on:

The woman, who wishes to remain anonymous, said she was too frightened to go near the animal. Some are saying the culprit is an unknown third party, while others accuse the woman herself of being the abuser. "How else could that poor thing have gotten into her yard?" said Twitter user @BlitzPounder1980.

Marty squinted at the picture. That wasn't a dog. It conjured the image of the *thing* he'd seen with the BOA agents. Marty's blood went cold, and he started to get the feeling the in-betweener was going to have a lot more victims. Why was he doing it? Was there a reason, or had he just gone insane?

Or was he angry? Marty had never considered that. After hearing Carla's description of a shambling man, Marty had assumed the in-betweener was apathetic. But if he was *angry*, then he'd be looking for people to hurt. Which meant he was more dangerous than Marty had first realized.

Another Twitter post, this time by a random user. It was a picture of two black vans and some familiar-looking meatheads around a creature under a blanket. The text read, *this is starting to get scary,* and they tagged the Mayor of Montréal.

And another news story on a separate site hit: *Sick family of raccoons scare locals. Nothing to worry about, say police.* But when Marty tabbed over to Twitter he saw a response to the article, *raccoons my ass, what the hell is this?* Attached was a shaky video of an undulating mass pressed underneath a backyard deck.

Holy shit. The in-betweener was losing it. How many more had he affected that weren't in these stories? How many ghosts had he put through this torment?

Marty needed to find the in-betweener before he hurt more people.

MARTY BOUGHT A stack of sticky notes and wrote everything he knew about the in-betweener and the locations mentioned in the articles on them, sticking them to his wall.

The articles and social media posts were becoming more frequent, going viral among locals. Marty wouldn't be surprised if the six o'clock news covered the story.

Marty slapped another sticky note to the wall just as his phone started to vibrate. The caller ID read *Steph*.

Marty's thumb hovered over the end call button. He realized he'd missed a day of work, and had no idea when his next shift was. Did it matter? He was doing something bigger, more important.

The phone kept vibrating in his hand.

They might be worried.

They might be angry.

Marty looked at his wall of sticky notes. It felt like progress, but it also felt like he was running in place.

He picked up the phone. "Hi."

"Marty? Are you alright?"

"Yeah."

"You didn't show up yesterday, and you went totally dark. No one could reach you. Alhad almost called your parents, he thought something bad happened."

Marty winced. "I'm fine, everything's fine."

"Fine? What happened yesterday?"

Marty switched the phone from ear to ear. "Um." He didn't

have an excuse. And I can't tell her I'm hunting ghosts. "Uh."

"Marty, what's wrong? Something's wrong."

"No, no. Everything's fine. It just, uh, I, was really tired. I think I have the flu or something." God, that sounded weak.

"Are you trying to bullshit me?"

"What? No, of course—"

In the background he heard Alhad's distant voice—"Is that Marty?"—and then louder through the phone: "Marty, what's wrong?"

"Nothing's wrong. I was just, like, tired and I think I have a flu."

"Flu? You sure that's it? You didn't answer our texts."

"I was asleep most of the day."

"Are you feeling better now?"

"Yeah, much better."

"Great, then get your ass down here."

The phone was returned to Steph. "Guess you can't weasel out today," she said.

Marty tried a friendly laugh that came out awkward. "Yeah, I'll see you soon, I guess."

Click. "Ah, shit."

"What happened?" Abbi asked.

"I have to go to work."

WALKING INTO CHESTER'S felt like the walk of shame. Joe gave him the stink eye the entire time. Marie—one of the other waiters—looked at him like something stuck to her shoe. Alhad hovered around Marty while he put his apron on, asking a thousand questions—seemingly for his own reassurance that everything was alright.

Marty got situated at his station, the sink drain staring back at him.

Steph bumped his shoulder. "We're all going to see a movie later, you should come."

"No, thanks."

"You sure?"

"Yeah, still kind of tired."

Steph ran her fingers through her hair and gave Marty a tight-lipped "Okay" before leaving the kitchen.

Soap up, swish-swish, rinse, repeat. An extravagant six hours for the new ghost hunter in town.

HANDS WRIST DEEP in spit scrubbing, Marty couldn't figure out *why* the in-betweener was doing any of this. Did he have some kind of plan? More and more it seemed like the actions of a rabid animal, with no intention other than to lash out.

Were the ghost victims connected in any way? Marty didn't know how to find out, but he doubted it. From what Abbi had heard, the person that Carla referred to as 'the shambler' was a roving, reasonless danger.

Who was the in-betweener? Marty hadn't thought to ask himself before. If he could figure out who he was in life, then maybe he could figure out what he wanted in death.

MARTY USED GOOGLE Maps to put pins on all the known locations of monster sightings. It was incomplete, but a picture was forming. The in-betweener seemed to be circling a certain neighbourhood, never going more than a few blocks away.

But how to narrow it down? He could wait for more news stories, or he could just go and take a look. Do a couple laps around the neighbourhood to see if there was anything there.

Marty grabbed a fresh hoodie and headed out.

Wallace sat with his back against Mrs. Hubbard's door.

"Going out at this time of night?" the old ghost asked.

"Just for a walk."

"Ah, right. Walking's good for you. I should've been smart like you. But what can you do?"

"Right, yeah. Not much, I guess."

Wallace wrung his hands. "You're not getting into trouble, are you?"

"Of course not."

"It's just, you had a guest, and I was worried."

"Don't be," Marty said. "I've got everything under control." He thudded down the creaking stairs.

"Are you sure?"

The door closed behind him.

Chapter Five

The In-Betweener

MARTY PRESSED HIS toe down on the curb, wondering if the next step would take him past some unseen threshold. An ordinary person would say that was ridiculous, but ordinary people didn't live with ghosts all around them.

And that was what Marty noticed. There were always ghosts, going this way and that. A couple in the street, some chatting on the sidewalk, leaning on doorframes.

There were no ghosts here. The street was quiet, barren. Was this what it felt like to be normal? Marty couldn't decide if he liked it or not.

He took a step forward. And then another. It wasn't monumental or life-changing, not in the way he though it should be.

There was a lot of neighborhood to cover. He couldn't do it all tonight. Maybe he should just go home. Figure something else out.

He kept moving, peering down lanes and around street corners. He spotted a few black vans: he wasn't the only ghost hunter in town.

The houses were mostly duplexes, with bungalows sprinkled throughout. Little plots of grass hugged walkways and front steps, dotted with shrubs.

Why here? It was so... plain. Nice, but plain. Why was the in-betweener circling this neighbourhood?

Marty caught sight of a silhouetted figure standing in a laneway. They leaned against a fence, hunched over, limping—no.

Shambling.

Marty froze, afraid to move, afraid to act.

The in-betweener heaved, his chest rising and falling with deep wheezed breaths.

Marty reached into his backpack and gripped his shark tooth dagger. Tentatively, he walked forward. I can do this, I can do this.

The in-betweener's face was pallid and green-tinged, his eyes bloodshot. Viscous black liquid bubbled from his mouth, dripping steaming dollops onto the ground.

Marty neared, only a few feet away from the in-betweener.

The in-betweener stepped forward, clawed-hand gripping the chain-link fence, his head tilting to look at Marty with his less varicosed eye.

"You see me?" the in-betweener said.

"Yes." Marty's voice shook.

"You're like me, like how I was." The in-betweener reached out a hand bloated with decay. "You have to help me."

Marty stepped back, grip tightening on the shark tooth dagger. "I can help you pass on."

"Pass? No, no, no." The in-betweener shook his head, ooze bubbling from his mouth as he started to cough.

"It'll stop, the pain. I just have to..." Marty held up the shark tooth dagger. "If you let me, this'll help you."

The in-betweener started breathing rapidly, his black-crusted nostrils flaring. "You don't understand you don't fucking understand, no one does you fucking—" He reached a grasping hand for Marty, grabbing a handful of his hoodie. "You don't know anything, don't know what's going to happen. It's not nice it's not pretty."

Stab him, said a voice in Marty's head, not his own. *Stab him now*.

The in-betweener shook Marty, baring his green-tinged teeth. "I can see now, you understand? I can see what happens, and I don't want it. Neither do you, nobody does. You just don't know it yet."

"Please, I can help. Just let me. It'll put you at ease. You don't want to live like this, do you?"

"You don't know, not yet." His grip tightened. "I didn't deserve it, you understand? I don't deserve it."

STAB HIM.

Marty raised the bone dagger over his head.

The in-betweener screeched, stumbling backwards and falling to the ground. He raised one hand to ward off Marty. "Please no. Please, God, please, no."

Marty held the dagger over his head. Just do it, he told himself. He's right there; just do it and this is all over.

The in-betweener wept tar-black tears. They rolled down his cheek, bubbling and boiling. He was muttering now, "Please no please God no I can't please why please please please."

Marty lowered the dagger. "I know you don't know me. But trust me, this will be better than how you're living. Just let me do it, it'll make everything better."

The in-betweener's face contorted into a snarling, angry visage. "Fix everything? Nothing will fix this, nothing." He spat the words, black oil spattering the concrete.

"This is how it has to be."

"Has to be?" The in-betweener scrambled to his feet. "You don't fucking understand, you can't, you won't."

STAB HIM, the voice boomed in Marty's mind, rattling his skull.

The in-betweener ran, shambling away. Marty followed, bone dagger clutched in his hand. He was catching up, and he reached out to the in-betweener.

The in-betweener grabbed one of the chain-link fences and pulled. A sickening squelch followed as the fence morphed into an undulating pound of vivisected flesh. Marty gasped, stopping in his tracks.

The in-betweener crawled through a hole in a fence, into a backyard.

Follow him, do not let him get away.

Marty ran, trying to ignore the writhing flesh beside him. He shouldered through the broken fence and saw the in-betweener limping down an alley between houses. Marty's legs pumped; the in-betweener wasn't fast, and within moments Marty would catch up.

The in-betweener raked his hand along the house's red bricks, and in his wake, they began to undulate and writhe. Marty charged forward. If he could just get within arm's reach...

The wall bubbled, forming boils that distended and popped. The slimy flesh grew and expanded, pushing at Marty's shoulder until he was pressed against the neighbouring house.

His heart hammered in his chest, fear urging him forward. The flesh was slick against his skin, and he felt it slowing him down, trying to grow around his body as though to pull him in.

The streetlights filtered through a membranous layer of ghost flesh above him, tingeing his world red and raw. He cried out, primal and terrified. He stumbled, grabbing a handful of flesh, which popped in his hand, covering it in yellow liquid.

The flesh pushed him to the ground, bearing down on him. He crawled, eyes wide, panicked cries burning his throat raw.

And then light, and the weight lifted. He crawled and scrambled away, standing in the middle of the street.

One half of the house had turned into a writhing mass of meat, bubbling over the top and onto the roof of the adjacent home.

Police sirens, flashing lights.

Marty ran home.

HE'D TORN HIS clothes off and threw them in the garbage. Another hoodie gone. Naked, he stood in the shower, letting the warm water wash over him for he didn't know how long.

The mass of bubbling meat replayed itself in his mind— over and over like a broken reel. He couldn't will it away, he couldn't think to try.

He never wanted to leave the shower.

He wanted to close his eyes and never wake up.

Marty cried in the shower, wracking sobs that shook his body.

As he cried he saw the bulging veins of exposed flesh, and he cried harder because he knew it would never leave his mind.

That he would never sleep the same again. That what had happened wasn't some nightmare he could wake from.

His crying rose from his gut, a deep wail that emptied his lungs with despair.

MARTY STARED AT his sticky-note wall in a daze, imaging the notes filling with pus like balloons. He was startled by the sound of his phone vibrating on the coffee table. Steph. He set the phone to silent and put it face down on the table.

He refreshed all his browser tabs, mechanically. The bright orange flames didn't register at first, but then he focused and saw the report. A fire in his neighbourhood had burned down one home and spread to a second. One dead.

It was the house the in-betweener had touched, Marty knew it. The only picture was from around the corner, catching a glimpse of the rising smoke and licking flames; but Marty knew it was the same house.

One dead. He stared at the screen. One dead because I didn't stab him. It was Marty's fault, how could it not be? He had the in-betweener right in front of him, and he was too chickenshit to do anything about it.

One dead.

He felt his skin catch on fire, his blood boiling. A tightness constricted his chest and his vision blurred as tears threatened to escape.

He closed his eyes, taking in deep shuddering breathes.

I couldn't do it, I couldn't stab him.

Someone knocked at his door. Marty jumped, unreasoning fear urging him to run. He breathed, calming himself as best he could.

He bent to look through the peephole, and remembered it didn't work. He wasn't sure how he'd managed to break a peephole. He unlocked the door and opened it.

Steph, rosy cheeked and bundled against the chill air, jabbed a finger at him. "Do you know what time it is?"

"Uh," he tried to guess based on the daylight, "noonish?"

"*Maudit câlice*," Steph threw her hands into the air. "Can I at least come in?"

Marty stepped aside so Steph could march past him. She took her shoes off and left them on the tiny carpet he kept near the door, and then wiggled out of her jacket, tossing it on the couch.

Marty glanced at the clock. *Well, shit.* It was 4:00 P.M.; he'd missed his entire shift. He was supposed to be on lunch duty today.

"Alhad is the only thing keeping you from getting fired," Steph said. She made a round of his coffee table, as though looking for evidence of wrongdoing. And then her eyes drifted to his wall. "What the fuck?" She stared at all the sticky notes, his makeshift corkboard. "Marty, what is this?" She leaned close, reading the sticky notes. "Are you *stalking* somebody?"

"What? God, no."

She thrust her hand at the wall. "Then what the hell is all this?"

"It's, uh. I'm into a conspiracy."

Steph groaned. "Have you cracked? Is this a call for help?"

"No, no. Just look," Marty pointed to the sticky notes. "There's been a trend of stories about weird creature-thing sightings. But they're all covered up as being, like, a sick homeless guy or a dog with a disease or whatever. And"—he pulled up some screenshots on his laptop— "these are screencaps of what people are actually seeing. There are even posts being deleted." He shoved the computer at her. "See?"

"Uh, okay. That's definitely creepy. But I still don't get the point?"

"The government is covering it up."

Steph rolled her eyes.

"Look! A screencap of a journalist's social media post about one of the creatures, and then—check their timeline—it's gone." Marty loaded up the profile and showed her.

"There are a million reasons why someone would delete a post."

"Yeah, but then never mention it again?"

Steph ran her fingers through her hair. "I think you're seeing things where there's nothing to see." She gestured to the sticky note wall. "This is insane, Marty. This is why you're missing work?"

"Maybe."

Steph looked at him, really looked, like she was trying to find the cracks. The broken parts of him. "This is fucked up."

"Yeah."

Steph tabbed through all his open sites, looking over the keywords he'd used to try and find posts related to the in-betweener's victims. "You really think there's some kind of monster stuff happening in the city?"

"Yeah."

"And you're trying to… track it?"

"Yeah."

"And you don't think this behaviour is bizarre and alarming?"

"Yeah—uh, well. Probably."

Steph set the laptop on the coffee table, sidled around it to the entrance, and started putting on her shoes.

"Steph?"

"I'm going to tell Alhad that you need some time, he can smooth it over with the owner. At least for a while. I don't know what's going on with you, but I think you should see a doctor. You can call me if you need anything, okay?"

"Okay."

Steph pulled on her coat and was out the door.

He collapsed face-first onto his couch. Fucking hell.

Chapter Six

A Favour

MARTY WOKE TO frantic knocking at his door. He groaned, rolling over and wincing at the kink in his neck. It was past midnight. Was it Steph? Maybe she forgot her phone or something. Marty waddled to the door and swung it open.

"What did you do?" Wallace said.

Marty rubbed the crud from his eyes. "What are you talking about?"

Wallace looked frightened and nervous. "There's a man outside who wants to see you, he's been calling your name."

"What, who?" The fog cleared from Marty's head. Could it be a BOA agent?

"He's a ghost. But, Marty, he's not right."

"Not right?" Oh, no. "Stay inside, Wallace, no matter what. Don't get near him, don't touch him. Stay away." Marty pulled on some clothes, grabbed the shark tooth dagger and stumbled his way down the stairs.

Wallace's voice trailed after him. "What did you do?"

Outside, the in-betweener leaned one shoulder against a

streetlight. Wet, rasping coughs shook his body. Black tar bubbled from his throat to patter onto the cement.

"Marty, Marty, Marty." He said it like a mantra.

"How do you know my name?" Marty clutched the bone dagger, but kept his distance.

"I hear things. I know things. Do you want to end up like me? I know you don't, but it'll happen. It always does. It's because we're scared. Aren't you scared, Marty?"

"You're hurting people."

"You're not listening, Marty. I need something, you can do it. Please, can't you do it?"

Marty edged closer. "Do what?"

"A pocketknife from my home. My father gave it to me decades ago. I'm scared, I don't want to go alone. You understand, don't you, Marty? Let me have him with me, I always needed him. I'm not strong. You see that, I know you see that." Coughing wracked his body, shaking him from the inside. "It's just a little knife, a little nothing. Please, it's all I need. Then I'll go, like you want, I'll find peace. No more hurting."

"You won't resist? You'll just pass on, no running, no fighting?"

"No running, no fighting."

He was within arm's reach of the in-betweener, Marty could lash out and hit him. "You promise?"

The in-betweener smiled, bile-crusted yellow teeth gleaming sickly in the streetlight. "I promise."

Marty relaxed his grip on the bone dagger. "Okay, I can do that."

The in-betweener reached into his pocket and pulled out a pair of keys. They gleamed, flecked with light like sparkling snow. Marty put out his hand, and the in-betweener dropped them into his open palm. Marty's ears popped, and for an instant he thought he heard a distant thunderclap. The keys looked more solid, more mundane in his palm.

The in-betweener's face grew sallower, his eyes more sunken, and his coughing more violent. The tar-like sputum poured from his mouth like a ruptured artery.

"Please, Marty. Let me go with a memory of my father, with a little bit of peace and strength."

"I'll get it for you. I promise."

The sickly ghost turned to hobbled away. "I'll be waiting. Thank you. Thank you, thank you…"

THE IN-BETWEENER HADN'T told Marty where his house was, if he could even remember. But Marty had a good idea of where it'd be and how to find it.

Fog had rolled in, in the quiet neighbourhood with no ghosts. The streetlights were muted beacons, fighting through the gloom. The only living creature Marty saw was a skunk, waddling from yard to yard.

Beside one of the streetlights stood a figure of flayed flesh with burning eyes. The Boneman stared at Marty, his head slowly turning to follow Marty's gait.

Oh, no.

And then the Boneman was in front of him, staring down with a skeletal grin. Marty felt the malice emanating from those emotionless sockets.

You made a deal with him. The Boneman's voice was like screeching crickets.

"It's part of the plan." Marty brushed past him, walking faster.

The Boneman's voice seemed to follow him, always in his ear. *You weren't supposed to make a deal.*

"I'm handling it." Shit, Marty, now's not the time to have a spine.

Marty's gaze was pulled to one of the houses, and the Boneman stared at him from its darkened window. *You're failing me, Marty. You had a chance, but you balked.*

"No, I just found another way." Marty's pulse quickened.

He rounded a corner, and the fog became red-tinged, the streetlights radiating black light. Marty's eyes couldn't focus, couldn't understand.

He was locked mid-step, unable to move.

You failed me, Marty. The Boneman's words were echoey and distorted, like whale song. From the mist, like a giant from myth, walked the Boneman. Taller than the streetlights, the red mists swirling around his arms. The buildings rolled, shifted. Marty's vision blurred as his eyes started to water and panic made his heart hammer.

"I'm going to get him. I promise. I just need to find his pocketknife." Marty yelped, his wrist was turning, and turning, tensing as it threatened to break. He cried out: "I'm going to do it, I promise."

His wrist snapped, tendons tearing, bones breaking. Marty sobbed, the pain shooting up his arm.

I cannot abide failure. The Boneman turned his fingers like he was opening a door.

Marty's head unwillingly followed the motion, his body immovable, until he felt the tension, the stabs of pain as he was forced to look over his shoulder.

"Please, I promise, I'll do it. No matter what, I'll do it." Pain shot through his neck, he grit his teeth but that just made it hurt more. "I promise."

The Boneman—human-sized—was now in his line of sight. He extended his hand to one of the buildings. *Do not trust him, Marty.*

Marty collapsed to his knees, sucking in gulps of air. The fog wasn't red, the streetlights were their normal orange glow. His wrist throbbed, but otherwise felt fine. Whatever the Boneman had done was just a warning. Keep it together, Marty. In front of him was the building the Boneman had gestured to, a pair of black vans parked outside it. Down the street he saw another two. This was the in-betweener's house.

Marty rose on unsteady legs, leaning against the streetlight; half to keep himself hidden from the vans, half to catch his breath.

I shouldn't have signed that contract.

The vans' windows were tinted: Marty assumed they were BOA agents staking out the place. The front door of the house opened, and a guy in a polo shirt and jeans walked out, making sure to lock the door behind him. He rushed down the steps, got into a beat-up silver car, and drove away. He didn't seem to notice the black vans, and the BOA didn't seem to care about him. Maybe a family member taking care of the house? It didn't matter now—Marty needed to get inside.

The house was dark, no lights, no movement. He gripped the in-betweener's keys. Front door was out of the question, the BOA agents would see him. Back door it was, then.

Marty backtracked until he was out of sight of the vans, dashed into one of the neighbour's backyards, *oomphed* his way over a pair of fences—his entire body ached—and dropped into the in-betweener's backyard.

The house was a bungalow, with one floor and a basement. The backyard was unremarkable, a square of grass with a chain-link fence and a stubby shed in the corner. A few lights in the neighbours' windows reminded him that there were still people here.

Marty walked up the three cement steps to the back door, and breathed a sigh of relief that someone had left the screen door open. He fumbled with the keys, but after a few seconds he was stepping into the in-betweener's house.

The back door led into a little horizontal room cluttered with rakes, brooms, shovels, and coats. An empty garbage pail sat nestled in a corner. Marty felt like an intruder, seeing the clutter and detritus of a lived-in home he was never meant to see. After everything that had happened, this was too normal.

This back room led into a modest kitchen. It wasn't big, and a circular table made for four people occupied the majority of the floor space. Marty pressed his hand to the countertop: smooth black and white marble. He opened the wooden cupboards, and felt silly for being surprised at finding dishes and cups.

Next was the living room, with a loveseat and a twenty-inch TV. There were old pictures on the wall, sepia or black-and-white: Marty guessed the in-betweener, his parents, and a brother. In the background of each was the same house. So the in-betweener had inherited it? Marty scanned the other pictures. It was hard to see the in-betweener as Marty knew him in the human in these photos; Marty had to guess. Most were of when he was a little kid, a couple from high school, a graduation photo, then nothing. Marty recognized one of the men in the pictures: the guy in the polo shirt he'd seen leave the house. That must have been the in-betweener's brother, taking care of his stuff after his death.

The second room's door was ajar, and it squealed as Marty pushed it open. A bedroom that was mostly bed. No closet, a nightstand, a dresser. The bed was made, and Marty got the sense it hadn't been used in a while, like months or years. The nightstand was empty, and the dresser only had spare bedsheets. Was this a guest bedroom? Marty figured the in-betweener didn't have a lot of guests.

There was one more room, its door closed. Marty didn't feel good about rifling through someone else's belongings, but he had to find the pocketknife.

The floorboards creaked as he walked up to the final door. It opened on less noisy hinges. A bedroom, more cluttered, slightly larger. This had to be the in-betweener's room.

There were clothes piled in a laundry basket, scattered books and magazines, odds and ends like a comb, hand moisturizer, deodorant. Marty took a deep breath, and then started opening drawers. Socks, underwear, T-shirts. Mostly plain colours, a few argyle patterns, some plaid. No pocketknife. He went through the closet, sweaters—mostly black and white, one red; jeans; a pair of shoes. He checked the pants and sweater pockets, no wallet. Maybe his brother had collected it? There was a small computer desk in the corner: a couple of cables, no drawers, no computer. That must have been it—the in-betweener's brother had taken all the valuables out of the house. Did that include the pocketknife?

Marty got on the tips of his toes and rummaged around the top shelf of the closet. There was only one box and an old lamp. Marty took down the box, set it on the bed, and opened it.

Photo albums, old ones. The whole family was in here, grandparents in black and white, parents in off-tone red, and the in-betweener and his brother in disposable camera colour, their eyes flashing a now ominous red. And then they were adults, the in-betweener—healthy and alive—starting to look sad. Inexplicably so. His brother stood with his arms around someone Marty assumed was his wife, two little kids looking miserable at the prospect of standing still.

They were nice pictures, but in each one Marty noticed the in-betweener was alone. Off to the side, at the back. There were no pictures of the in-betweener that didn't have his brother's family in them. Except one, where he wore a janitor's outfit, mop in hand, his trolley beside him. Marty squinted at the picture so he could read the nametag: *John McKinsey.*

Marty riffled through the papers at the bottom of the box—tax papers, pictures of a dog, high school diploma—no pocketknife.

For fuck's sake, *John*, you couldn't tell me where you kept it?

On a hunch, Marty got down on his hands and knees and looked under the bed. Nothing but dust bunnies.

There's still the basement.

Marty never liked basements, especially when he was alone. He didn't know why, or when it started. It didn't matter if it was at his parents' house, his grandma's house, or a friend's house; going into a basement alone made him jittery.

And now he had to go rummage through a dead man's basement.

Marty set everything back the way it had been in the box, and gingerly put it back on the closet shelf. He didn't want John's brother to freak out. It's weird, thinking of the in-betweener as a "John." From what Marty could see, there was nothing remarkable about John. He didn't have any dungeons or secret compartments, no villain's lair, no shrine to a dictator or some other shit.

Marty thought of his sticky note wall: right now Marty looked a lot more unstable than the in-betweener.

He brushed his hands through his hair, letting out a slow breath. To the basement. He gripped the doorknob and opened—Ah, shit. That's a closet. Wrong door.

The last door had to be it, and as Marty opened it he stared down the length of a darkened stair, leading into blackness.

The wooden stairs screeched as Marty stepped down them. They were backless, which gave him renewed visions of thrusting hands grabbing his ankles. He used the light on his phone to look around. The basement was unfinished: concrete floors and walls, exposed pipes in the ceiling amid cobwebs. Boxes were stacked on top of each other. The entire place had a smell of mildew. Marty hoped the pocketknife wasn't buried in one of those boxes.

He made a slow tour of the basement. The place was filled with junk. Lamps, kid's toys, a rocking horse, a mattress leaning on the wall, a bike unreachable behind an air conditioner unit.

There were two doorless doorways. One led to the furnace room; Marty had to duck under piping and steel thingamabobs. Nestled in a corner were more boxes, *Christmas lights* written on their sides in sharpie.

The second doorless room was the laundry room. A washer, a dryer, stacked laundry baskets. He opened the closet: old dishes and tablecloths. Marty assumed this was where things went to be forgotten. The layer of dust and the millipede saying hello meant he was probably right.

Marty went back out into the main floor area, passing his light over the boxes. If the pocketknife wasn't upstairs, then it had to be down here somewhere.

He started sidling through the stacked boxes, bending this way and that to get a look behind them or for any labels. He felt like he was searching through three generations' worth of crap.

A typewriter. A lamp that looked like a woman's leg. A clown doll? Eek. A box of G.I. Joes. A toolbox. A box filled with fishing stuff; must have been his dad's or something. Old crayon drawings. Elementary school certificates. Dog toys, aww. More pictures of grandma and grandpa. A baby's crib covered in a tarp, a little creepy. Tricycle. God, John, throw some of this shit away.

Marty sat on one of the boxes, exasperated. This was impossible. There's just too much shit. But a chest pulled Marty's attention. It was rectangular and padded with leather. It had been hidden under one of the boxes Marty had moved. He wiped away a layer of dust and flipped the lid open. More junk.

But sentimental junk?

There was a plastic jar filled with marbles. Pins and buttons with odd patterns. A binder with loose papers and a leather notebook. Marty flipped the notebook open. Oh. It was a journal, the first entry dated 1955. Did it belong to John's dad?

There were more pictures, all of John and his dad. One of them fishing, where a young John looked miserable. Another of them in a zoo. One of them at the Statue of Liberty, and a few others taken around Times Square. A plastic bag filled with brightly coloured fishing lures, a toy boat, a travel book about New York, and—Marty's heart stopped—a pocketknife.

He picked it up, holding it like it was made of glass. Engraved on the wood inlay was, *To John, from Dad.*

This is it. He put the pocketknife in his pocket, and started for the stairs. Movement in his periphery snapped his head around; a figure stood in one of the doorless doorways. Tall, thin, clean shaven. The ghost who'd been with the BOA agents.

"Marty, right? I didn't think we'd find you here." Light arced in from a small two-foot window and the ghost stepped into it, revealing his pallid complexion and sunken eyes. He wore a tailored suit that was ragged around the edges.

"How do you know my name?"

The ghost smirked. "Just a guess. I'm Gil, nice to meet you. You've really fucked up."

"I'm fixing it. I'm going to take care of everything."

Gil, hands in his pockets, stepped forward. "I'm sure you think you are. But you're in over your head, Marty."

"That's what everybody keeps telling me." Marty edged toward the stairs.

"Maybe you should listen to 'everybody.'"

"Or maybe everybody should have some faith in me."

Gil laughed, a half-concealed throaty chuckle. "Doesn't matter how much someone believes in you, jump out of an airplane without a parachute and you're dead."

"It's not that bad, I've almost got it."

"And you trust the Boneman?"

"The in-betweener needs to be sent away. He's hurting people."

"He is." Gil stepped between Marty and the stairs. "But why do you think you can do it?"

Marty bit his lower lip, gnawing the question in his mind.

"The Boneman is using you," Gil said. "Why else would he pick a deadbeat nobody to do this job?"

"Maybe he saw something in me."

Gil bent at the waist, barking a laugh. "If you're really that fucking stupid then we're all dead."

A shadow swept past the window and then was gone. Was that a person? Shit, they're closing in.

"Because the BOA has been doing a great job at dealing with this." Marty edged closer to the stairs.

"Listen, you little shit—"

Marty bull-rushed Gil. The thin ghost couldn't hold his ground against Marty's weight and went tumbling to the floor as Marty clomped up the stairs.

"You're going to regret this, Marty," Gil called from the basement. "The Boneman is going to fuck you over."

Subtlety forgotten, Marty thrust the back door open and ran for the neighbour's yard. He heard raised voices from the house, but he was already turning a corner and out of sight.

It's almost over. I can do this.

MARTY TRUDGED UP the stairs to his apartment. Wallace was there, pacing, muttering to himself.

"Wallace, something wrong?"

Wallace's head darted in Marty's direction, his expression going from angry, to sad, to angry again. Wallace pressed himself against Mrs. Hubbard's door, like he was trying to sink into it.

"What's the matter?" Marty had never seen Wallace so agitated.

A coughing, bent over figure limped from around the upper landing. "Did you get it?" the in-betweener—John McKinsey—asked.

Marty held up the pocketknife, a surge of triumph in the way he brandished it. "I told you I'd do it. Now you have to keep your promise."

The in-betweener limped down the stairs, bubbling black tar dripping from his mouth to the floor. "Yes, I will, I will." He reached out a hand, his fingers bent and stiff. "Give it to me."

Marty gripped the shark tooth dagger in one hand, the pocketknife in the other. He held out the pocketknife.

Stab him, The Boneman's voice rattled inside Marty's head. *Do it now.*

Marty's hand hovered over the in-betweener's. John's red-rimmed eyes were wide, desperate.

Do not give it to him.

"Please," the in-betweener stifled a cough, "just give me this memory of my father."

Stab him, Marty.

Marty's grip on the shark tooth dagger tightened.

Don't trust him Marty. Stab him. Stab him now.

Marty let go of the pocketknife.

NO!

The knife tumbled end over end, landing in the in-betweener's palm. Marty's ears popped, and there was a distant thunderclap.

The in-betweener clutched the pocketknife close to his chest. His pallid skin grew rosy, his coughing subsided, and with a strong arm he wiped away the last of the bubbling tar from his mouth. His eyes were no longer bloodshot and yellow-tinged, but a healthy white. He looked more like John McKinsey and less like the in-betweener.

John breathed deep, and when he breathed out, there was no wheezing cough. "Thank you, Marty. I feel so much better now."

STAB HIM STAB HIM STAB HIM!

Marty held out the shark tooth dagger. "Okay, that's good. Now it's your turn."

John stepped away from Marty. "No, no that's not happening."

"But you—"

"Promised? Kid, you know what? Fuck you. You're not sending me anywhere." John was walking backwards, toward the stairs that led outside. "I don't have to do anything you say. Not now. I'm not going to hell, understand? I'm not going." John turned on his heel and ran for the stairs.

Marty followed, but as John passed Wallace, he raked his fingers through the old ghost's chest. Wallace screamed, a guttural horrifying sound. Marty stopped in his tracks, seeing John running down the stairs in his periphery.

Wallace started to change. His ribs distended, pustules growing between each one, popping as more flesh oozed from the boils. His face tore in half, a coruscating display of tendons shifting and moving as his skull was crushed and reformed into a lopsided shriek. It—Wallace—writhed on the floor as meat popped and squelched and slurped. There were too many mouths, all vomiting pus-filled blisters. Too many eyes, yellow and bloodshot. Too much movement beneath the mound of flesh that had once been his friend.

Marty pressed his back to the wall, afraid to go near the monstrosity, afraid to move. He screamed. He couldn't help it.

The monstrosity slowed, frozen in time. The hallway's lights grew red, and behind the creature stood the Boneman.

"I told you not to trust him," the Boneman said. "This is the consequence. It will happen again, and again."

Marty couldn't find any words. His eyes were locked on the

frozen form of what had been Wallace. He wished he could look away.

"You made a deal, Marty. A favour is owed."

"I'll do it." Marty's voice broke.

The red light faded with the sound of stomping boots. As Marty returned to reality, the grotesque creature before him let out a keening wail of pain that rattled Marty's teeth.

A pair of burly men in suits came up the stairs. Mrs. Hubbard's door started to open, and one of the men grabbed the handle and held it shut. The other stood in the path of the upstairs residents as the voice of the landlady rose in concern.

Another pair of men came up the stairs, carrying hooks attached to chains. They thrust the hooks into the undulating flesh of the thing that had been Wallace, ignoring its scream of pain, and dragged it slopping and squelching down the stairs.

The man holding Mrs. Hubbard's door looked at Marty. "You Marty?"

Marty nodded.

"Get the fuck out of here."

Marty ran down the stairs, slipping on the trail of blood and meaty chunks left behind by the *thing*. He heard the man saying to a worried Mrs. Hubbard, "I'm a police officer, nothing to worry about, please stay inside…"

Marty stumbled out the door, the night's crisp air giving him solace that he wasn't in hell. He saw Wallace's tarp-covered form being stuffed into the back of a van.

The two BOA agents were there: the blonde woman with the buzz cut and the doughy guy.

"Don't you fucking run—" The woman was cut off by Marty dashing away.

He turned to climb over a fence, but a pair of arms wrapped around him, locking his own arms against his torso. He was lifted off the ground, his feet kicking at the air.

"Not this time, fucker," the woman said into his ear.

She tossed him into the back of a van, where a couple of meatheads glared at him.

Marty curled up into a ball and closed his eyes.

Chapter Seven

A Deal's a Deal

MARTY DIDN'T KNOW where they took him. They spoke, but Marty didn't hear any of it, the words distant and muffled by the fog of his mind. He didn't resist when they hauled him out, pushed him through a door and down some stairs, then thrust him into a chair.

They didn't even tie his hands or feet.

The walls and floors were cracked concrete. Overhead, a single light buzzed. It made the room feel sterile. The room was maybe four feet by four feet. No windows, no light switch, no mirrors. Marty scooted his chair back and realized a dark stain rimmed a grated drain set into the floor.

The old, rickety door opened on squeaking hinges. The big buzz-cut blonde woman walked in, dragging a chair behind her. She thumped it in front of Marty and sat with her elbows on her knees.

She held up the shark tooth dagger. "The hell is this?"

"A shark tooth."

"It's a big fucking shark tooth."

Marty shrugged.

She popped her knuckles one by one. "Listen, Marty, we know who you are and that you're fucking around with the Boneman. Make it easy for everybody and just start talking."

Marty thought, maybe in a delirious arrogance incumbent of all humanity, that he was made of tough stuff. That he couldn't be pushed around by a suit, by the government, by anybody. In his mind, he'd puff out his chest, clench his jaw, and not give the coppers a damn thing.

Marty wasn't tough.

He told her everything. At first, his voice cracked, and then it poured out of him in a stream of bleary-eyed tears. He told her about the deal with the Boneman, about the in-betweener, everything.

Most of all, he told her about Wallace. How he'd always tried to be helpful but didn't quite know how. How Marty was sure that if someone said, "This is the right thing to do," Wallace would've done it without thinking. How Wallace was afraid of the same things as the living.

Her glare softened. She leaned back in her chair, her thumb toying with the shark tooth dagger's edge. "This thing paralyzes the 'in-betweener' so he can be sent on to ghosthood?"

Marty nodded.

"And anybody can use it?"

"Uh, I don't know."

She frowned, got up—taking the chair with her—and was out the door. Leaving Marty alone again.

I really fucked this up. A part of him thought the Boneman would answer, but there was nothing. I should've just stabbed him when I had the chance. No deals, no bargaining. Stick it right in his gut, and move on with my life. Not that there'd be much life to move on with after this. Marty bet that Steph and Alhad would never look at him the same again. They'd just see a weird, flaky conspiracy nut. Joe would transcend into a hate-filled deity who could stink-eye so hard Marty would explode.

I hope Abbi's okay. He hadn't had a chance to see her. In a way, he was glad. Better the in-betweener not know that she was associated with him.

The door swung open, and this time it was the doughy guy. He hadn't bothered to bring a chair, just pulled the door shut and stood there. He scratched at a couple days' worth of stubble, looking at Marty like he was roadkill.

"Must have been, uh, rough seeing what you saw," he said in a thick French accent.

Marty didn't answer.

"Why'd you run?"

"I don't know. You had guns and were standing around one of those *things*."

"Yeah, guess so." He tossed Marty's bag at his feet. "Consider yourself off the case. Go home, try to pretend none of this happened."

Thank God. Marty grabbed his bag.

And the memory of a voice reminded him, *You made a deal.* Marty rifled through his stuff: no dagger. "Where's the shark tooth?"

"You're not getting it back."

I made a deal. "I need it."

"You can't handle this. Just go home, forget about it. We're doing you a favour."

I signed a contract in blood. Marty couldn't let it go: he'd signed a contract with a demon, with a hellish arbiter of ghostliness. If he reneged... I don't even know what will happen because I couldn't read the fucking thing.

Marty needed to get his shark tooth dagger back, to fix this. Not because he was the only one who could, but because he'd signed a fucking contract like an idiot and now the thought of failing made his bowels turn to soup.

And he'd just told the BOA everything he knew about the in-betweener, and how to stop him. That meant the BOA was going to try and stop him first. Holy shit. I really fucked this up. Marty's chances of competing with an agency like the Bureau of Otherworldly Affairs was less than slim.

But fuck, he had to try.

There was a bang on the door, and the woman's voice said, "Hurry up, Beaulieu."

"Alright, alright," Beaulieu said. He gestured for Marty to get up. "Don't dally, or Cavanagh will skin you." He chuckled to himself.

Beaulieu opened the door for him. The woman—Cavanagh—her arms crossed, glared at him as he walked back up the stairs into what he assumed was BOA headquarters.

It wasn't much. A large open room of concrete stacked with boxes, crates, barrels—wood, plastic, and steel. People with laptops propped on top of stacks of boxes or papers, exposed wires trailing all over the place.

He scanned the entire mess, but his dagger was nowhere to be seen. Had they already put it in one of those boxes?

Cavanagh grabbed his arm and pulled him toward the exit. In her belt was the shark tooth dagger.

Shit.

He could grab it and run, but he was sure Cavanagh would squish his head with one hand. But there was no other option: he had to do it now or resign himself to the Boneman's wrath.

They were at the exit, Beaulieu holding the door open, Cavanagh pulling Marty along. He could feel the crisp night air on his skin; see the streetlight pouring into the entranceway.

He had one foot past the threshold. Just do it.

Marty shoved his shoulder into Cavanagh, grabbing the dagger at the same time. Cavanagh grunted, caught off guard, and Marty dashed through the door and into the alley. Beaulieu leapt to follow, tripped on the step, and fell face first onto the ground. By the time Cavanagh had lumbered over him, Marty was around the corner and running into the centre of the Place des Arts square. Marty ran around the fountain and made for the metro entrance. He had a lead on her: if he could get inside a Metro car before her he'd be home free.

Cavanagh reached the edge of the fountain, but instead of running around it, she stepped onto its ledge and leaped. She landed with a thud on the other side, only feet away from Marty.

Marty ran through the doors into the Théâtre Maisonneuve, pushing people aside as they cursed at him. He heard an *oomph* as Cavanagh knocked a guy on his ass.

He ran through a tunnel of holographic eyes, all shifting and twirling, covering the floor in shifting threads of light. A look over his shoulder showed him Cavanagh close behind, almost within arm's reach.

Marty's legs pumped, and Cavanagh's hand extended. She grabbed a handful of his hoodie, but he shrugged out of it, running as fast as his pudgy legs could take him.

For a second, Cavanagh stood there, the hoodie in her

clenched fist; Marty swore he could hear her teeth grinding.

Marty ran down the tunnel of little stores, the sound of pounding boots just behind him, yanking his wallet from his pants pocket. He hit the turnstiles, slapping his wallet onto the Opus reader, and stumbled through the bars to the stairs.

Cavanagh didn't bother with an Opus card: she vaulted over the turnstiles.

The Metro car's doors opened, and people piled in. Marty was halfway down the stairs, Cavanagh just reaching the top. He hit the bottom as the doors started to close, and with the last bit of strength he had, he lunged into the Metro car, the doors clipping his shoulder.

They closed behind him just as Cavanagh reached them.

Thank God.

Cavanagh started to pry the doors open.

Holy fuck.

But the train started to move, squealing its way down the tunnel. Cavanagh backed off, and Marty breathed for what felt like the first time in a year. He expected to hear a thud on the Metro's roof, only to look up and see Cavanagh tearing the ceiling open.

Everyone in the Metro car stared at him. He pressed himself into the corner, head down. And after a few minutes everybody forgot he was there.

Chapter Eight

I'm Fine

MARTY WENT TO his parents' house. It was all he could think to do. The BOA probably knew about his parents, but there weren't any black vans in the neighbourhood, so he figured he had a day or two. Or not. He really didn't know. He just couldn't go back to his apartment.

His mom, Izzy, gave him a big hug. She shuttled him inside and insisted he sit and eat, even though he just wanted to go to bed. Her salt and pepper hair was tied into a bun, and as she put an apron on she yelled, "Pat, Marty's here for dinner!"

Marty's dad, Pat, walked out with the loping gait of a wary animal. He hiked up his pants. "What happened?"

"Nothing," Marty said.

"Nothing? Then why are you here? There's got to be something, eh."

"He just came to visit, he's allowed to visit," Izzy said.

"Visit?" The kitchen's light gleamed on his dad's balding pate. "You mean he wants to eat our food. I see how it is."

"Pat, stop it."

Pat quieted, pulling out a chair. "You just going to stand there? Sit down, I'll make some coffee."

Marty sat, hunched over with his elbows on the table. The flower-patterned tablecloth was rough on his skin. He wiped away breadcrumbs.

He kept his head down while his parents had a mumbled argument by the sink. About why the coffee wasn't in the right spot, about how they weren't expecting him and didn't have anything prepared, about why he was there at all. Marty pretended not to hear any of it.

His dad sat down with two cups of coffee, cream, and a porcelain sugar holder. "So, how're things?"

"Fine."

"Fine? Just fine?" Pat sipped his coffee. "You hear that Izzy, everything's fine. Oh, sure, sure."

They were silent. Marty sipped his coffee while his mother prepared a pan of lasagne.

"We should've waited until after to have the coffee," Pat said. "Izzy, why didn't you say something? Now what are we going to do."

"You'll be fine," Izzy said.

Pat leaned in toward Marty, and in a conspiratorial tone said, "Don't blame me."

Marty forced a smile.

They were silent again.

Whiskers jumped onto Marty's lap. Feline eyes rimmed in bright orange fur regarded him, followed by a meow. He scratched her neck and she head-butted his stomach, purring.

"Whiskers missed you," Izzy said.

"Guess so," Marty said.

Pat turned on the TV, and for a half hour they watched *Pawn Stars*, barely a dozen sentences exchanged between them.

The lasagne was good. Marty didn't realize how much he'd missed it. He stuffed it into his face with abandon: it was the only thing that made him feel like things might be okay.

Whiskers kept trying to paw at Marty's food; it used to infuriate him, but now it felt familiar and comfortable. When Pat shooed her away, Marty felt exposed.

When they were done, Izzy made more coffee and they all sat around the table, sipping and watching more TV. Marty dreaded what he was about to ask, but he couldn't go back to his place, at least not for a while.

Whether because the BOA were after him or because of Wallace, he hadn't decided.

He blurted out, "Do you mind if I stay the night?"

Pat glared knives at Izzy, like it was somehow her fault.

"You can stay as long as you want." His mother said it as if she was anticipating an argument.

Pat turned away. "Really, huh? That's how it is. Wow."

Izzy pushed herself away from the table. "We still have some of your old clothes. Give me what you're wearing and I'll wash it."

"You really don't have to," Marty said.

"It's no trouble at all."

"I can just stuff them in a bag and wash them at home."

"Please, just give me your damn clothes to wash."

Marty raised his hands, acquiescing.

Pat slapped his hand on the table. "Good, more work, eh? Because it's not enough, it's never enough."

Marty ignored him and tried not to see the way his mother

flinched. Instead he went upstairs to his room. After a moment, his mother followed, proffering a stack of clothes.

A minute later Marty was wearing a pair of TMNT pajamas that stopped at the shins. Izzy scurried off to wash his clothes.

He sat on his bed, wondering if it had been a mistake to come home. It always turned into an issue, a problem he didn't know how to fix. He gazed at his walls, still plastered with comic book heroes and pictures he'd printed himself. He'd cut them up to make a hodgepodge fresco that looked like the heroes were fighting each other.

Out the window he could see their small backyard. A squirrel pranced along the fence, stopped to look for danger, then continued prancing along. From behind the shrubs emerged a shadowed figure, his body thin, eyes sunken, scalp clean shaven.

It was Gil, the BOA ghost. Gil looked right up at Marty, and shrugged.

The fuck?

Marty didn't have any run left in him. Instead, he went downstairs and slipped on his shoes. Pat was snoring like a diesel engine, slumped on the couch.

Izzy was in the kitchen doing the dishes. "Where're you going?"

"Just the backyard, to get some air."

"I have a sweater you can wear."

"No, I'm fine like this. I'll just be a minute." Marty opened the rickety backdoor, the hinges complaining.

Gil was pacing in a small circle. He didn't look up as Marty made his way down the cement steps and across the yard.

"What are you doing here?" Marty tried to fill it with anger at a stranger stepping onto his parents' property, but it came out whiny.

"We have a file on you. I've got to be honest, it doesn't say much. I suppose that'll change now."

Marty looked over his shoulder, trying to spot the black vans and BOA agents. "I guess I can't hide. So, are your meatheads going to haul me away now?"

"Meatheads, that's funny. No, not yet. Cavanagh hasn't thought to look through your file, and Beaulieu hit his thinking quota last week." Gil smiled to himself. "You're safe for a minute, mostly because you're an annoyance, not a suspect."

"Have there been," Marty swallowed, "more of those monster-things?"

"Haven't checked the news? This one's trending, hot stuff. So far, the theories are"—he counted them off his fingers—"viral disease, escaped mutants, radiation experiments, aliens, and diseased alien mutants."

"Can the BOA stop him?"

"Of course we can. The question is, do you want us to stop him?"

Marty's hands got clammy. "What do you mean?"

"Well, we know you're not working with McKinsey."

"That was a possibility?"

"Sure, couple of ghost talkers want immortality. One helps the other along, the other helps the one prep for his death." Gil shrugged. "Makes more sense than 'idiot man signs deal with ever-living hell spawn.' Seriously, no one warned you about ghosts from the deep?"

"It never came up."

Gil whistled. "Wow, I guess this is what happens when you keep your head in the sand."

"If you're not dragging me away, then why are you here?"

"Why'd you make the deal, sign in blood? It had to be something good. Did he promise you immortality? A comfy spot in ghosthood? To let you see a lost loved one?"

"Um…"

Gil tilted his head, waiting.

"Um…"

Gil whistled. "Nothing? You got nothing. Well, kid, I've been working with the BOA for eighty-four years and you're only the second chump to get weaselled this bad."

"I'm helping people," Marty said under his breath.

"What was that you said? Helping people? Somebody died in a house fire, your apartment friend got transformed into the physical manifestation of eternal torment, and now McKinsey is out in the wild with rosy cheeks and a taste for the everliving. You're not helping anybody."

Marty knuckled tears from his eyes.

"If you cry, I swear to God I will punch you in the mouth."

"I can still fix this," Marty sniffled. "I just have to find the in-betweener."

"There's one reason why I came here by myself." Gil jabbed his finger at Marty. "I know that if you aren't the one to send McKinsey to the afterlife, then the Boneman is going to turn you into sushi."

Marty gulped.

"I'm starting to regret this. But, shit, kid, nobody else cares." Gil stuffed his hands into his pockets. "Cavanagh and Beaulieu aren't on your side, not really. You're an inconvenience, something hampering them from putting McKinsey down. It'd be easier with that dagger, but we have our ways of doing things. That means you're on a timer, kid. Cavanagh's decided it's not worth chasing you around for the dagger. They're going to brute force McKinsey into the afterlife. Good for us, good for ghosts, good for the city. Bad for you."

"So, you're the only one on my side?"

"I'm not on your side. I'm here to tell you that McKinsey's hanging around downtown, don't know why." Gil started to walk away. "Good luck, Marty. I hope you find him before we do."

Gil hopped the fence and sauntered down the lane.

Why was the in-betweener roaming downtown? Maybe Abbi had some clues. He'd go see her in the morning. He also wanted to make sure she was alright. And Carla, and the half-face guy who sold them tea, and everybody else he saw walking the streets.

The back door opened, and Izzy poked her head out. "You're going to catch a cold."

"I'm fine." Marty walked up the concrete steps, letting his mother usher him inside the house.

"I can make you more coffee?"

"No, thanks."

She frowned, wiping her hands on a towel. "And how's work?"

"The same."

"Meet anyone new?"

Translation: Am I getting grandkids soon? "No."

"You're not very talkative."

Marty shrugged. In the background Pat's snoring filled the house like off-key industrial music. "How're you and Dad?"

She waved her hands dismissively. "The same old."

"He still getting on your ass about everything?"

"He's stressed."

"Right."

The conversation petered out from there, and Marty excused himself and trudged up the stairs to his childhood room. Whiskers curled up next to him on his bed. And for the first time in the last couple of days, he dreamed of nothing.

UNTIL HE FOUND himself standing in the middle of a field of black waist-high grass. The sky burned red, the sun a dark-veined dot of orange, the mountains jagged scabs. He heard the Boneman's voice, felt it like the caress of a breeze.

"He has broken it," the Boneman said. "The space between us and you is widening, stretching, consuming. It cannot. This will destroy your world, Marty. It will upend mine. It is unacceptable."

"I'm working on it."

"You've failed twice. Once more and the consequence will be unbearable."

"I know where he is. I'm going to find him."

"Marty, you cannot fail, or there will be nothing left of you."

The voice whispered behind him. He turned instinctively, and his heart hammered in his chest. Hanging from long-dead trees were bodies, flayed and carved and cut open. Marty's eyes trailed the red meat that slopped out of them, the way the eyes stared at him, the way each face looked a mirror of his own.

He woke with a strangled scream. Whiskers mewled at him, rolling over. It was morning, but his room was dark, the sky overcast, and a pitter-patter of rain slapped his window.

Marty reminded himself to breathe, just breathe.

Chapter Nine

Closing In

"What did you do?" Abbi kicked her cart at him. It banged against his shins.

"Ow."

"What did you do?"

"Nothing. Well, maybe something. I was trying to help."

"And?"

"The in-betweener wanted something from his dad, a pocketknife or whatever, and then he'd go willingly. So, uh, I got it for him and he bailed on me."

Abbi glared at him. "Are you serious?"

"Yeah." Marty pulled up his hood. He was standing on a corner just off St. Catherine, and people were staring at the guy talking to himself. He was glad most folks had their heads down and shoulders hunched against the rain.

"I don't even know what that means." Abbi paced around her cart, her intestines looping around themselves. "I mean, you gave him a physical object, and he kept it? I... I don't know what that means."

"Is that not normal?"

"It's really not normal. When you said the Boneman gave you something, I thought it was just because he was from the deep, I didn't—ah shit Marty. I think this is really bad."

"Like how bad?" A thunderclap boomed, and ten seconds later there was a flash of red lightning, illuminating the entire sky. "Is lightning supposed to be red?"

"I don't think so."

"Ah, shit."

"That BOA guy, what did he tell you?"

"Just that the in-betweener was roaming downtown, I don't know why or where."

"Things are tense here, and nobody's talking about it. Everybody's spooked and no one wants to admit it. There's a lot of us who hang around here, and I'm starting to see people freak out."

"Have you seen Carla? She always knows what's going on."

"I've…" Abbi wrapped an intestine around her finger, and then unwrapped and rewrapped it, "I've been freaked out too, okay. I haven't been going far from the café."

"I don't get it. Freaked out how?"

"It's just in the air, Marty. I can feel something bad. Like I'm being watched by a wolf."

"Okay, okay." Marty paced in a small circle. "The BOA is after him too, so we have to find him before they do. We go to Carla and get all the gossip we can, and then… I don't know. We'll look around or something." Marty brushed his hand through his hair, grabbing and pulling as he did so.

"Maybe we should just let the BOA deal with it."

"Abbi, I signed a contract *in blood*. If the BOA deals with it,

I'm going to get carved up."

Abbi rubbed her eyes. "Right, right. I'm sorry. You're right. We can do this, we can do this."

"Um, I mean, you don't have to if you don't want to."

Abbi kicked her cart against his shins.

"Ow."

"Let's go find Carla."

THINGS WERE GETTING weird. The storm clouds overhead had turned a dark inky black, roiling like a sped-up video. Thunder cracked, red lightning following it, and each time the skyscrapers were bathed in a blood-red tinge.

If Marty believed, he would've thought this was the end times.

Carla was eating a bagel from a closed down bagel shop. There were no humans but a pair of ghosts still worked the ovens, a stack of blue-tinged bagels on their counter. The rain pattering on the windows was loud enough to hear inside the building.

"It's scary, you know," Carla said between mouthfuls. "People are disappearing, and after Jean, well, we're afraid to go looking."

"Something happened to Jean?" Abbi asked. She nibbled on a bagel, and Marty cast glances at her intestines, trying to see it travelling its digestive path. He couldn't.

Carla's brows knit, her wrinkled face sagging. "He got turned. It was horrible, all screaming meat and the like. None of us have the stomach to go looking now, we're all huddling in our corners."

"Where was this?" Marty asked.

"Just around the corner on Crescent. You know how Jean likes to mill around with young people, makes him feel less old." Carla stared off at nothing. "I guess I should say liked, he's not around anymore."

Can ghosts die? Marty didn't want to think about it.

"Have there been others?"

"Yes, unfortunately. Those black vans have been driving around like crazy, and all the live people are starting to ask questions and gather around with those phones to try and take pictures."

Marty took out his phone; he'd barely looked at it recently. Eighteen notifications from Steph and Alhad and oh, shit. A missed call from the owner. Marty decided not to listen to the twelve voicemails, and instead opened up his social media. He didn't have to search hard—a bunch of hashtags were trending locally: *monsters, aliens, Montréal Invasion*. They all had posts of people scared, some freaking out, others making jokes (and people self-promoting stuff?) But when Marty went over to the local news sites, there was barely anything. The only mention was the police statement that there was nothing to be worried about, and to stay away from sick animals.

"I guess we're going to have to go looking for him," Marty said.

Carla puffed up her cheeks and harrumphed. "You are not. Whoever's doing this is dangerous."

"I have to." Marty got out of his seat. "Maybe you should stay here," he said to Abbi.

She shot him a scowl and started for the door.

Marty was glad to not be doing this alone.

* * *

MARTY AND ABBI crossed in the middle of the street, ignoring the car honking at him. Everything was dark, the inky black clouds making the store signs shine like beacons. Marty's gaze darted to one side: he'd thought he saw something scurrying. Maybe it had been a mouse.

The black vans were everywhere, parked on corners and driving amidst the traffic. Marty put his hood up and hunched his shoulders.

Crescent was busy like always. The crowds pressed together, students ignored the rain. A pack of too-loud guys shouldered past Marty. There weren't that many ghosts here. Usually they were sprinkled among the people, but now only a few pallid faces bobbed through the foot traffic.

Near the lip of an alley a small crowd had gathered, their phones out. A gaggle of meatheads stood in their way. Marty and Abbi neared. Echoing between the buildings' walls was a shrill, keening wail. Marty peered past the crowd and saw a wriggling tarp half concealed by a dumpster. He looked away. He knew what was under it. If he'd needed any more confirmation, Gil was loitering nearby.

"This must be recent," Marty said. "They haven't hauled it away yet."

"So that means the in-betweener is nearby."

Where would John McKinsey go?

Walking from behind the dumpster was Cavanagh: she cast a wary eye over the crowd.

Marty's eyes hit the floor. He hooked his arm around Abbi's and dragged her away from the crowd.

"What's the—"

"Cavanagh. BOA agent. Big. Scary."

Abbi looked over her shoulder and raised an eyebrow. "Damn."

"Flirt later. If she's here, then the in-betweener has to be nearby. The trail's hot."

"Except we don't know how to follow hot trails."

Marty brushed his hand through his hair, grabbing and pulling as he did so. I don't know either.

"What if we follow the BOA guys?"

Marty looked over his shoulder. "That'd be risky." But it's the only chance we have. "Okay, but we have to stay out of sight, which includes you. I'm pretty sure they can see ghosts."

Marty and Abbi crossed the street then hunched near a car and kept their eyes on the alley. Cavanagh and Beaulieu were having a heated conversation. Both had bags under their eyes.

Gil stared at the monstrosity, hands in his pockets. His gaze passed over the crowd and locked on Marty. Gil's brows knit, his mouth a tight line; he needed to get it done or get out of the way.

Marty's eyes drifted away to the nearby wall. It was shimmering. The bricks rippled like water, and a thin membranous layer began to stretch. A silhouetted inhuman form pressed on the film, claws trying to carve through it. Another flash of lightning, a wash of red, and the wall was just ordinary brick again.

"Did you see that?" Marty asked.

"What?"

"Nothing, never mind."

Cavanagh and Beaulieu left the alley, shoving past the crowd of gawkers. The meatheads remained on guard duty.

Marty and Abbi followed at a distance, weaving around the pedestrians that were roaming the bars and restaurants for a place to unwind, or get drunk, or whatever. The BOA agents turned onto a quieter street. Marty and Abbi watched from the opposite corner, staying near a gathered crowd. Just beyond them were some orange traffic cones and a length of police tape. Marty could guess what was beyond the tape.

"The in-betweener's really been losing it lately. Was all this just today?" Marty asked.

Abbi peered over Marty's shoulder to see the orange cones. "Yeah. What's wrong with him, Marty? Why would he want to do this?"

"Ghost reasons?"

"I've never seen someone this unstable. This shit is on a whole other level."

"Maybe they just didn't have the power to do this."

Screams from down the street, and a surge of bodies tried to run in the opposite direction, pressing Marty against the wall as they pushed past.

Marty turned to see a skyscraper writhing and bubbling over. Thick vivisected chunks of meat bulged from its windows, spilling onto the street. Cars squealed out of the way. The undulating hell-mass stretched right the way across the street, creating a wall of nightmare fifteen stories high.

"Holy fucking shit." Marty started backing away.

A black van screeched to a halt. Cavanagh and Beaulieu jumped in and the van peeled away, toward the writhing mass.

"That's where he is," Abbi said.

Marty's eyes followed the trail of meat at the hell-wall's base.

It spilled over the buildings, into the alley, and to the next street over: St. Catherine.

"Oh fuck." Realization dawned on Marty. "Oh fuck, oh fuck."

"What?"

"That's where Chester's is."

"Oh no!"

Marty shoved his way through the crowd, Abbi just behind him. He tripped on a foot and toppled halfway before Abbi shoved her cart forward in time to catch him. He went face first into wet, cold intestines. If he'd gone over in the surging crowd, he wouldn't make it back up.

Marty ran, huffing and puffing as he reached Chester's back door. Overhead he could see the writhing blister-covered flesh seeping over the roof's lip.

He dashed inside in time to see Joe dart out the front door without looking back.

"Steph? Alhad?" he called.

"*Help!*" Steph called from the kitchen.

Marty ran through the small storage room and into the kitchen, where piles of the flesh had spilled in through the windows. Alhad was trapped from the waist down under a mound of meat. Steph was trying to pull him out, but he was too heavy.

"Oh fuck please fuck no please." Alhad's face was red, his voice tinged with terror.

"Marty, help!" Steph had her arm hooked under Alhad's armpit.

Marty stumbled forward and hooked his arm under Alhad's other pit. His heart hammered in his chest at being this close to the wall of flesh. Each rippling undulation sent electric pings of remembered pain through his body.

Together, Marty and Steph pulled, dragging Alhad free of the mass. Alhad climbed to his feet and backed himself into a corner, his eyes trained on the wall of meat.

"Out, out, everybody out," Marty said. He had to push Alhad toward the back door.

Alhad resisted, trying to run away from the door. And then Marty saw a thin layer of membranous film covering the back door. It was slowly thickening, the encroaching flesh solidifying. Over his shoulder, he saw that the front door was worse. Blisters like stacked boulders were wedged into the doorframe.

Marty realized Abbi had followed him in. "We have to go through it," she said.

"I don't think they can do it."

"They can, and I'll help them."

"Are you sure?"

"Who the fuck are you talking to?" Steph asked.

Marty ignored her. "Okay, do it. I'll be right behind."

"Marty?" Steph said, but then seemed to lose her train of thought. Abbi grabbed Steph's arm and pulled her toward the back door. Steph started walking as though of her own free will. She gripped Alhad's wrist, pulling him along. "You're going to be right behind us, right?"

"Yeah," Marty said.

Abbi went cart first, the rusty metal parting the viscous film. It pressed all around Abbi, and then Steph who shivered, and finally Alhad. Marty had to push him to make him go the whole way. He could see them through the film, distorted but whole in the alley.

He took a step forward, and remembered how it had felt when the walls were closing in on him. How they'd pushed him to his knees, threatened to smother him, consume him.

"Marty, come on." Abbi's words were muffled through the thickening film.

Marty took a deep breath that did little to still his hammering heart, and stepped into the film. A surge of revulsion tempted him to step back, but when his head entered the clear air of the alley, and he saw his friends waiting for him, he stepped through to the other side.

Steph grabbed Marty's arm and started to pull him toward the street.

Abbi grabbed Marty's other arm to hold him still. "Marty, I think the in-betweener is on the other side of this."

Marty's head tilted, up and up and up. The flesh wall was higher now, casting a long shadow over them.

"I can't," Marty said.

"Can't what?" Steph was yanking at his arm.

"I can guide you through, Marty," Abbi insisted.

"We can go around, find another way."

"Marty what's wrong with you?" Steph was smacking his arm, like trying to knock him out of a trance. "Come on."

"If we wait, the BOA will get to him first," Abbi said.

"Fuck." Marty pulled free from Steph. "Fuck."

He took Abbi's hand and let her lead him toward the wall.

"Marty?" Steph was hysterical now, her words borderline screams. "Marty, what the fuck are you doing? Marty, stop! Please stop!"

Abbi's cart plunged into the mass, the vivisected tendons spreading just enough to press against all its edges. Then Abbi stepped into it, and Marty focused on the pale hand in his, leading him toward the undulating wall. As the flesh closed around his fingers, he wanted to pull away, to turn and run, but he kept stepping forward. He felt the pressure on his arm, his shoulder, his torso, and finally his head.

He was submerged, writhing, throbbing flesh pushing on him from all sides. His chest seized. He was suffocating, dying.

"Breathe," Abbi said.

He did, and found the air heavy and moist, but filling his lungs all the same.

"Don't stop moving, don't step backwards. Just keep following me." He could see Abbi's form beyond the pressing blisters. She was distorted and shadowed, but still there, just a few feet ahead of him.

The walls pressed, forcing Marty to slog through the sinuous goo. It parted just enough to let him through, but still squeezed. He tightened his grip on Abbi's hand and reminded himself to breathe.

A raking at his shoulder.

"Don't look," Abbi said.

But Marty turned his head, and through the flesh wall saw a black clawed hand pawing at him. He recoiled, trying to back away, but only pressed himself further into the meat wall.

Abbi quickened her pace, pulling him along faster and faster, too fast. Marty lost his grip, Abbi's hand slipping out of his.

The claws groped at his shoulders, grabbed handfuls of his clothes, and started to pull him toward them. He cried out, "Abbi!" But the throbbing flesh muffled his call. The hands hauled him into the wall, blisters popping and reforming against his body, each sickening squelch making him nauseous.

A pale hand reached through and grabbed hold of his hoodie. "I've got you," Abbie said. "I won't let you go, but you need to step forward."

The black hands were clawing and pulling at Marty, holding him still, threatening to drag him deeper. "I can't."

"You can. One step, and then another. I'm not letting go."

He was afraid to move, any step threatening to shatter his precarious balance, letting the hands overpower him and drag him deep into hellish flesh.

One step. Marty's leg moved like it was being forced through sludge. He felt his foot touch concrete. Abbi's outline was clearer now, her brow creased. And then another. Marty's limbs were heavy under the wall's pressure, but finally he broke free, stepping into the same space as Abbi.

She led him forward, hand still gripping his hoodie. "I'm not letting go."

And a minute later Marty stepped out into open air, gasping as he breathed in.

Abbi stared upward, and Marty followed her gaze. The ghost flesh had spread in a lopsided circle, cutting off this small area from the rest of the city.

"He has to be here," Marty said.

A keening wail filled the alley, joined by a dozen others. It was a guttural cry of pain, primal in its terror. Its shrill shriek was inhuman.

Marty and Abbi walked forward, slowly, tentatively. They saw the first creature around the corner, its body pressed against a wall as though it could retreat within the bricks. The monstrosity wailed, its hundred eyes bloodshot and twitching. As they walked by it, it shrunk within itself like a deflated ball.

Its keening wails became wet whimpers.

There were two more in the street. One vomited innards, and Marty dipped his head behind a car to empty his stomach.

When he turned back, Abbi's eyes were trained on something down the street. "He's there," she said.

Thunder cracked, and the roiling inky black clouds lit up with red flashes of lightning. In the light Marty saw a dozen shapes twisting on the ground. He and Abbi approached slowly, walking past the shrieking mounds of flesh. They were concentrated in a small courtyard between buildings, slurping and sloping on the ground, their distention slapping the pavement.

Sitting in the middle of the courtyard, his head in his hands, was McKinsey—the in-betweener.

Marty gestured for Abbi to stay back: one touch from McKinsey would turn her into one of those monstrosities. He reached into his backpack and drew the shark tooth dagger, clutching it until his knuckles turned white. He walked forward, stepping around the shrieking globs of flesh.

McKinsey raised his head from his hands, eyes going wide with anger at the sight of Marty. "You fucking shit. You little fucking shit. You think you're going to fix this?" He gestured to his victims, to the roiling black clouds. "You don't understand anything."

He got to his feet and marched back and forth, his eyes trained on Marty. "I can hear them, you understand? Whispers coming from the deep. You don't know what it's like, you don't know how it is. I don't have anything, you little fucking shit. I don't fucking have anything. I never have." Spittle ran down his chin, his eyes bloodshot.

"And so it's worth all this? Pain and screaming and torture. It's worth it because what? Because you never got out of your parents' house?"

"You keep your fucking mouth shut."

"Was it really that bad, John? Was it really worth getting this angry?"

McKinsey's hands balled into fists. "You don't fucking *know*. Understand? You just don't. I had nothing, I died with *nothing*. With nobody. I clean other people's shit and all I got for it was nothing, fucking nothing."

"Is that why your brother is taking care of your stuff now? Because you had nothing, because you had no one?"

The veins in McKinsey's neck bulged, and he spoke through clenched teeth. "Why him, eh? Why the fuck does he get to have every-fucking-thing while I clean piss and shit. He didn't deserve it, he didn't fucking deserve anything. No one does, no one gets it. You fucking fuck."

Marty was getting closer, walking slowly. Fifteen feet away, twelve, ten...

"You think you're some kind of hero? Some kind of good guy? You're just another piece of shit living in a shitty apartment like the fucking scumbag motherfucker you are."

"It doesn't matter what I think, John. You're hurting people and you won't stop. So I'm going to stop you."

"It's going to happen to you. I know it will, I can see it. You think you're going to be somebody, but you're a nobody, just like me. And when it comes, you're going to cling just like I am. You're going to understand then, you're going to see what happens." McKinsey's face went red, his eyes wide, his words tinged with untamed rage. "Come on and fucking do it, fucking try."

Marty lunged, dagger upraised.

McKinsey caught his wrist, Marty grabbed McKinsey's shirt, and the two of them grappled with each other. Marty trying to force the dagger into McKinsey's flesh, McKinsey trying to wrap one grasping hand around Marty's throat. They pushed and shoved to the sonorous screeching of the tormented around them. Thunderclaps beat like war drums as lightning painted them red.

Spittle ran down McKinsey's chin as guttural, rasping grunts hissed from between his teeth. Marty's back and arms ached, his muscles tensing, trying to push the dagger just close enough to McKinsey's flesh.

The sounds of a tree trunk snapping, tendons tearing, and wet plops of meat hitting the ground followed by twisting steel and squealing tires. A black van burst from the wall of ghost flesh, skidding to a halt at the courtyard's edge. The doors opened, Cavanagh and Beaulieu barrelling forward.

Oh no.

McKinsey twirled Marty around, holding him like a shield. "You want me, then you have to go through—"

Cavanagh pointed her gun at Marty and pulled the trigger. Searing pain tore through his bicep, and McKinsey let him go, reeling with a cry of surprise. Marty fell to his knees, staring at the blood trickling down his arm. He felt dizzy; even more nauseous.

Beaulieu stood over Marty, gun pointed at his chest. Cavanagh ran past them; in her hands was a wooden spear with a stone blade protruding from a skull's open jaw. Its eyes glowed red with each lightning strike.

Cavanagh's hand outstretched trying to grab McKinsey, and

Beaulieu's head turned away from Marty to watch. Behind him, he heard Abbi calling his name, before her voice was drowned out by the shrieking monsters.

Marty lunged at Beaulieu's knees. He cried out, falling over. Before he could right himself Marty was running for Cavanagh, hoping she wouldn't stick him like a pig on a spit.

McKinsey caught Marty's eyes, and he smiled a knowing smile that seemed to say, you'll do the same as me.

Ignoring the searing pain from his bicep, Marty wrapped his arms around Cavanagh's waist, the entire weight of his body forcing her off balance. She stumbled, falling to the ground, giving McKinsey a chance to run. "You idiot!"

Marty chased after the fleeing in-betweener, reaching out his injured arm and clutching McKinsey's shirt, pulling him to the ground. He raised his shark tooth dagger.

"Please, Marty, don't do this to me. Please." Tears streaked down McKinsey's cheeks, terror in his eyes.

Marty plunged the shark tooth dagger into McKinsey's chest, feeling the sickening way it grated on rib and sank into the meat underneath. Marty let go of the blade and staggered backward.

For a moment, McKinsey didn't move, staring at the hilt protruding from his chest. A crack of thunder and a flash of red that hung in the air like bloody mist. The Boneman stood behind McKinsey, his arms outstretched like a puppeteer. The in-betweener turned, a strangled cry escaping his throat when he saw who was there.

The Boneman flicked his wrist, and McKinsey's arm struck out, ramrod straight. Another flick, and McKinsey's other arm followed suit. The Boneman spread his hands, and McKinsey's arms pulled in opposite directions, stretching his torso wide.

Tears streaked his cheeks; he was begging, pleading, anything but this.

The Boneman twirled his hand, and McKinsey's back bent at the waist with a sickening crack as his spine broke. The Boneman's long skeletal fingers slid between McKinsey's ribs, and he splayed open McKinsey's chest like a boiled lobster.

McKinsey's cries were wet and guttural, burning his throat raw as they were lost among the shrieks of the monstrosities. The Boneman tore out McKinsey's heart, arteries snapping. With a delicate wave of his wrist, the heart disappeared.

A flash of lightning, and McKinsey's body thudded to the ground. Marty blinked, and there was nothing there but a red smear. The Boneman was gone.

Then the blood loss hit him, and Marty fainted.

Chapter Ten

Overcast

BLEARY-EYED, MARTY took in the room. A hospital bed, an IV drip, some monitors, no other beds. *Fancy, I get my own room.* Marty struggled to get up, and a pale hand eased him down. He realized the cart in the corner filled with guts wasn't his. Abbi smiled at him.

"You're fine," Abbi said. "I think they're going to let you out in a day or so."

"Where—"

Abbi shushed him. "There's a meathead outside the door. He can't see me though." She smiled. "I've been eavesdropping. They're going to get the record wiped so nobody knows you were ever shot."

"Goodie."

She shushed him again. "Cavanagh and Beaulieu brought you here in one of their vans, and you should've heard them. I thought they were going to shoot each other. Apparently, you're a pain in the ass."

"And McKinsey?"

"Gone, just… gone."

The door opened, and the meathead peeked in. "You awake?"

Marty groaned. "Yeah."

"Don't be a baby about it, it's just a bullet. You're staying for a couple days and then I'm taking you home." He closed the door.

"Friendly," Marty said.

"Yeah, well, shit almost hit the fan."

"I'm pretty sure it did hit it a couple times." Marty propped himself on his elbow, the one that didn't hurt. "And what happened to all the"—he waved his hand—"stuff."

"Check the news."

Marty reached over to the corner table and grabbed his phone. Local news sites were already reporting a large fire due to an "unusual weather phenomenon."

"So they burned it all?" Marty asked.

"Pretty much. Although," Abbi fidgeted, "they loaded those monster-things into their vans. I can't think why."

Marty didn't want to think about it either. Instead he thumbed through the messages on his phone. Forty-eight missed calls, mostly from Steph, a couple from his parents. He opened his messages, and immediately felt like shit. From Steph:

Just fucking answer me.

Marty please

Marty?

Why the fuck did you do it?

Marty.

And so it went. Marty typed *I'm fine*, and then deleted it. It felt insufficient, and he didn't want to try explaining anything. Instead he set his phone face down on the corner table.

"I guess this means we won?" Marty said.

"I guess. It doesn't feel like it."

They were silent for a time, until Marty said, "I'm fucking hungry."

Abbi laughed.

The door opened, and the meathead peered in. "You say something?"

"No."

He grumbled and closed the door.

Out the window Marty could see that the roiling black clouds were gone. Instead, the sky was simply overcast, rain pitter-pattering on the window. *That's it, I did what the Boneman wanted, I'm free.* He'd fulfilled his contract, signed in blood, and now the Boneman had no hold over him. *Never again,* he promised himself. Only now was the memory of walking the flesh passage coming back to him, of Wallace wailing in the hallway. He wasn't hungry anymore.

"Marty?"

"Hmm."

"You said you did it because you wanted to help people, is that, well, is it true? Or were you just scared?"

"I mean, sure I was scared, but of course I meant it. Why wouldn't I want to help people?"

"Well, you know, we're ghosts. Already dead. Why would you want to help us?"

"We're friends, aren't we? We help each other, that's, like, a thing."

Abbi smiled, brushing hair behind her ear. "Yeah, we're friends."

*   *   *

MARTY, CARLA, AND Abbi sat in their corner on the second floor of Second Cup. Marty sipped a latte, as did Abbi, and Carla had a steaming cup of tea. The burned-face barista who served them seemed to be in better spirits, all the ghosts did. Like a weight had been lifted off their shoulders.

The living were hushed and morose, talking to each other in low whispers and casting nervous glances over their shoulder to the sounds of honking cars or police sirens.

"Fucking clouds, really?" Marty said.

Carla chuckled. "I suppose it's more believable."

The story that had been trotted out by news sites and television pundits was that the whole incident was a unique weather phenomenon. The amorphous ghost flesh a result of 'low lying cloud formations.'

"It's a load of fucking shit, are you kidding me? *Fucking clouds.*"

"Would you believe that it was hell-spawned goo?" Abbi asked.

"There's video!" Albeit, grainy footage with poor light from the storm clouds.

"This is easier for people to understand," Carla said. "They need to reconcile with it, make it sensible. Otherwise, they won't be able to handle it."

The worst part was when people started arguing about it online. Anybody who brought up the idea that it might not be natural was shouted down as a conspiracy nut. They usually got bombarded with images of the ancient alien guy with captions like *clouds, they're made by aliens.*

"It's only been four days and nobody's talking about it anymore," Marty sighed. "I thought it'd have at least a week of staying power." But everybody had moved on to the next viral story.

"It's probably better this way," Abbi said.

Marty ran a hand through his hair. His arm still ached, and it would take a while until it was healed, but he already felt better.

"I think you have to go soon," Carla said. "You don't want to keep the boss waiting."

Marty groaned. The owner wanted to meet with him before Marty's shift.

"You think he's going to be mad?" Abbi asked.

"I don't know. I hope not, but I can't blame him if he is."

Carla patted Marty's hand. "I'm sure it'll be fine."

Ugh.

Carla started to get up. "I could use a refill."

"I can get it for you." Abbi gestured for her to stay seated.

Carla shooed her away. "I can do it myself, and it gives me an excuse to chat up that barista boy." Carla shuffled around the table, taking the stairs slowly, one at a time.

Marty and Abbi sat in silence, both looking out the window and watching people walk by. There'd been a question nagging at the back of Marty's mind.

"Before, when we were talking about ghosts from the deep making deals, I asked if they'd ever approached you."

Abbi hugged herself. "Does it matter?"

"No, I guess not."

A silence stretched between them, one that felt heavy. Finally, Abbi gesture to her cart piled with her innards. "They offered to get rid of that."

"They can do that?"

"They can do a lot of things."

"And you said no?"

Abbi leveled an annoyed stare at Marty. "You saw what making deals with the deep gets you. It's not worth it."

"Right, yeah. Of course."

Abbi rocked her cart back and forth with a toe. "Anyway, I like my cart."

"Yeah, me too."

THE OWNER—MORDECAI—was seven feet tall and nearly as wide. His stomach poured onto the desk, and even sitting down he had to hunch to keep his head from hitting the low-hanging light. He shuffled the myriad of papers on his desk and furrowed his comically bushy eyebrows at Marty.

"You hurt your arm?" Mordecai asked.

"Yeah."

"And you had to go to the hospital for it?"

"Yeah."

"And they kept you for a few days, because you hurt your arm?"

"Yeah."

"Was it broken?"

"No."

The creases in Mordecai's face deepened. "So then why did you have to go to the hospital?"

"Fell on it pretty bad."

"But they kept you there?"

"Yeah." The BOA meathead had made it clear that Marty wasn't supposed to tell anyone he'd been shot, and Marty wasn't in the mood to start breaking rules.

The owner leaned forward, hands clasped on top of the desk. "You know, my father built this place." Technically his father bought it, but whatever, right? "And he trusted it to me, to take care of it. I'm following in his footsteps, see, and I can't let him down." His dad had been the chef and owner. Marty had never seen Mordecai so much as chop vegetables, but he was going to keep his mouth shut. "Now, I need the people working in this restaurant to respect it, to understand that they have responsibilities. It wasn't just the hospital, Marty, you were missing time before then. I know Alhad likes you, but I can't have someone who doesn't respect my business."

"I understand."

"If you can't come in on time and when you're scheduled, then don't come in at all."

"It won't happen again, I promise."

"I don't take promises lightly," Mordecai said. "And I want you to know that if Alhad didn't have a soft spot for you, you'd be gone."

"I understand."

Mordecai turned his attention to his papers, dismissing Marty with a wave.

Marty turned on a heel and left the cramped office.

SOAP UP, SWISH-SWISH, rinse. Marty scrubbed and lathered and scrubbed some more. Alhad was uncharacteristically quiet, and he hadn't said much to Marty since they'd pulled him out from under a pile of blisters. Joe stomped into the kitchen and thrust a pile of dishes onto Marty's station so hard they threatened to crack. Marty gave him the stink eye: he wouldn't forget how Joe had run, leaving Steph and Alhad behind.

Soap up, swish-swish, rinse. It had been a little over a week, and now Marty had realigned into his place of nobody going nowhere. Like a planet orbiting the sun, this was Marty's trajectory.

Soap up. Things could be worse, he could be tormented in some unnamed hellscape by a flayed dude. *Swish-swish.* Washing dishes was pretty easy, though it messed up his back and he had to use embarrassing amounts of hand moisturizer. He felt okay. Not great, not bad, just okay. *Rinse.*

Steph walked up to him, standing about a foot away, leaning on the countertop. He'd mustered a text that read *I'm fine, don't worry. Everything's okay now.* It seemed like she didn't want to talk about what had happened.

"We're going to see a movie," Steph said. "You should come."

Marty was tired; he wanted to go home and collapse into his bed. But Steph had an earnest, worried look. Like they shared a secret and she was afraid of being alone with it.

"Yeah, sure. Sounds cool," Marty said.

MARTY WAS WAITING for the Peel Metro. It was just past midnight and there was still a decent-sized crowd waiting around. Ghosts walked among the living: one a beggar hollering at nobody, another an STM guy who acted like he was on guard duty. Amid the faces Marty glimpsed sunken eyes and a clean-shaven head, but only for a moment.

He spent the train ride looking at his feet until he got off at Jolicoeur. On his way home he caught sight of a familiar-looking beefy dude lingering in front of a *dépanneur*: it was a BOA meathead.

Great, they're following me. This realization didn't shake him to his core like he thought it should. He just wanted to get home and sleep.

Movement in his periphery made his head snap around. Standing behind the window of a duplex was a flayed figure with a skeletal grin.

And then it was gone.

It's the stress, Marty told himself. I just need time to calm down, get myself together.

He walked home with his eyes pinned to the ground.

Marty unlocked the door to his building, holding the handle in place to keep it from wiggling. He trudged up the stairs, trying not to see the wet marks that stained them. As he approached his door, he stopped mid-step. Wallace was staring at Mrs. Hubbard's door.

"Wallace!"

Wallace turned to Marty, his face haunted, impassive. His mouth moved, but no words came.

"Wallace, are you alright?"

Wallace's rheumy eyes grew bleary, deep-set recognition trying to fight its way out. But he just turned back to staring at Mrs. Hubbard's door.

Unsettled, Marty went into his apartment, his mind occupied with thoughts of ghosthood and death as he kicked off his shoes.

He flicked the light on, and a familiar figure sat in his

favourite spot (which was the whole couch). Cavanagh.

She thumbed through her phone, glanced up at him, and then back down to whatever business she was doing.

Finally, Marty said, "You shot me."

"And I'd do it again."

"Is that why you're here?"

Cavanagh smiled at him, bitter and cynical. "You scared?"

Marty didn't answer.

"No, I'm not here to shoot you," she said. "I'm here to tell you a few things." She counted them off on her fingers. "One, we know where you—and everybody that knows you—lives. Two, you're going to stop partaking in any kind of vigilante business, even if it's helping an old ghost lady cross the street, nothing. Three, you hear from the Boneman again you come straight to us. No detours, no handling it on your own, no trying to be a good guy. And four"—she reached into her jacket and took out the shark tooth dagger—"you get anything else like this? You bring it to us, right away. No questions, no stalling. Right. To. Us. Understood?"

"Yeah."

"Give me a little more commitment, Marty."

"Yeah, I understand," he said, a smidge louder.

"I know guys like you, Marty. You want to be the hero, the tough guy, the big dick in the room."

"That's not—"

"Shut up and listen." She pointed at the door. "Your friend outside, what's his name?"

"Wallace."

"You messed him up really bad. You know what happens when a ghost 'dies'?" She didn't wait for an answer. "Neither do we. But I do know that they go somewhere deep and have to crawl their way back out, if they even can. Wallace isn't going to be alright for a long time, maybe forever, and that's on you." She got up and walked toward the door. "Remember, the Boneman comes to you with literally anything, you bring it to us. Otherwise, your little guts-girl might be the next Wallace."

The door thudded behind her.

Marty let out a breath.

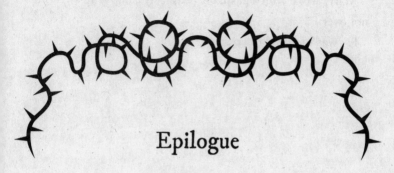

Epilogue

The Deal

BLACK WAIST HIGH grass touched the horizon. The sky burned red, and all around Marty were gnarled trees, their dead branches reaching up, splayed fingers of pleading hands. John McKinsey, the in-betweener, hung from them. His innards spilled onto the grass, blood gone black a long time ago.

The Boneman loomed like a mountain, his body blocking the sun. The bones around his neck rattled like tree trunks in a tornado.

"I'm done, I did what you asked. Deal's over," Marty said.

"It is not over."

Marty felt tremors threatening to shake his body. "I got McKinsey, just like you wanted."

"A favour is paid. Another is owed."

"That's not…"

"You signed the contract, Marty. A favour you have paid, and another is owed."

Marty's heart hammered in his chest. "And then that's it, I'm free?"

Marty woke with a gasp, his bedsheets damp with sweat. It's not over.

He was too tired to cry.

Matthew Marchitto

Matthew Marchitto lives in Montreal, where he spends his time creating fantasy worlds both bizarre and unsettling. His favourite stories are those that can convey a lot with a little. He has self-published two novellas, *Moon Breaker* and *The Horned Scarab*, and is currently working on an epic fantasy novel.

UNMASKED

By Martin Hall

Chapter One

I WAS SILENT and alone, dark against the morning sunlight. The smell of smoke clung to me, as it always does when I retreat to my deepest self.

The dark-haired man strode through the door, hands in his pockets. He walked alone, and no stiff-limbed Cousins stumbled before him smelling of camphor or clove oil to announce his arrival. He came to see me, on his own, and knowing that I was not then myself. It was an act that went beyond daring, a foolhardy thing to do, and he knew it.

It was almost Fifth Bell, when the Sun was at its highest, and I was at my grandfather's old desk. The last of the morning's letters lay at hand, the ink drying on the curls and loops of my grandfather's signature. The pen still rested in my left hand. Looking up at the man in the doorway, my chest tightened. An unease not my own settled with a chill in the pit of my stomach. It was not, understand this, because the man was handsome—though he was—but because his face was bare. I gasped in a voice that was only in part mine, and my hand reached up to touch fingertips to the lacquered and carved dirgewood mask that sat firmly over my own face, leaving only my mouth and chin bare.

"I hope I do not intrude," he said, though the smile tugging at the corners of his mouth told me that he was not sincere. "I come with respect in my heart, and no sword at my hip." Slowly, he held up his hands to show that no weapons were concealed in the tightly fitted sleeves of his tunic. With studied and deliberate formality he turned around, acutely aware of where he stood and how much his life depended on being able to show that he respected the Claimant's office, and that he bore no threat or malice—either from himself or from his kin. He bowed deeply. "I represent myself at Sun's height today, and not the Esteemed House of Verocci."

Numbly, my hands pushed the day's correspondence aside. I steepled my fingers and tilted my chin to stare down my mask's nose at the intruder. My jaw stiffened in contempt at his bare-faced presence. I was unable to escape the voice deep within the dirgewood that dug sharp, cold fingers into my soul.

He is young, the voice hissed, *and he is well-dressed. He has come with silks on his back and rings on his fingers*, it whispered in my heart. *His chosen colours are red and black*, it said, rising like bile in my gorge.

"Verocci," he said out loud through my lips, the first word spoken since the man pushed open the door. The word was a revelation to him—he did not, could not recognise the man bare-faced. Elders rarely concerned themselves with anything beyond colours and masks.

The man in the doorway bowed low to hide a grin. "Perro, of the Name." He straightened his well-tailored jacket with mock solemnity. I let my hands drop to the table, maintaining an air of casual regard as I fought off the nauseating pulse of the Vetruvi Claimant's rage roaring through my blood.

Verocci, he hissed in my own voice-that-was-not-mine, *have no place in the houses of the Vetruvi.* His outrage pounded in my ears. I struggled against the urge to vomit. I reached up to adjust the silken straps that held the dirgewood mask tight against my skin.

"Please," the man said, holding up a hand, "no need to introduce yourself. I speak with Carra Vetruvi, and am honoured to be in her office."

A sharp pain stung the inside of my cheek and I tasted blood on my tongue.

"Verocci dog! You would dare disrespect me so in my own place of business?" I spoke the words unbidden, the thought voiced not my own, as was the custom. I would not speak in the presence of my elders. The fact this Verocci came here, bare-faced, and dared to address me in his presence was insult enough for my family's Claimant. He bid me stand, his hand that was mine hauling open the drawer of my desk that was his. "There is nothing I have to say to you or to your kind," he snarled through my lips.

With some satisfaction he picked out a pistol, easing back the flint as he levelled it at his visitor. Perro was unarmed, and kept his hands respectfully raised as I readied the vicious little weapon. "Leave now," the mask said in my voice, "or I will inform your Advocates where they may find your body. Let them bury you on solid earth, and let what trees grow strive to gather what little wisdom can be found in your empty head." He gave a dismissive snort. The taste of blood was sharp on my tongue, bitter and strong above the numbing distance of dirgewood.

Perro Verocci stepped back. "Peace, honoured Elder. Peace. I came not to speak with you, and certainly not to challenge you. I respect the Vetruvi. I came to you at Sun's height. There is no formal business I wish to conduct, and no challenge I can issue." He looked down for a moment as if uncertain. "I simply came, in my own capacity, to speak with Carra. Please, Per'Secosa of the Vetruvi—I wish to talk to her as a citizen, not as a Claimant." He held up a hand to frame his perfectly sculpted chin. "I wear no mask."

"Claimant." I snorted, the scorn in his voice translating to an ache in my jaw. "As if any Verocci can lay honest claim to the Title." He turned, and I watched from within as he shot a glare at the yellowing map that hung in a heavy frame from one wall. Visible within were the original boundaries of the Dukedom, criss-crossed with amendments and agreements and divisions and secondments.

"As you say," Perro said. "I am no Claimant—I am merely a man."

Young, his voice said inside me. *Young and foolish and Untrusted.* The last word stung: I was Untrusted myself, as were so many others of my family. I felt my skin itch beneath the smooth wood of the mask. I was still for a moment, mastering the anger I felt at his condemnation.

Were he in any other room, Per'Secosa would not have hesitated to pull the trigger and have a detail of servants drag the body away. This office, however—at the Keystone of the Grand Canal, perched over the gates and high enough above the city to be stirred by only fresh breezes—was precious to him. The vases that might be disturbed by the dying man's fall, brought by his ships from countries far beyond the Sun's rising and setting. The carpet where Perro would bleed his last, that he himself had chosen and laid down when he had been courting his first wife, back when he still drew breath. The wallpaper on which the man's blood might spray, exquisitely crafted at great expense to match that which hung on the walls in his own lifetime; he had demanded it be stripped away when its deep blue lustre had faded over the long years.

Deep in the grain of the dirgewood, I could feel the regret and pride of the man who had been Secosa Vetruvi. Behind my eyes a headache gathered, storm-like in its fury. I began to formulate an excuse for getting a drink. Elders were frequently inattentive to the physical requirements of their hosts, and could only be roused from their own interests by a plea for food, water, or rest. Many of them resented their bearers' physicality, scorning their endurance as weakness.

"Per'Secosa." My voice sounded reedy and thin in comparison to my voice as his, as uncertain as the steps of an invalid long confined to their sick-bed and learning to walk anew. He was silent, without and within, biding his time to hear my unwanted words. "Per'Secosa, you see he is unmasked. He is here to see me." The sentiment was alien. It tasted peculiar on my tongue—or on the memory of my tongue, at least, for my words were seldom heard by any but the mask I wore.

The Claimant sniffed. "You say you are here as a citizen?" He cocked my head to one side, looking through me down the length of the pistol at Perro.

"Honoured Elder, I am." His hands were spread wide. Habit kept them away from his hip, though he bore no sword.

Per'Secosa took in the rings he wore—none large enough, nor bearing a sharp enough edge, to deliver a venomous scratch. The experience of centuries of assassinations—successful and unsuccessful, prosecuted and defended—had made the mask quick to see any threat. Yet those years had also made him willing to push at any opportunity.

"So you have no Claim?" I could feel his thin hope that the young man, bereft of his elders' guidance and dominion, would stumble into saying something foolish. Three hundred years separated my ancestor from his flesh—in all that time, neither Vetruvi nor Verocci had managed to mumble our way into forsaking the Claim, at least in any way that the Advocates would support. There were less than five instances, in the entire span of the Dispute, of such a renunciation even being taken as far as Court.

Calaviri, for one, had renounced the Vetruvi Claim in living memory—after he had spent twenty years unmasked in a lightless dungeon. No tree grew over Calaviri's grave, for his kidnapping and the loss of Per'Letoro was seen as his own fault. The Verocci's plot came to nothing, for even the most generously bribed Advocates viewed Calaviri's kidnapping as coercion.

Perro laughed. I was impressed, looking on, at how little he sweated, even with the pistol levelled between his eyes. "I would make no such statement on behalf of myself or my family, living or crafted. Today, honoured Elder, I attend your office to seek a meeting with Carra Vetruvi in her own person as a citizen. I would view it as a boon granted, and would be happy to discuss repayment through our Advocates."

I bridled at his last sentence—I was not some favour to

be haggled over. My own anger brushed against that of Per'Secosa—though his was the centuries-deep indignation that a member of his enemy's family would dare to set foot in his private chambers. My anger was immaterial to him, a lesser thing of little concern. My anger, at least, was my own, and felt for myself. I gritted my teeth, numbly aware of the tense ache of my jaw. "Carra is family," he hissed in my voice. "She is not property. For that insult alone I should kill you."

Inwardly I laughed. Per'Secosa viewed me as he had viewed my father, and generations of Vetruvi-born before us: little more than a frame on which he could hang his enduring ambitions. I swallowed the thought before it could work its way into the grain of the mask. There were secrets we had from each other, of course—we were trained to the masks from infancy, schooled in sharing our worlds with another, far older soul. We learned to keep a little of ourselves back, or we would be like poor Naryana Vetruvi who was lost in the depths of the Elder's memories and emotions. Naryana could tell nobody what day it was, and often called our family by their fathers' names. She spent too much time among the Cousins, whispering secrets nobody else cared to know to those who simply listened mutely, bobbing their heads in a pantomime of agreement.

It amused me that the mask should show such outrage for one it viewed with less enduring affection than it did the furniture in its favourite dining room. I was a component whose ageing and replacement was regarded as nothing more than an inconvenience. If my Grandfather-Looking-Out cared much for our family beyond his devotion to the Dispute, he did not show it, unless he stood to gain by doing so. To him—to all the Elders and the Crones—the families were nothing but a legal requirement, like the filing of a Petition or the seeking of an Opinion.

I twitched in impotent silence, locked inside myself as he glared at Perro Verocci, bare-faced in the house of his family's enemies. I knew my arm was getting tired from holding the pistol rigidly levelled at him; I knew Per'Secosa would barely notice, and certainly he would not care. When I finally slept, the ache would be mine alone to bear.

In the world beyond my little silence, Perro had further prostrated himself. He wove an intricate web of flattery—it impressed the mask, which in turn impressed me. Per'Secosa gave ground, harking back to the shared history of our clans, of how we had made our homes within the Agreed Districts and how we could yet meet on amicable terms, despite all that had passed between us. He puffed out my chest as he would have done were he making a donation to an orphanage or a monastery, and opened the palm of my empty and gloved right hand.

"Speak your terms, then," he said. The words were hardly more than a whisper, my throat dry.

"My terms would not be other than fair—I seek only to trade," said Perro, suddenly returning to older, more formal terms.

"Trade?" The mask's interest was piqued. Regardless of his aspirations, Per'Secosa had been a merchant before he had been anything else. Bargaining ran deep into the grain of his soul. "There are no Contracted terms for trade between us." A sniff, a tightening of the jaw. "You expect me to deal with you without letters, without the involvement of your family's Advocates?" the mask snapped, Per'Secosa's patience fraying.

Perro held up his hands. "True, there are no terms. I am newly arrived in Terazzio, and had I known I would be here before I decided to take a walk through her beautiful streets… Well"—he made a contrite gesture—"I would certainly have written to beg a meeting. My ship"—he paused, cleared his throat—"is tied up at the docks." Perro flashed a grin. "We arrived, as I say, this morning. I came here on my way to announce myself at the Ve… at my family's offices."

"And you sent no word ahead that you would make port here?"

A shrug. "We saw no sails for three days; we took the coast, to catch the trade winds. I carried but little cargo."

"Yet you seek to trade it here."

"At a favourable rate, I assure you."

I could feel his interest tug and gather, my Grandfather-Looking-Out. He was curious. More than that, he was hungry. "What does your ship bear, then, Perro Verocci, and from where?"

The young man's expression was a perfect replica of humility and embarrassment, arranged so as not to betray the triumph he felt. "Calveros. Raw, I'm sorry to say—from Altamiri. Forty weights."

The spirit within me shivered. Per'Secosa could almost smell the spice, mingled with the harbour air of all those years ago when he had walked the City's jetties and wharfs on his own feet. It still thrilled him to strike a deal—particularly for such a large quantity of spice that had not passed through the hands of incompetent Altamiri smoking-houses, thus ruining its value.

"I would be interested," he said. My voice did not suit his flat, affected indifference. "Were you to seek a speedy sale of your goods. If we are to deal, I would know your business with Carra. I would know why you come to me before you come to any House that calls itself friend to your people."

"It would allow me to spend more time at my ease in your city. The Dances are soon, and I am young. Carra and I need to make sure we complement each other well. I could return to my people and say that I was able to unload my goods to a reputable and trustworthy buyer." Perro's eyes flitted from my own to the dull silver barrel of the pistol. My hands sensed the tension in the device, wound to breaking-point, needing only the trigger to be pressed to set the rasp spinning and fire the shot. "But I would have to know such a buyer could be trusted."

So I was to be bartered, then, and for forty weights of discounted spice. The mask was already musing on how and where he would take delivery of the Calveros. I could almost smell it.

The Grandfather-Looking-Out lowered my arm before restoring some semblance of sensation to my limbs. My left arm throbbed, aching and stiff. In my right hand there was only the itch, and Per'Secosa was adept at pushing that away. "Very well," he said. "We will discuss the matter of your Calveros, in this office, at the first Sounding tomorrow morning. You may rest assured you have a dependable buyer. I give my word as Grandfather of the Vetruvi." He drew himself up to his full height—my full height—a less than imposing five feet. Perro betrayed no sign of amusement.

"You are most obliging, Honoured Elder." Perro visibly relaxed.

"Remember that when next your own Elders choose to wear you."

A bow, low and solemn. "I shall, venerable one." The mask—used to centuries of flattery, lies, and betrayal—still loved to soak up praise. The corner of my mouth ticked up in a brief smirk.

My hands reached up to lift the long, heavy curls of my hair and undo the clasp at the nape of my neck. Slowly my senses began to stir as I held onto the straps, reverently cradling the cheeks of the mask in the palms of my hands.

As it fell forward, and I felt the cool air of the room on my skin, I sighed. I closed my eyes for a moment and allowed myself to enjoy the room—the scent of Perro's perfume and of my own, chosen for Per'Secosa's fond memories of the scent rather than for how well it suited me, filled my nostrils. The ticking of the heavy clock in the corner seemed richer when heard with ears that I did not have to share. I opened my eyes and turned to look around the room, moving with the clumsy gracelessness unique to those who spent most of their days masked. I lifted my hand and looked at it in a beam of sunlight, smiling at the motes of dust that drifted aimlessly by. I held up the mask in my right hand, studying its neatly crafted lines and contours, its idealised likeness of our family's deathless patriarch. I stretched, letting loose a long groan as I awoke from his grip and steadied myself against the solid polished wood of his desk.

"Carra?"

Perro Verocci stood expectantly before me. I shook my head and placed Per'Secosa's mask gingerly down. The dirgewood settled on the desk with a bone-hollow click, draped in the black ribbons my attendants had laced behind it that morning. The clock chimed heavily, the drawn-out sound marking the fifth Bell of the day. Across the Grand Piazza, the Civic Carillon took up the song, its high clear notes driving a flock of pigeons off the red tiles of the Collegia's roof.

"I'm sorry," I said, feeling the Sun's gentle warmth on my skin. "It takes me a while to find myself when I lose contact with him. It is not unlike seasickness, and it takes me a moment to recover."

He nodded. "How do you feel now?"

I seized his arm, yanking him forward and pulling him, stumbling, into my arms. I turned my mouth up to his kiss. We held each other in silence before parting, one step back, neither willing to let the other go.

"Better," I said, smiling.

I fell back into his arms again and we held each other in the sunlight, cheek to cheek, no one but ourselves. We spun around, laughing, giddy with who we were.

"I'm sorry," he whispered. "I'm early, I know, but I couldn't bear to stay away from you any longer. Carra..."

"Shut up," I replied, a feral smile on my lips. I pushed Perro back against the heavy wood of the desk and brushed away the papers, sending them fluttering to the sun-streaked carpet below.

We had nothing more to say to each other.

Interlude

The Blood Summer

WHEN I WAS young—no more than seven summers, by my remembrance of it—the last major attempt against our family's lives by the Verocci took place. They moved quickly against each branch—the Senior lost his life out on the Stone Sea, swallowed along with his cargo as his ship burned down to the keel. Mothers, fathers, daughters, and sons—none were safe in those days. The Verocci were pitiless. We all were. No. *They* all were.

Per'Secosa's memories of the Blood Summer, as the gravetenders took to calling it, are entwined with my own half-recalled whispers, the rumours and exaggerations of horrors and outrages that were brought to our doorstep every day.

They said that the Verocci had slaughtered the Patriarch of the Casparians, casting him and his sworn guards into a ravine while still in their coach. It was not long before I learned that it was in fact my family that had done this terrible thing, after the Patriarch met with Antonos Verocci. They also said that we, the Vetruvi, had barricaded the doors of the Monastery of San Arcosa, where

Santos Verocci had claimed sanctuary, before burning it down. That too was a lie, spread to cover the Verocci's looting of the monastery, and Santos' death at the hands of its defenders.

In his grain Per'Secosa felt closer to a settling of the Dispute than he had for two hundred years. The Verocci felt the same way, and so between us our Houses seeded many graves as we grasped at the Dukedom.

The masks, when the Blood Summer was done, felt the price they had paid was too high. Too many of their kind—enemy and kin alike—had been touched by fire. Too many souls had been scattered in ash.

I was playing in the study of my father's summer house at Villa Anora, spinning the globe and studying all the far-off lands that traded goods with us in countries that paid no tribute to our King. It was a red-skied evening late in the Blood Summer. Swordsmen lounged in the porticoes, drinking in silence. I remember little of that night, after the attack—little but shouting, servants and family members running back and forth, and the smoke.

So much smoke.

They said it was one of the servants—one trusted for many long years, yet one able to be turned against their masters. The masks, both Council and Crone, cannot agree on how this happened. A sliver of dirgewood driven into the base of their skull, some say, would make a Vetruvi servant as pliable as a Verocci Cousin. Others presume that the unfortunate's family was used to force them to turn the knife on their masters. None will countenance that perhaps the servant simply despised us. It would be dishonest to claim the Vetruvi were kind and generous masters, and I have learned to save my dishonesties to be used when they will have the greatest effect.

The fire started in the kitchens. Like poison that spreads through the whole body from the smallest of cuts, the Villa Anora was turned from a fortress to a killing floor through the kitchens. The swordsmen sitting out at the gates slumped insensible, drugged by their own wine. Verocci men flitted through passageways burrowed into the Anora's walls to save my family from people like them. Behind it all, the fire burned, hollowing out my father's house and plucking away strand after strand of my people.

I was lost in the villa, deep within halls and passages I did not know, as it filled with smoke and heat. It seemed as if I would never escape, never find my way out to the lush green gardens and never sit beneath the night-blooming flowers that curled their way around my bower. The smoke and flame shrouded the places I remembered, turning my home against me. I ran with tears hot on my cheeks.

It was in the receiving room where my father met his associates that I first felt cool air. The bookcases were already licked by flame, books buckling as the lacquered wood singed beneath them. I had screamed—screamed until my throat was raw, and I fervently believed there could be no more voice left in me to scream. I had never been more afraid. Sniffling, I saw a darkness that promised a way out of the heat. A window had been left open. Smoke probed it hungrily as I ran over to it.

The floor was slick. I fell, hard, and tripped against something heavy. A body slumped against me in the darkness. Fire licked around me. As if in a nightmare, I remember that moment from two perspectives—a frightened child, her hand in the flames, and a dying man, spurred on to a last act by the mask he wore. The stink of smoke and iron was everywhere as the man—as my father—reached out to me. Howling in pain, I reached out with my right arm to a man who had been little more than a silent presence in my life. I screamed louder, my voice cracking, as he pressed the bloody mask into my hand.

As children we were taught to always treasure our Elders. We respected them, even when their voices were not ours to hear. In that moment, as my injured hand gripped the mask and my father slumped back into the smoke and flame, I first knew the silence that would come to dominate my days as the first whispers of my Grandfather-Looking-Out, Per'Secosa Vetruvi, crawled through my skin and into my heart.

I often think back to the moment I burst from the window of the Villa Anora and the smoke peeled away from me. I held the mask in my tiny hands, shaking and alone and frightened, but it felt so good to breathe the clean air as, behind me, my playthings and my home burned to the ground.

I lost four relatives that night. We mourned my father, who had served as Per'Secosa's bearer for over thirty years, as well as Uncle Secorro, who ran back into the house moments before it collapsed, and the masks of Liberi and Papiro, which had been hanging in state for three days following the deaths of their wearers at Court. The loss was bitter, and the pain of losing almost total use of my right hand was hard to bear, but what I recall most of that night was the feeling of breathing free air—of being all but suffocated before a moment of liberation, of life springing once more back into me as I stood on cool grass beneath the stars and knew that I would not die.

I feel it again, every time my own hands take the mask from my face.

Chapter Two

WE FIRST MET years ago, at Court. We were both children without a childhood. I was twelve summers, and had been bearer of the Vetruvi Claimant for five years. I was still getting used to his ways, but in many ways, it is easier for a child—you are cowed, silenced by the mask, and you retreat to a world of your own dreaming, and play there, muffled from the outside while the Elder makes the decisions. You learn something akin to respect. There is little else that you do learn—the Claimant rarely indulges in the business of spending time with their bearer's immediate family, and your education is considered of little consequence when all that the Vetruvi have ever known is at your fingertips.

After the fires and the killings of the Blood Summer, Per'Secosa was left as Ranking Claimant and Grandfather to the Vetruvi clan. Two older siblings, twins whose graves lay beneath the roots of the same tree, had been lost that year. One, Aldanisti, had been struck down by my cousin Valeria, his own bearer— of course, the Curse claimed poor Valeria almost immediately afterwards, withering her away to ash as her spirit was claimed by the blooded dirgewood.

As Grandfather and Claimant, Per'Secosa had a right to be heard before all other family members, living and dead, in legal disputes and diplomatic matters. His Claim—and the Claim of my branch of the family, as he had bonded with me after that night at Villa Anora—had seniority. So it was that we found ourselves at Court, flanked by dusty-robed Advocates bearing rolls of stiff parchment and heavy glass pots of ink. Perro was young and nervous-looking, flanked by a pair of burly, slack-jawed Cousins silent behind cheap porcelain and slivers of dirgewood. Perro's face was entirely hidden by the cumbersome enamelled mask of Antonos Verocci—a crudely carved grey oval with no real attempt to capture the family patriarch's likeness. The only concession to individuality in the Verocci style was the dead man's personal coat of arms picked out in bright shining paint on one cheek like an ornate beauty mark. A spiderweb of cracks spread out over the lacquered surface, mottling the age-old personal sigil of Antonos Verocci. Behind him stood his family's advisors in mute attendance, their own smooth masks embellished only with abstract designs that denoted to which of the Verocci estates they belonged.

I had no idea how long Perro had been bearing Antonos; after five years, I already moved with a confidence that mirrored Per'Secosa's in life. It was a far cry from Perro's clumsy stiffness as bearer of Antonos. None of our family or our retainers had been able to determine beyond doubt whether Antonos' awkward gait was a sign of weakness or a deliberate feint. Antonos had been bound into his sleek grey shell for so long it had been rumoured he was starting to forget things, and that the use of his limbs was largely given over to his bearers. A minor scandal to be sure, but even the hint of blood in the water can rouse the vindictive interest of the Vetruvi. Any advantage, once it can be placed in our hands, is greedily seized upon.

Our family's old motto—*In All Things Can Be Seen the Blade*—was never spoken aloud these days, but it still shaped the thoughts of our Elders. It cut the course of the only decisions that mattered to the Vetruvi.

Perro and I stood before the Judge, each of us flanked by our guards, each of us resplendent in fresh silks dyed in the colours of our families. Through me, Per'Secosa studied the Judge as he blessed the proceedings—a public servant in a bone-white mask with no eyes and a carefully neutral cast to his mouth, he counted off conditions of the Accord on shaking black-gloved fingers as the sunlight passed carelessly over polished dark wooden benches. I was bored, and Grandfather-Looking-Out shared that boredom. He was far more concerned with Antonos than with the bounds and details of the proceedings at hand. Perro, with Antonos' soul clasped over his face, shuffled fitfully and cast furtive glances around the room.

One such glance caught my eye—mine, not Grandfather's—and made the hairs rise on the nape of my neck. My cheeks flushed for a second before I was able to pack the strange feeling away. In the long winter that followed I would take out the feeling and turn it over in my mind when I lay alone at night, the mask safely on the stand beside my bed. I knew in that glance that the young boy wearing Antonos was looking at me. We have ways to tell, though we may be behind the mask. The Untrusted have learned to read each other.

The Judge mediated between the two Houses, adding

conditions and formalities to their interactions. The intention was to reduce our dealings to the most formal manner possible, to avoid a repeat of the Blood Summer. We would have no more of the treachery, as we put it, of the Verocci, nor even the just but brutal retaliation of the Vetruvi for the deaths of our kin. Grandfather-Looking-Out thought our actions the more noble—at least by his standards. While the Verocci had used paid killers and their empty-eyed slaves to bring low our people, we had taken revenge ourselves, and been unafraid to get our hands dirty. As the Judge spoke, Per'Secosa's voice crowed inside my head, reliving the deaths of Verocci scions he had been pleased to cause himself in the days before he had been bonded with one so small and slight as myself. The sensation of my own hands around a man's throat crawled through my fingers, and I fought back a wave of nausea.

"A ball." The words cut across Per'Secosa's murderous daydreams, and he looked over to where Antonos' muffled voice echoed out across the court. "Why not a ball?"

Grandfather-Looking-Out sniffed. I felt the muscles of my back knot and tighten as my lips curled in a sneer.

Antonos spread his hands wide in a fashion that reminded me of the marionettes dancing for street puppeteers. "A ball, every year, at the Royal Court. The expense to be shared equally by both families." It was hard to tell how Antonos thought or felt. The old man's expressionless voice rose from the throat of young Perro Verocci, a dreamer in a trance.

"Why?" My voice had the snap of Per'Secosa's authority to it. It pleased him to see the Verocci guards jerk reflexively forward, hands gripping sword-hilts, at the implication of threat in his word.

"Because we are friends now. We have put the terrible events of our past behind us and must go into the years ahead of us as amicably as possible." Antonos tilted his masked head slowly to one side. As he stepped forward, a trick of the light made the threads of his doublet seem older and more worn than they were. A sheen of scuffed fabric rose from the elbows, and frayed threads danced like ghosts around the buttons. He looked tired.

"Withdraw your Claim, then!" I snapped in retort; Per'Secosa was always ready to twist an imaginary advantage into something with a legal backing.

The Judge raised a black-gloved hand, palm out, to silence us. "The Claim is not under discussion, Per'Secosa Vetruvi. These proceedings are convened to bring an end to undeclared hostilities between the Verocci and Vetruvi clans." His voice was flat, mechanical. Centuries spent studying the law had washed all uncertainty away from him, wearing the rough edges of the Judge smooth and featureless and paring away his doubts. Where others might hesitate over a word, the spirit driving the Judge had no doubts about the legal weight of his every utterance. His every motion was calculated, minimal, measured. Impatience burned in me at such a dismissal.

My fist crashed into the wood of the pulpit. "Yet you allow this to be a fit subject for our discussion? A ball? To what end? That we hold hands and dance? Gossip and eat dainties like womenfolk? Do I need to remind you of my station?"

Perro—Antonos—stood straighter. "I need no more be reminded of your station than of my own. My end, as you put it, is that our children learn to resolve their differences without bloodshed, Per'Secosa. My end is that one day our families will live as friends."

Grandfather-Looking-Out crossed my arms and gave a chilling, mirthless laugh. "You've changed, Antonos. Remember that you killed my son."

"As you killed mine." Antonos drew himself up to his full height. I noticed one hand pressing hard against the carved wooden railing that separated his family's booth from ours. Perro's knuckles were white against the wood. "Yet more killing will not make it better. Let it end here, today, with us."

"I remind you both that you stand in formal Court. This is not the place to openly discuss your vendetta." The Judge shifted in his seat, heavy black robes whispering as he moved. "In the spirit of friendship I will disregard your previous statements. They will be struck from the record." He held up his hand again, and the scraping of a razor across parchment filled the air. "Per'Secosa, Antonos, please. We are old friends. We know each other well. There are more years in us than in all the Untrusted in this court." The Judge stretched out his arms and I saw the pale ancient skin beneath, so totally at odds with his deep, sonorous voice. "Put away your knives, and let the Court attend to the Claim in its course, as the law decrees."

Both men raised their bearers' chins at that—they both knew how easy it was to bribe Arbiters, and how little their work in the Courts had achieved. The Claim was as old as Secosa Vetruvi himself—older yet, and never had the Courts handed Per'Secosa his prize. I could feel the old man's thoughts, angry and implacable, grind their way through my mind. Per'Secosa reached a conclusion that allowed him to twitch my lips up in the ghost of a smile. My hand rose up to stroke and smooth the polished and lacquered moustaches of his mask.

"Very well, Antonos. I accept your terms. Let there be a

grand ball, and let us carry the expense between us. Let the King see that we can be as brothers to each other, and that we are second to none in generosity."

Antonos' featureless mask inclined towards me, and I could feel Perro's eyes on me once more. "Nothing would bring me greater joy, Per'Secosa of the Vetruvi."

The advantage of the Truce Dances, as they became known, lay in the simple fact of the splitting of their expense. In theory, this was meant to accustom the two families to working together, to co-operate in hosting the ball without throwing themselves into debtor's prison. In practice this meant that the organisation of the Dance became another weapon in their age-old war, with both Vetruvi and Verocci laying on ever more sumptuous and extravagant affairs with the hope of humiliating or beggaring their enemies. This was something that the old men—the stewards and treasurers of the Estates—complained bitterly of, though it delighted the young Untrusted who were eager to dance and drink and eat well and flirt dangerously with their peers.

The Truce Dances were masked balls, of course—even the Cadet branches and Lesser Families came in masks, though theirs were simple wood and porcelain and gauze rather than the heavy dirgewood worn by the Noble Houses and the King himself. I sometimes envied them their breezy masks and light, revealing clothes as I stood at the Grand Dais sweating in my buttoned collar and ostentatious dress, knowing that in hours my neck would be stiff and sore when feeling returned to my limbs and I was once more myself.

Aside from everything else the Truce Dances allowed us a brief chance to be ourselves. For a moment the masks were laid aside and the young scions of the Families—the Untrusted—could dance together as themselves. Though I was always careful to hide my excitement from Grandfather, it was the highest point of my year. I was little involved in family feast days and festivals, and the holy days of the High Gods were attended, of course, by Per'Secosa. Any day worth honouring required the Claimant's presence. If there was feasting to be done, I would only taste the memory of the food. At the Dances, however, I could run. I could swing my arms. I could walk on my own in public, unmasked and Untrusted. Once a year, before the eyes of all the Court, I could be free to be simply Carra Vetruvi. For a moment, I could forget what that name entailed. I could enjoy the candlelight and the music until the moment my eyes turned to the Grand Dais and the mask sitting nestled in its velvet-lined case. The candles revealed the watchful eyes and wickedly sharp swords of the King's Guard. Behind them, on the highest level, the King watched from behind his elegant, gleaming golden mask, always silent and all but motionless.

Each year I danced with Perro—never the same dance, and never at the same time. We danced the zarabanda, the musette, the walse—elaborate folies and pavanes that Per'Secosa despised. Perro and I did not formalise our meetings, at least not before the Court. We danced as was polite, and after a while we became old enough to recognise what we meant to each other and bold enough to whisper those words as we spun, hiding them beneath the delicate strains of the music. On the night of the fourth Truce Dance we each excused ourselves separately from the festivities and walked away, eluding our guardians until we came together in a dark, forgotten corner of the Palace.

I was shaking when I pushed open a dusty door and came face-to-face with Perro: of course, Per'Secosa and Antonos had met many times, but Carra and Perro had never spoken privately to one another before. I had no way of knowing if he was being honest, or if his invitation to me was a pretext to kidnap the young and sheltered bearer of Per'Secosa Vetruvi.

The room was dark. A single shaft of moonlight made its way into the chamber, split into jagged arrows by thin and frayed curtains. The furniture, all piled into one corner, was decades or centuries out of fashion.

"Hello?" Ever since I was young—since I took on the mask— my own voice, heard out loud, has seemed strange to me. Whenever I speak my own words, I feel as if I am letting the world hear some great secret that is for me alone. The room echoed with my improper voice. I swallowed, fearing I had been betrayed and angry at myself for slipping too easily into the suspicion that guides every action of my family.

I heard the quiet scuff of a slipper's sole on the bare boards behind me. I spun around, eyes wide. I had not brought a dagger with me—even in the concealed sheath within my bodice that usually held one of the long, slender knives our women habitually carry. There was movement in the darkness. An arm circled my waist, held me gently but tightly. I felt breath on my neck.

"You're trembling."

I closed my eyes and swallowed, willing my childish fear to leave my body. I leaned back against him, feeling the pressure of his arms around me. My hand traced his cuff, slipping beneath the kidskin of his glove to stroke the back of his wrist. I noticed his skin was cold, his body shaking. "So are you."

He laughed at that, a hushed expression of genuine amusement so different to the barks of the centuries-old masks Per'Secosa spent his days talking with. I turned in his arms, the rustle of my skirts sounding unbearably loud amid the dust and greying wood of the small room.

"I didn't think you would come."

I decided to be honest with him. "I feared you would not come alone."

He sagged with relief. "I feared that too." He held out his hand. "Perro."

I smiled. The moonlight turned his dark curls to silver. "Carra."

"Carra." My own name on the lips of another. I turned my chin up to catch his mouth with my own.

"Perro," I murmured as he pulled me close. My eyelids fluttered as his lips traced their way up the bare skin of my arm to my wrist.

We tumbled to the floor together, spluttering in the cloud of dust that our fall brought up. Apologising through covered mouths and in between harsh coughs, we laughed in the dust and then we were silent for a moment, each studying the other intently. I was remembering all the little motions that were his—his and not of the mask—as he was drinking in all that made me Carra and not simply the current bearer of Per'Secosa.

We shuffled across the floor, scraping a path through the dust as we made our way over to an ancient chest decorated in sea-nymphs that were unfashionable even before Antonos Verocci was born. Leaning back against it, we held each other and spoke. We spoke with unfettered honesty and the wild drunken urgency of those long silent. We bared our souls to each other on that night before beating the dust from each other's clothes and heading back along separate darkened corridors to the clamour and heat and light of the Truce Dance.

We met up at the next dance, and at the one after that—though it was on that first night together that Perro and I fell in love.

Chapter Three

YEARS LATER WE lay together on the floor of the Vetruvi family Claimant's office, limbs tangled beneath the great window that looked out over the Grand Canal. I allowed myself a smile, drawing lazy shapes on Perro's chest with my fingertip and feeling the warm sunlight as it traced its way over my feet.

"This is dangerous," I whispered. Beneath the excitement and joy of seeing him once more, of being with him again, was the knowledge that the dark-lacquered mask still sat heavy on the desk above us. In the few nights we had taken together—in all the precious little time that we had—we had never discussed our Duties. Yet, for all we did to live in those moments when we were together and unmasked, I could never shake the feeling of those cold empty eyes fixed on me—on us. They were eyes that could not see without stealing my own sight, home to a soul that would have me cut from the family if I allowed myself a moment of weakness and let him see a memory, or even so much as a daydream, of Perro.

"I know." I curled tighter around Perro as his chest rose and fell with a sigh. "Meeting like this, here…" He encompassed the austere, dark walls of the office with a half-hearted flourish of one hand. Musty shadows gathered in the corners, made darker at each tick of the clock and the glow of the sunlight on our skin.

"No." I cupped his cheek, chiding him gently. "It is dangerous that we meet at all. We know who they are—who *we* are. They cannot tolerate this." I shifted on the floor, my discomfort making a cold knot in my belly. "They will not."

Perro was silent for a long moment. His eyes went to the edge of the desk above us. "Maybe they won't need to tolerate us, Carra. That's why I came. What I wanted to talk to you about."

"I thought you came for me." I almost laughed, despite the gathering sorrow in the room. Even the sunbeams, cut into little columns by the window's frame, grew cold.

"I did." He cleared his throat. "I had something to ask you, Carra—something to say." His tongue darted out to lick at his lips. It struck me that I didn't know Perro well enough to tell if that movement meant he was nervous, and I wondered whether or not even Perro knew.

I became still, like a startled animal unsure whether to bolt or hide. I could feel the words before he said them. I had felt them gather around us for years. I knew they were coming. We had both known, ever since our first dance. I had never figured out whether saying them would be bravery or cowardice.

"Run away with me."

I still gasped. Waiting for years, and it somehow managed to shock me.

"I mean it," he said, putting an arm around my shoulder and cupping my chin. "Carra, my heart… I see you for one night a year, and hardly even that. I see you through his eyes so often.

I feel my heart break when I look on you, when I see your face bent in one of his scowls, or see his curses tumble from your lips. Run away with me, Carra. Come with me to Akasria, or Essenbahr. Somewhere dirgewood doesn't grow, where the King has no power, and where our families will never reach us."

I could feel a tear sting the corner of my eye. I turned away from him. "They'll reach us. Nobody turns against the family—not a bearer, and certainly not the Claimant's bearer. You know there's no way they can allow us to get away. They can't show that kind of weakness. We never have."

Perro slumped back in disgust. "They treat us like a suit of clothes, Carra. We are Untrusted. We mean nothing to them." He pushed himself upright, gathering his clothes and dressing himself as he perched casually on the edge of the desk. "They'll find other bearers if anything happens to us. We don't matter." He turned, pulling his tunic down over his head, and glared down at Per'Secosa's mask. "Carra, without us they're nothing. Without them, we can live."

Scrambling up from the floor, I covered my mouth at his words. My eyes flicked anxiously to the mask sitting in the afternoon Sun.

"He can't hear us," I said, though I all but whispered it. "They are clever, Perro. You know how they think." I folded my hands together, studying them intently. One, smooth and clean, the hand of a young woman of exemplary station, and the other twisted and scarred by flame, marked by my family's legacy. "They will come for us. They know how. They have lived for so long—they have wisdom we don't."

Perro finished fastening his breeches and straightened his stockings. One hand scooped up a neat slipper of the type fashionable among the merchant families of Valtua. "Wisdom?" He uttered a short bark of laughter. "Antonos can barely remember how to walk. If they're so wise, then why have they been killing all of their children for the past three hundred years?"

I couldn't shift my gaze—couldn't look away from my hands. The mottled fingers of my right adjusted the gold chain looped loosely about my left wrist. In my heart I knew it was so— death was all the Families knew, death and the fear of it. Perro saw the Dispute as it was. Two families—two men, in truth—so driven by hatred that even their deaths had not stopped their vendetta. That hate had changed my family, and Perro's. It had changed the world.

"I cannot leave with you now," I whispered. I gathered up my shift and slipped it over my head, fiddling with the knots as I met Perro's gaze. "The guards would never let me away from here bare-faced. They have their orders." I almost smiled. Even now, dishevelled and in a state of undress, I felt safer and more clothed than I ever did while I wore the mask.

"I know." He tilted his head to one side. His dark, mischievous eyes watched me with mournful joy. "I miss you, Carra."

"And I you." I looked him up and down once more—another thought, another memory to keep me company. He had dressed swiftly, and was as impeccable and dashing now as he had been when he first strode through the office door. Pulling the heavy brocade of my formal dress up and into place, I turned my back on him and lowered my head, baring my neck. Instinctively he moved to stand behind me. I felt his breath against the skin of my neck and my resolve almost crumbled.

"I need your help with the laces," I said, my voice cracking.

"Are you sure?" His fingers danced at my hairline, brushing against bark-brown ringlets. "Isn't there anything else I can do? You know my skills lie in the unpicking of knots—not in their making."

I held my breath as his fingers inched around my shoulders. I swatted back at him. "Perro! We've already been too long. Lace me up." I tapped at the back of my bodice and Perro reluctantly set to work.

As he worked I thought in silence, staring out of the window at the narrow barges as they made their slow way upriver from the docks, wallowing under the weight of their cargo.

"When do you want me to come with you?"

He stopped for a moment. "Will you come?"

My shoulders slumped. "I want to. You know I do. I just..."

"You fear you will be caught and punished." I thought of my mother, vanished for years behind some Elder's mask that she could never again remove, locked forever inside herself for a moment's foolishness in defying the Claim. I thought of her dark hair matted beneath buckles and locks, her eyes looking out but never seeing, until all that had been her was worn away like stones in a riverbed.

"Yes." There was no harm in honesty. It was like strong liquor; speaking from my heart, speaking as myself, was intoxicating.

Perro took a deep breath as his nimble fingers threaded the bright colourful laces through my bodice, tightening my dress with a seamstress' care. "As do I, Carra." I felt a tremor run through him. He swallowed. "In three months, Carra, it will be high summer."

"The Truce Dance." I fell silent, trying to coax the words out of him.

"Yes. At the Dance..." He cleared his throat. I could feel the tension, the fear in him. He was torn between telling me everything and bolting for the door.

I had never seen this side of him before.

"That night, when next we see each other, meet me in the kitchens. Bring him." He jabbed a finger at the mask on the desk before us. "I will bring Antonos."

I shivered once more, though the spring sunlight was warm on my bare arms. I knew what he proposed. Each of us could not harm our borne masks without harming ourselves, but a mask that belonged to our enemy's family had no blood connection with our own.

Our enemy's masks—those we could destroy. Those we could burn, casting their dirgewood ghosts out forever.

Perro pulled my laces tight. I gasped as the air was driven from my body.

"Let me think about it, Perro," I said.

"What time is there to think? We will not meet again before the Dance, Carra."

I closed my eyes. Perro was right—there was no time. Our pleasant afternoon together was an aberration of the sort neither of our families would allow again. Per'Secosa's greed would not often overwhelm his caution, and it was unlikely that he would ever allow me so long out of his keeping again. Nor could I see Antonos or the Verocci Crones permitting Perro to walk the streets without at least a pair of Cousins looming over his shoulder.

"Yes." The word made my heart beat faster. Perro's arm circled my waist. "Yes, Perro. I will meet you in the Palace kitchens, on the night of the Dance."

I spun to face him. He planted a gentle kiss on my forehead. "Come at Tenth Bell, at the fullest of the night."

I looked back over the desk—the papers were tidy once more, the Claimant's world back in order. It was as if Perro and I had never been here. To make a place look undisturbed is one of the first skills a bearer masters, though we keep that from our elders. My fingers strayed toward the mask. I turned back for one final glance.

"I love you, Perro."

He bowed his head, a tear glistening in one eye. "And I you."

I touched the mask and the spirit of Per'Secosa rushed impatiently into me. My limbs grew numb as he snatched them from me one by one. My senses dimmed, and my world was once more dark and quiet and small. Within Per'Secosa, Carra looked out on her beloved as the Claimant took his seat.

"Are you still here?" I said, in the voice that was not mine. "Did you get what you wanted?" Grandfather's tone was a vicious barb, my lips rolled back in a cruel smile. "Will you be quite the complement to my bearer at the Dance?"

"My apologies, Per'Secosa. I had a most enlightening talk with Damma Carra Vetruvi. I assure you, we did not speak of family business, and the Claim was not raised."

Per'Secosa rolled my eyes. "That at least is something. The young are full of all manners of idiocy—to throw away so much simply to speak to another foolish child." He wrote out a small slip with a flourish, pushing it across the table at Perro.

"I will expect to take receipt of your forty weights of Calveros, Verocci, at Lightfall on the docks. Our inspectors will be very thorough."

Perro bowed low. "Duly noted—they will find nothing

amiss, and the shipment will not want for a feather of weight, Per'Secosa Vetruvi."

He withdrew with a final flourish, and once again the office was silent apart from the scratching of the pen and the ticking of the clock. Per'Secosa looked down at his papers, his attention drawn to my right hand. My jaw tightened as he turned, looking around the desk for the single black glove he always bade me wear.

It itches, I whispered. The ghost snarled and tugged the glove into place over my fingers, rolling it up past the elbow to cover the puckered, burned flesh. "You are of a Family, Carra. To show such a mark to our enemy..." He trailed off, glaring at the door.

"Disgraceful," muttered Per'Secosa, shaking my head in disgust at the thought of a scion of a Family—even one as despised as the Verocci—making his way bare-faced through streets built on Vetruvi wealth.

If I could have, I would have smiled.

THERE ARE FEW wonders to equal the sights of Terazzio at night. This is as well, for night is the only time I ever get to experience the city as myself—though, of course, such things are not permitted.

The city is grand—impossibly so. Even for one such as I who can lay curdled memories of other, older cities in far distant countries over the place of my birth, and who has hundreds of stolen hours recalled on far shores beyond the Duchy's reach, there is nothing to match Terazzio. The city spreads over the countryside for miles—on a clear day, she is a mosaic of brick and tile, of garden and river and stone and copper that reaches out and grasps her hinterland like a diva drawing back a velvet curtain. At night, those colours are replaced by a shimmering sea of warm, ruddy amber that paints the clouds above with silver and gold. Terazzio is a city of the earth, but her touch is felt among the Heavens themselves.

Terazzio is a city built on trade—at the mouth of the Largo, it straddles the wide delta in a web of bridges and locks and dams. A network of canals, cut by nature and hard work, ferry goods upriver to the Summer Cities. They in their turn bring down wine and olives and cloth from the mountain country that our own family's ships spirit out into the far seas, only to return to port months later, their bellies heavy with Calderan wine and Saskaran pepper.

In the days when Per'Secosa was a young man and alive, Terazzio was already an old city—I sometimes see his memories of it when a scent or a half-familiar face stirs his deep, ancient mind. The Elders in dirgewood have struggled long against the effects of time and rot on the mansions and townhouses and temples and public piazzas of Terazzio, and it surprises me not how little has changed—for very little has, and the city is a place where dirgewood can be happy with life as it once was—but that anything has changed at all. It secretly thrills me that, despite the Elders' efforts to stop time and to keep the city as it was in their day, Terazzio nonetheless grows. The new harbour at Porto Cassare—with its fragile wooden bridges that are pulled up on rude pulleys during the spring flood-tides and its streets that still smell of timber and paint—is one of my favourite places in the city. Per'Secosa hates it—the sharp-roofed little buildings with their high dormers and painted lintels are, to him, squalid and cheap, a blight on the civic honour.

He is forever writing letters to the Commune, offering all sorts of rewards to them if they would but acquiesce and tear down Porto Cassare or the little Church of Alcaron at Novamira, or whatever structure happened to capture his scorn on that morning. It pleases me that they are—to the greatest extent that decorum will allow—politely ignored.

The night after my respite in Perro's arms I was allowed some time to myself. Something was displeasing the Claimant, and he had been grinding his teeth ever since he had finished his letters and contracts for the day and made the journey upriver to the Estate.

Per'Secosa ordered the gates to the Vetruvi grounds locked before passing his mask away to safekeeping deep in the family vault and letting me rest for the night. The ghost needed no sleep—dirgewood is always restless—but he had learned centuries ago to at least show the impression of caring for his bearer. He had no interest in our nights, and forcing us to keep moving despite our exhaustion was considered an act of a low-station Elder.

The last memories of Tollio, who had starved to death while Per'Secosa wore him, were strong enough to etch themselves into the old man's wooden soul. I had felt them myself once, on a dark and lonely night when I was tired and my guard was down, and had no wish to ever experience them again.

Per'Secosa had ordered bedclothes laid out for me, and a fresh bowl of scented water by the dressing table. I splashed the faint aroma of roses onto my cheeks and brow, blinking in the chill as I dabbed at myself with a cloth. When I was sure I was alone—that the guard outside, thinking I had retired for the night, had retreated to the kitchens to raid the cook's supply of brandy—I slipped quietly across the room and opened my wardrobe. Silently I brushed my dresses aside and pulled out a bundle concealed behind my winter hats and scarves. I heaved it up onto the bed and undid the leather thongs that held it shut.

With some pride and pleasure I smoothed out my costume—a battered weatherproofed tricorn, a heavy cloak, a nondescript tunic and breeches, and a pair of scuffed, solid shoes. After dressing I drew out a dark wig, curled and pomaded in a style fashionable a few years ago among the city's young men. Carefully smoothing down my hair, I fixed and pinned the wig in place and let the neat little ponytail stick out from beneath the brim of my hat. I shrugged on the cloak, scooped up one of Per'Secosa's old timepieces, and undid the latch on my window. Catching my foot on a toehold in the vines outside, I pressed myself tight against the wall and climbed quietly and patiently down.

In the distance, I heard the bell in the family's chapel chime four times—Four Bells since Moonrise.

I smiled. If I was lucky, I had four hours. I set off at a sprint for the orchard behind the glasshouse—with a whirl of my cloak I was gone, beyond the family's walls and into the sprawl and noise and clamour and stink of the city at night.

He had not told me where he was staying, but my guess was that Perro—or rather Antonos—would decline to lodge with his cousins in the Casa Serafina. It was well known that Antonos loathed the pious Verocci Crones, and his taste for refinement and music would likely steer him to the Roscovi in the old Harbour district where he could listen to Calimbe's quartet in the evenings.

Now I was well away from the family, I was in no hurry, so I took a longer route over hulking old stone bridges and newer ones of rope and wood that swayed alarmingly high above the canals. I ate a fresh pastry stuffed with honey, cinnamon, and rich stewed apple while dangling my feet over the bank of the Silver Canal at Novamira and drank cheap wine seasoned with cheaper spices in a smoky tavern full of cursing dock workers. I danced to music teased from old fiddles by young sailors and fended off the advances of pretty girls and old men alike.

There is nowhere in the world like Terazzio at night. My hesitancy to rush to Perro may be hard for some to understand, but the world beyond the mask's interests is one that does not exist for the Untrusted in the way that it does for those allowed to live their own lives. Should an apprentice to a miller decide to drink a glass of beer, gulping it hungrily down on a hot summer morning, they can do that. Should a young woman in love dance with her paramour on a sawdust-strewn floor, they can laugh together and enjoy the music and the fire and each other's company. One of us—the children of Vetruvi and Verocci—cannot freely do any such thing. For us, being able to escape, even for a few hours, is a hard-won and rarely spent coin. It is, for us, life.

Besides, dancing and eating and drinking—in short, living a short moment of life as I would want to live it myself—only made my heart race all the more at the thought of seeing my Perro.

I left Novamira contented and warm, with the chill of the spring wind on my cheeks and the fire of the spiced wine tingling in my belly. I took the narrow winding back streets around Altavestra, crossing the sluggish waters of the Septava Canal by the Prayer Bridge. Stopping at the tollbooth under the bell tower of the Temple of the Holy Flame, I slipped a silver coin that had been rubbed as smooth as a pebble into the devotion box. It was supposed to bring me blessings, though in truth the only blessing it brought was a shortcut and a fine view as the fire-monks unlocked the door and parted before me, bowing as I stepped up out of the booth and onto the high bridge.

From the peak of the Prayer Bridge it is possible to see the lights of the Harbour district spread out beneath you like diamonds on velvet. Craning over the parapet I could make out the lights burning in the Roscovi. Carriages—a rarity in Terazzio's cramped streets, and a sign of new-family vulgarity— pulled up alongside to deposit fat, smug-looking merchants whose faces would no doubt be mercifully hidden behind the common oak and ash masks they wore as an affectation. Stifling an excited giggle, I wondered which light in its ornate facade marked Perro's rooms. As I jumped back from the parapet to the walkway, I adjusted my scarf and hat. The Roscovi was busy. I would have to be more careful there than I had been in Novamira, where members of my family rarely ventured among the little low buildings that clustered along the banks of the canals and tidal streams there. I touched a hand to my forehead, absently moving to adjust Per'Secosa's weight against my nose, and almost laughed as the wind tugged at my cloak.

Of course. Without the mask, there was little chance I would be noticed at all. Even my own family members would be hard-pressed to know me without it. Few would claim to know Carra Vetruvi so well—perhaps even none, save for Perro. My cheeks burned at the foolishness of thinking I might be recognised for myself, even if my disguise were anything less than magnificent, which I was unwilling to admit.

I all but skipped over the bridge and down the slippery steps that led to the Harbour district.

The cramped streets that wound through the canalside boundary with Altavestra stank of wharf and fish and the coal that fed the soot-wreathed Saskaran ships that bumped heavy against their stone jetties. I walked with a light step and hat pulled down low, trying not to draw any attention to myself. It was better to appear suspicious on the docks at night than to look innocent—such attempts to defray attention only make it appear you have something to hide.

The night air was heavy and thick around the Harbour, and my wig itched. Choking fumes of Saskaran coal tore at my throat, and the scent of fire caused me to scratch the mottled flesh at the back of my right hand. Hurrying on, I slipped around a lounging group of dock-workers. One of them—a young man, scarcely older than myself—shouted to me, and I felt a prickle of sweat between my shoulder blades.

"Patriciar!" A ripple of laughter rose up from the group. "Patriciar, it's a good night."

It took me a moment to realise the honorific was directed at me—a moment longer than that to understand that the porter raising a bottle by a brazier meant it in earnest. The man raised his eyebrows and beckoned me over to the fire.

"It's been a good day for us, Patriciar. Will you share our fire?"

I counted eight of them—an auspicious number. "Thanks," I said, my voice higher than I would have liked. I kept my hat over my eyes and my cloak hunched over my shoulders as I made my way back to them. They were red-cheeked and laughing—evidently, the bottle of wine they were finishing was not their first of the night.

"How is it with you, gentlemen?" I winced inwardly. My greeting was stiff, formal—the sort of phrase you might consider using to open conversation with a clerk in a counting-house while waiting for the Master to produce your accounts. The porters laughed. I balled a fist, hoping my hands would stop shaking, that my nerve would hold.

"It goes eminently well with us, Nobilus—eminently well." The man holding the bottle performed a loose bow that made him look like a broken marionette. "We have been given a full slate of ships to unload tomorrow, and have done well enough today to earn ourselves a compliment." He raised his eyebrows as his foot tapped at the pile of empty bottles by his feet.

I rubbed my hands together, favouring my chilled left at the fire. One of the men pressed a bottle into my hand. I considered wiping it on my cloak, before dismissing the idea as rude. In a quick motion I brought the bottle to my lips and took a swig.

"Gods!" I all but jumped back from the fire, my eyes watering. The porters burst out laughing as I sputtered and spat, running my tongue over numb lips. "What in—what in the name of the High Ones is that?"

"Strong, isn't it?" I glanced over at the porter to my left—a burly sack of a man with a weather-worn face and eyes that watched me with sharp, focused intent. "Given to us by the House of Verocci this morning, for a job well done." He nodded over at a vast shadow, its spars swaying high above the docks. "Tied up their ship today, brought her cargo ashore—

even picked up a shipwright to attend to the hole she picked up on the way here."

"Hole?" I squinted over at the silhouette of Perro's family ship, noting the intricate tangle of rope and wood that held her in place.

"Run her ragged up the Coast, they did." Another man spoke up, shaking his shaggy head in disbelief. "One storm and they'd be on the bottom."

"And we wouldn't be drinking their whiskey." A third joined in, raising a bottle. "Or whatever this is."

I cleared my throat. "It's not whiskey."

"We bow to your palate, Patriciar."

"Don't defer to me—I don't know what it is." I laughed with them that time, and the drink—whatever it was—unwound the strings that were stitched through me, muscle and bone. "Listen—did they say where she was torn?"

"Torn?"

I looked down. "Holed." Holed—that's what they say now. Nobody speaks of a ship's tearing anymore.

"Close to here, from the looks of her—no further than La Migna, the rocks there." He eyed me, shrewdly. "Why—looking to get trade gossip? We've taken their liquor, we can't spill a word on their cargo."

I held up my hands, the crooked fingers of my right itching inside the glove. "No—nothing like that. I'm just taking to sea in a few days, and it would be good if I knew where I might be in trouble running a light ship."

"Light?" The first man—the one who called me over—snorted. "Who said it was light? Hours we sweated over that ship."

"It was…" I caught myself before I repeated it, before I said something stupid. The ship's master himself had told me he was only running a small cargo of Calveros. "It was just a guess." I held up a hand, passing the bottle along. "I'm not trying to draw it out of you—just idle talk. I thought—if she was running the coast by La Migna…"

"You thought her a smuggler? Her? The *Holy Light?*" A long, drawn-out whistle. "Gods, you're far from your home, sir. What's your trade? Clericus? I bet there's nothing but ink under those gloves."

The *Holy Light*. Ancient as Antonos Verocci, and revered among his clan. Why would I think Perro would be voyaging in any less a vessel? Why did it unsettle me that Antonos' ship lay in our harbour? I nodded, accepting the bottle back and bracing myself for a drink. "You have me. I'm a child of the counting-house." I winced, grimacing as the burning liquor traced its way down my throat. "I'm out for adventure tonight." That much, at least, was true.

In the distance I heard Chapel bells chime, taking up their tune from the Civic Carillon. I wiped my mouth on my sleeve—a motion remembered rather than studied—and passed the bottle back. "Gentlemen, you have been hospitable, and I thank you for that, but I have somewhere I need to be." I produced a stack of jealously hoarded silver coins from my purse—eight, piled neatly one atop another—and held them out. "I return a gift, to thank you for your fire and your good company."

The porters bowed slightly. "Your company and your gift are welcome to us." They murmured the phrase like a prayer, in quiet unison. I weighed the purse in my hand, ensuring that I would have enough for the customary drink of simmering heated wine on top of the gratuity paid out to the hotel's doorman to gain entry, and took my leave of them with a light step, building a path in my memory that would lead me to the warm doors of the Roscovi.

I was scarcely three streets from the Roscovi's doors when I was accosted.

The first fear that anyone of Birth has when travelling incognito is that they have been recognised—prior to the dirgewood, we wore masks in public to ensure that our enemies would not know who we were when we walked abroad on the family's more discreet business. When we travel in disguise we are alone, and we are vulnerable. We do not have the strength and expertise the masks lend us in order to fight for their lives, and we do not have the protection of our guards and servants. All I had was a long-bladed dagger I kept belted at my hip. Should I be attacked, it would not be enough.

I turned a corner, slipping between the crumbling wall of a warehouse and the narrow stem of a guttering street lamp that hissed noisily, like an angry cat. As I walked I heard a sound behind me, hidden beneath the drone of the broken lamp—a sharp rasp of drawn steel cut across the hubbub of the night. Ahead, I could almost make out the strains of the quartet at the Roscovi.

"Fair night." The voice behind me was ragged and deep, an uneven growl that had spent too many years enjoying pipes of ersatz tabac and heavy liquors valued more for their strength than their quality. I sketched a thin, tight smile in place on my lips and turned slowly, my arms at my sides.

"Fair night indeed," I said affably as I turned to take in the two men who stood in the shadows of a nearby alley. Two lengths of sharp iron glinted in their hands, outlined by the weak and stuttering light of the lamp. "Gentlemen." I tugged at the brim of my hat, subconsciously deepening my own voice much as the mask did when it spoke through me.

The shorter of the two stepped forward. He wore a ragged dark scarf bound around the lower part of his face, leaving only his eyes—bruise-dark, worn and desperate—glaring over it at me. "Might be you can make it fairer, lad." His accent was provincial, and his eyes were too much like the taller man's to be coincidental. Brothers, I guessed, and from the hinterland, come to Terazzio to seek their fortune only to crawl inside a glass when they found there was no fortune here to be had. Not for them, nor for any living. All the city's wealth, pouring in and out of the canals and docks and warehouses and counting-houses day and night, was guarded, directed, and ruled by the dead.

Despite the sweat on my gloved palms and the panicked racing of my heart, I almost laughed. Masks alone made money in Terazzio; the footpads' crude scarves hid their features, and they might be their only avenue of income. Masks make money. As above, so below.

I held up my hands. "Peace, friends. I want no trouble."

The tall man shifted, exposing to the lamplight the blade of the old and clumsy-looking sword he carried. It was of poor quality—Per'Secosa would have been outraged to see a length of iron so poorly worked—but it was, above all, long. Long enough to reach me if I bolted.

The little man gestured to my belt. "If you want no trouble you'll hand over any coin you're carrying." He sniffed loudly and raised his own narrow sword. "No notes, no papers."

I held up my hands, keeping them tucked in at my sides. "Of course." I reached over slowly and undid the drawstrings of my purse before drawing it out of the inner pocket of my tunic. I held it up, making sure my hand trembled so that the coins clinked and rattled against each other inside the little anonymous bag of dark kid leather. I held the purse out, trying to make the shaking of my hand appear natural as I looked up and made sure both men were watching it.

"There, look," I said, quietly, as I teased the purse open and let the streetlamp reflect on the thick, old gold coins that lay within. As I spoke the two men edged closer, the points of their swords dropping slightly as they relaxed their guard. I was young, I was obviously frightened, I was compliant. They had no need to fear me. "Here—there's ten of gold and at least twice that much in silver." I licked my lips nervously. "More than enough for you to share." As Per'Secosa had in so many discussions and negotiations through the centuries, I took care to weight my words so my meaning was clear. They both saw the gold, both heard the word 'share'. Both, if my thinking was right, would enjoy sharing such a haul as little as a merchant of my own family would enjoy dividing the profits from a voyage with a partner of upstart or Untrusted status.

The big man punched his comrade in the shoulder. "Told you he was rich."

The little man narrowed his eyes. "Little enough for one dressed finely."

I smiled. "Please." My voice was carefully measured— plaintive, fearful, but not pitched so that my assailants would find it contemptible. Just enough for them to dismiss me. "Please, it's all I have." In truth, I was still wearing a locket around my neck that concealed a miniature portrait of my mother—two facing illustrations, masked and barefaced. Were it to be taken from me, it would mark me out as a Vetruvi and as a woman.

I did not know which fact, if revealed, would put me in greatest peril.

The little man gritted his teeth and swore. I saw his knuckles whiten on the hilt of his sword. I took that moment to relax my grip, and the purse spilled onto the hard cobbles of the street. Gold and silver rang out and flashed as it scattered its load into puddles, mud, and cracks. As the footpads' eyes followed my purse down I didn't waste a moment. I took to my heels and fled down narrow alleys and the unguarded hallways of damp tenements, hoping to wind my way back to the main thoroughfare without being caught. Behind me, I heard muffled curses punctuated with the sound of a single meaty-sounding punch being thrown.

I did not dare to stop, to turn and look. I simply chalked up the loss of my squirrelled funds to bad luck and ran, cloak flapping and lungs burning, until I reached the Roscovi.

Interlude

Interlude

Cassamaura

I OFTEN DREAM of sand, of the harsh Sun, or the grey ocean, or winds that tear at my eyes and throat. I can feel the wind, smell the cook-fires of peoples long vanished; I can squint against a Sun that never blinded me. To me—to Carra Vetruvi—these places do not exist, and all I can remember of their textures and sounds and smells in my own right is the smooth, age-worn lacquer of the lopsided globe that sat on the heavy oak desk in the scholars' room at the Villa Anora against a child's fingertips. Yet still I dream, even bare-faced and at night, of places where I have never been, of memories that are precious to Per'Secosa Vetruvi and which sit heavy and sour and cherished within my soul.

I came of age after the Blood Summer, living a life under guard. As bearer of the Claimant, I have left Terazzio's jurisdiction only twice. I have journeyed to the Palace to pay tribute to the King on the passing of a bearer, and spent three nights within the narrow confines of its lightless, sepulchral passages. The screams that herald the coronation are terrible to hear, and they echo for hours through Palace, reaching even the Visitors' towers.

My other trip beyond the marches of the City was to the Silvia Torranto, when Per'Secosa took it upon himself to attempt a hunting expedition. Being by inclination right-handed and by nature disinterested in the tall pines of the Torranto, the Grandfather-Looking-Out had little success as a huntsman in my body, and allowed me some time to walk the woods while flanked at a discreet distance by a number of the Vetruvi huntsmen in their red brocade coats. I think fondly of the woods, of coming unexpectedly upon a stream and wading barefoot into it—I remember the feel of the smooth stones against the soles of my feet, and the cold spring breeze against my cheek. The scent of the pines was sharp in the air, strong enough to ward away the more familiar tang of gunpowder and blood. There was sunlight, and for a moment I could almost forget everything.

Yet it is not the Torranto's pines my soul walks among in dreams, nor is it the deck of the *Cavalleri*, the family's treasured flagship. When I sleep, I dream of Cassamaura, its houses white and smooth as pearls strung out along the Southern Cape. I can see the tall pillars, representations of the Cassari gods carved along their length, that guard the sharp rocks pulled tight around the harbour mouth. At the Arch of the Honest Man, by a cramped little booth hunched at its roots where a single monk sits and passes out a spoonful of salt to visitors, I rub my hands together and feel the grains against skin that has never been my own. As I step into the city proper and away from the harbour, the scent of salt and fish and wood is swept away by the smells of the city—of beasts, such as camels and horses, rarely seen in Terazzio, of roasting meat and fresh fruit, of perfume and sweat and life—life unseen among the children of the Great Houses. Sunlight on walls of white stone and the far-off chimes of temple bells.

If I am lucky, that is the extent of my dream. If it is my own soul that walks Cassamaura's streets, that climbs moss-lined stairs to stand on the roof of a trading-house and calls out to the sunset, I see no more.

The ghost hates Cassamaura, more than he hates any other city. He hates the Whispering Bowls that sit by the wells in each District of the city—carved drums of smooth black stone where Cassamaura's ghosts come to counsel anyone who can spare them a drop of blood. Per'Secosa, if he scents Cassamaura in my thoughts, will turn his remembered steps away from the Sun and the scents I find too enticing and bring our shared mind to darker places—to courtesans bedded for sport, to drunken fights and punches thrown as a young sailor on the saffron streets. Often he thinks back to the Moon on the waters of the Eternal Bay.

It was a night, some hundreds of years ago, when Per'Secosa was dirgewood but his memories have muddied and lost the face on which he perched, and the old man sat hunched over a rough wooden chest. Around him, Cassamaura slept—the inhabitants fasted, and prayers were being said for the procession that would begin at sunrise. A dagger gleamed in Per'Secosa's hand, and two Cousins stood silent beside him, the moonlight glinting from the stylised noses and mouthless shovel-wide jaws of the masks that drove their stiff limbs. Per'Secosa's blood was high—it was a good night for murder. He had lost face in the market of Cassamaura that morning—

had to withdraw from a bargain, been painted a liar and a cheat, red-faced and with his nose to the ground.

In the chest, held uncomplaining and low to the ground by the two straining Cousins, lay a Vetruvi's revenge.

"Well met," said Per'Secosa—in his memory his voice is his own, as it was in his life in the flesh. Whoever bore him in those days was long gone, washed away by the dirgewood's heart. As, no doubt, would be my fate.

He levered the chest open. Within lay a single stone bowl, carved without a single chisel-mark and smooth as a river-pebble. It seemed to drink the moonlight. The dagger gleamed silver above it, yet the shadows only grew thicker around the bowl. Per'Secosa drew out a purse from his belt; I can feel the simple felt of it, stiff and wet against his fingers and heavy with its smell of iron. On that night, when the people of a far-off city fasted and prayed, Per'Secosa Vetruvi took a severed finger from the purse—a human finger, paler than it had ever been in life, its end dark as sealing-wax, a bone pink and splintered jutting from the ragged edge. With a careless flick of his wrist, he ran the finger around the lip of the bowl, daubing the stone with clotting, dark blood, and hunched low over the Whispering Bowl as it hissed and murmured to life.

The bowl spoke Cassari—they all did, keeping only to their own kin much as our own Masks do—and the susurrating words were lost against the tide. Per'Secosa grinned, the blade of his dagger tapping against the black stone.

"I know your tongue, spirit. You blackened my name in public. You put the name of Vetruvi beneath a cloud. The Vetruvi name—my name—does not go unavenged." He spat over the side of the jetty, a silent jet of thick, blood-tinged phlegm. Wiping his lips on his sleeve, he turned back to the chest and scraped an insolent furrow along the sacred untouched inner surface of the Whispering Bowl.

"This is how you choose to revere your dead—with offerings of blood and muttering stone. Helpless to do anything but whisper at your Untrusted. How was it that this place was once thought great?"

The bowl spoke, its words little above the moan of a breeze over open water. Per'Secosa laughed, shifting to place his weight on one boot and lean heavily over the bowl. "We are blessed, spirit. We walk, we think, we live again and again." He punctuated his sentence with well-timed heavy stamps on the rim of the bowl. "I can see things, sad creature, that you cannot. Do you know what we Vetruvi believe?" He brandished the dagger as if it were evidence in court, rather than a threat. "We believe in the blade. But what good would the blade do against you? All the blade can do is open the skin of the living to feed you."

Per'Secosa tossed the severed finger carelessly into the bowl, where it was swallowed by the deep shadows gathering in the heart of the cold stone. "But there is more than one blade, creature. We believe in the blade because the blade is cruel. All that will protect our family—our Claim—is cruelty. So think on that, whisperer. Think hard on it, for you will have a long time to consider my words."

He stepped back, his flesh face as impassive as the dirgewood perched upon it. In Per'Secosa's memories—in my dreams—it is the cold satisfaction of this moment that brings bile to the back of my throat. The old man turned to the two Cousins flanking the chest. "Row this out beyond the rocks, and let the sea have it." Removing a glove, he placed his hand palm-up on the forehead of each attendant's mask in turn. "I am understood."

"Yes." The Cousins' voices were dry as reeds.

In my dreams, Per'Secosa doesn't watch as they take their leave, dragging the heavy stone bowl with them, wreathed in its chill and whispers that push away the promise of summer in the night air. He looks back over Cassamaura and feels a sadness—a regret that the voice which insulted his House and his Name cannot beg or cry out for a mercy he never cares to give.

Per'Secosa has made the House of Vetruvi strong. But out beyond the harbour rocks at Cassamaura, in the cold depths of the ocean, a bowl of smooth black stone is being worn slowly away by sand and tide, and I know that it feels fear.

Chapter Four

THE ROSCOVI HOTEL is considered one of the finest establishments in Terazzio; perched advantageously close to one of the oldest and most prestigious docks in the city, the Roscovi began life as a clearing-house for smugglers operating along the coast. When Per'Secosa drew breath, traders from other countries frequently mistook it for the harbour offices—indeed, it was said that more trade was conducted in the Roscovi's dining rooms than in the harbourmaster's chambers. Eventually it became too prominent, too much of a feature of city life, to exist as home for a collective of fences and suppliers and it became respectable. The hotel's owners had gold enough to make it tasteful and were more than daring enough to make it fashionable.

The hotel's owners, as it passed down through generation after generation and its status rose from grubby to questionable to necessary to respected, maintained a reputation for discretion. Their particular gift was for ensuring that a deal made on the Roscovi's premises was respected, and that even rivals had cause to meet in its cosy, well-appointed rooms. Deals had been made between Vetruvi and Verocci at tables laid with dainties first made fashionable centuries ago, and no blood had been shed on its floors. To both families—to all of the monied dead of Terazzio—the Roscovi was considered sacrosanct. Better, it was useful.

It has not remained as bold and vivid as once it was, of course—the masks like things to be as they were, and unfamiliar music and strange food unsettle them, for they have no place in their wooden memories. The vibrant, striking façade of the Roscovi became no place for innovation—as less fashionable establishments aped its style to attract its clients, it faded into the city's landscape, cementing its place by being first and grandest among its peers. So the Roscovi has become the place where quartets ply their trade, and is recognised as the finest establishment in the Duchy for a talented musician with a knack for breathing new life into treasured pieces like Alca'ir's *Shivernacht* or Demerek's *Fifth*. Calimbe's players had been in residence at the Roscovi for a year—a feat almost unheard of within the memory of the living. As neutral ground, I had visited it on many an occasion. Even Per'Secosa, less given to sentiment than was usual among the dead and with little taste for music, was known to dally in the chamber when Calimbe took up her viol.

I watched the grand entrance, propped up against a streetlamp on the other side of the street, my cloak and hat painted with its greasy yellow light. The Roscovi fronted the Boulevard—the street had never needed another name, for it was the only one wide enough in the city for a wagon to pass down unhindered.

The strains of one of the lesser-known of Velmet's pieces were barely audible over the rumble of iron-shod wheels on the cobbled road. I frowned and tapped the toe of my boot against the iron base of the lamp.

There were two keys that would open the doors to the Roscovi for me—my coin, and my name. My coin was behind me, already being spent by either one or both of my assailants. I did not regret scattering it, and was not angry at myself, but I was not fool enough to think that my plan for the evening had not been complicated by its loss. My name, unfortunately, was even more lost to me than the money I had tossed at my feet. All I had to do was slip the locket out from beneath my scarf and I would once more be Carra Vetruvi. Doing so, I could easily breeze through the great archway of the Roscovi to be met by the building's illustrious proprietor, who would bow before me and escort me to their finest table and gift me a bottle of their finest wine—all for the honour of having me walk through their door. I could sit at the heart of the establishment, with a fine view of the performers and my head held high as one of the City's most prominent figures.

Of course, there would be some supposition as to why I was there without escort. There would also be curiosity as to why I was dressed in man's clothes. Indeed, gossips would be unable to do anything but consider, on top of all the other outlandish aspects of my presence, why my face was bare—why I was there as the social unknown Carra Vetruvi rather than as the Claimant and Patriarch of the Vetruvi Clan, honoured Per'Secosa.

It would have been at least moderately beneficial to the Verocci to make sure I met with an accident—either just outside the Roscovi's doors, or at some point on my way back to the Vetruvi Estate. That same Estate, of course, was where my family and Per'Secosa's retainers currently supposed me to be held, resting before the mask took me up again at sunrise tomorrow.

So I could not pay for a table—nor even for a glass at the long lacquered bar—and I could not trade on my reputation. The night was mild and starry, and the taste of apples and spiced wine had long since curdled on my tongue. In truth, I was not sure whether I could go on and look for Perro in the Roscovi, or if I even had courage enough to turn back and slink away to my cold, dark room above the rambling vines. So I sat across the Boulevard with my hat pulled down low over my eyes and watched the carriages come and go while I fought against my own nerves and waited for fate to make my decision for me.

After five minutes or so by the hotel's lamplit clock, I cursed quietly under my breath, furious at my own timidity. Tugging my cloak close around my shoulders I swept over the Boulevard, weaving between revellers and carriages as I slipped around the side of the Roscovi and into the tangled alleys that piled up behind it.

My nose led me to the kitchen door—the sharp-sweet smell of mouldering rubbish mixed with the warm aroma of vanilla-laced cakes baking. I stepped gingerly through low mounds of rotting grey waste, navigating the vermin that were too bold or too hungry to flee at my presence. Pausing as I raised a hand to rap on the door, I considered whether it would be better to charm my way past the cooks or to gain entry by arousing their sympathy. I rapped weakly on the door, drew my cloak up around my throat and hunched my shoulders, affecting a wide-eyed desperation as I shivered amid the establishment's

trash. Sympathy, I figured, would get me substantially further than charm.

I had no illusions about my skill as a lothario. My life is more sheltered than a Veldrish priest's—the sect who spend their every waking moment copying out a mad god's sing-song prophecies, only to stack them dusty and unread in their Great Library. I did not seriously entertain, despite my courtship with Perro, that I would be able to charm a kitchen-servant into letting me warm myself by their fire.

The door swung open and I was confronted by a woman not much older than I; harried and grey-faced, with a sheen of sweat and untidy dark hair crammed under a tight-fitting cloth cap. She looked askance at me as I coughed and shivered in the night.

"Please, miss—madam." I remembered my place and touched the peak of my hat. "I heard music. May I sit by your fire a moment and rest?"

The kitchen maid drew back. As she stepped into full view I caught sight of a heavy thick-bladed knife in her hand, but her eyes were not hard. She gave the faint ghost of a smile. "Have you found some bad luck, lad?"

"You might say that." I nodded miserably, feeling an angry shame curdle inside me. After my masquerade tonight, I would return to my home and sleep in clean sheets and eat well. She would go home to cold and hunger.

I reached up and my fingers brushed against my own skin. She would be cold and hungry, but she would never know the weight of dirgewood on her brow. She would never understand what it was to be pushed into darkness and silence by those who had died long years ago.

Perhaps my lot was not so much better than hers.

"May I come in?" I dared to sound hopeful.

She gave her assent and drew back. "Come on. I'll get you a hot drink." I slipped past her into the narrow unpainted hall and she closed the door behind me. "You're lucky I was passing," she said. "I hardly heard you."

"I wasn't sure if I should knock."

She thought for a moment. "Probably not. This is a respectable place—the quality come here." She jerked a thumb up at the low ceiling. "Three masks in tonight. Four if you count the one who brought his in a bag." She raised her eyebrows.

"He wasn't wearing it?" I sounded scandalised.

"It would be a crime if he did. He's a handsome-looking man." She shook her head ruefully for a moment before remembering she was speaking to a stranger—a stranger, further, who was incapable of hiding how pleased he was to hear of a handsome man staying at the Roscovi with a mask he did not wear. The servant clapped her hand over her mouth. "I misspoke. Your pardon."

I held up a hand and coughed, using the excuse to try to regain my composure. "I heard nothing," I said.

The woman looked at me uncertainly. For a moment she seemed to remember the heavy kitchen knife she held. "I'm Serra." She held out a hand uncertainly.

I bowed low. "Carrym." My coachman's name—I had used it before, and it came easily to me. "Thank you for your hospitality."

Serra smiled as I took her hand and held it for a brief, formal second. "Let's get you something to eat. I'll ask Kellyk. Maybe there's work."

I glanced down uncertainly at my tunic, still clean despite the night's misfortune. "I owe you much," I said with a nervous grin as I rubbed my hands together.

Within a few minutes I sat on a creaking wooden stool by the heat of the Roscovi's great stove, a comically dainty cup of warm milk in my grubby hand. I held it gingerly and watched Serra, the cooks, and the serving staff come and go in a loud, chaotic whirl of sound and scents. My stomach grumbled as I remembered how little Per'Secosa had taken for his dinner— and how bland his meal was. I had done little more than look for treats; nothing I had taken had really filled my belly. The kitchens at the Roscovi were a dark, fire-red labyrinth of spices and roasting meat by comparison with Per'Secosa's austere diet. I gave serious consideration to putting a heavy, satisfying dinner on my family's account at the establishment.

Instead I sipped my milk quietly and watched and waited until I had become just a bedraggled, quiet feature of the corner of the room. Serra forgot about me in time, and I heard her laugh loudly, joking with her friends about the foibles and demands of the nobility. One of the footmen had her doubled over in gales of laughter, wiping tears from her cheeks, as he mimicked Pater Achenaris's laboured nasal style. Achenaris was three generations past his prime, his mask bearing signs of worm-rot, and utterly lacked the moral fibre his fortune was based on chastising his flock about. He had had several meetings with Per'Secosa to solicit funds, despite the Vetruvi having no interest in his faith or his help. I hated the way he leered at me.

I enjoyed the footman's mockery of the stumbling old lecher. Were it not likely to result in his public strangulation, the man could have taken it to the stage. It was all I could do to bite my lip and let it wash over me, to not laugh and draw attention to myself as I wished them to forget me.

I took a sip of warm milk and wondered if anyone had a similarly cutting impression of Per'Secosa. I wondered how he would be seen and mocked by the people he saw as beneath his notice—not even Untrusted, but rather invisible. I doubted that anyone would want or be able to impersonate Carra Vetruvi.

Time passed, and the fire burned low. My heart raced—I could feel the minutes cutting into my precious time. Were I to be discovered abroad in the city, the family might feel it would be safer to have me kept under house arrest when I was unmasked. Per'Secosa would certainly have preferred it. I peeked out from under the brim of my hat. Serra was gone—only one member of the house's staff remained in that dim corner of the kitchens, absorbed entirely in polishing the thin-stemmed crystal bowls from which the sharp tongue-biting liqueurs of Varkos were drunk. I stood slowly and slipped off my cloak, hanging it on a peg behind the stool. I left the hat behind, smoothing my wig into place. By the kitchen's light, I judged it adequate—I had no idea how well it would look under the Roscovi's lamps. The hat, on the other hand, would see me ejected immediately for disrespect. With quiet steps I drifted through the Roscovi's narrow servants' passageways until light and music led me from dusty grey to brilliant gold. Quietly pushing wide one of the green-grey servants' doors, I shielded my eyes against the glare of gaslight on crystal and staggered under the hubbub of music and the slippery weight of a thousand conversations.

The great hall was thronged with masked faces, most of them

made of fashionable silk and porcelain, leather and lace rather than the formal dirgewood of the city's forefathers. Even those few daring enough to imitate dirgewood made sure to brightly colour and decorate their masks of Torranto pine, setting them apart from and far beneath the city's masters.

I bit my lip as I passed them. They would never know what the masks entailed—all that they brought with them as they stifled their bearers, filling them with lives and memories not their own. I had heard them speak, in days past, in hushed and excited tones of what it would be like to be a noble of the Duchy—to have the right to a grave beneath dirgewood, to rise again from death's dreams and walk among the living.

They dream of a deathless life, the aspirants and hangers-on. They dream because they do not know. It took all my will not to spit the sour, curdled taste from my mouth. I kept my head down, mouth twisted into a nauseous grimace.

I made my way to the staircase that swept like a waterfall in dark red carpet from the hotel's upper floors and cast around, straining to catch sight of Perro's dark curly head among the crowds. I pushed through a sea of masked faces, unrecognisable and unrecognised even by those of the Vetruvi in the Hotel that night, until I climbed up and through to the landing beyond.

I sighed with relief to breathe in air a little less thick with perfume, smoke, and sweat. I was dizzy, head pounding and mouth dry. On my own, unmasked, among the lights and sounds and tastes and scents of Terazzio's night, with empty pockets and the risk of discovery always at my back. I was halfway between retching and bursting out laughing, my hand on the warm dark oak of the sweeping bannister.

"Rough night, boy?" A lean, thin-faced man straightened up

from the opposite wall. He tucked a slim volume of poetry beneath his arm.

I forced a wavering smile. "You could say that, sir," I said. I took him in—he was sharp-eyed and unmasked, entirely absorbed in studying me.

"Are you well?" His eyes narrowed as he took me in from wig to boots. "Were you announced at the door, lad?" I pulled up my collar, wished him the best of the evening and slipped past him along the hallway. Daring a glance back at the man, I could already see him summoning one of the Roscovi's white-jacketed waiters with an impatient gesture.

I was not welcome in the Roscovi, even among those who wore no mask. I ducked around the corner and made for the back stairs, angry at myself for being stupid enough to dare a walk through the great hall.

The servants' stairs were dimly lit, ill-smelling, and coated with rough slashes of peeling, sickly green paint. The higher I went, the dustier and more neglected the staircase became. Climbing the stairs made my head ache, much like the experience of stumbling across a rotting memory—one that the ghost in the dirgewood had shunned for too long, one that had been reduced to reed-thin strings of recollection. Nervous and shaking I clambered up the narrow staircase, hand tight on the rough ship's rope that hung down in place of a handrail. I closed my eyes for a moment, listening to the distant buzz of the hotel. The staff weren't after me—at least not yet. It was my guess, informed by Per'Secosa's knowledge of Antonos and of the Roscovi, that Perro would be staying in the suite of rooms that occupied the hotel's topmost floor, far above the stink of the city and with a commanding view of the canals that I knew the masks loved.

They may not have called themselves gods, but they nonetheless enjoyed looking down on their domains from on high.

I slipped silently through the door, careful not to let the tread of my boot echo in the upper floor's deserted hall. I heard laughter in the distance—a small group of men, their voices raised in drunk and brash praise of themselves, puffed with bravado and wine. I held my breath as I walked, feeling foolish for doing so. One hand steadied me against the wall as I approached the voices. Laughter sounded like the bursts of a ship's guns, the full-bellied, red-cheeked roaring of men pleased with who they are. I heard little else—high above the streets, even the sounds of the quartet playing below were muted by the thick floors that lay between us.

I realised then that Perro would not be alone. He would be flanked by blank-faced Cousins, and surrounded by Antonos' retainers. In all likelihood, he would be Antonos. Sweat ran cold down my back at the thought that I had risked too much—that I had placed myself into the hands of my family's enemies. A life lived in silence was all that kept me from cursing loudly at my own recklessness. As I stood in the stuffy quiet of the Roscovi's upper floors, I felt the familiar chill of disgust at myself settle like an uneven lump of carved ice in the pit of my stomach.

I balled my hands into fists and crept forward, exhaling silently as I stepped out and around the corner, drawn by the sound of voices. All but hugging the wall as I crept, like a child playing hunt-the-mask, I spied a shaft of heavy honey-dark light spilling across the quiet polished boards of the hallway. Warmth followed it, seeping into the cold and gloom where

I waited. I crept closer only to stop at every burst of laughter, every muscle in my body as tense as a viol's strings. A pool of absolute cold settled in the pit of my stomach, and the icy memory of Per'Secosa's voice bled into my bones, chiding me for the mistake of rebelling against my family—of coming to this place.

I shivered, trying to draw a breath and calm myself against the exhaustion I could feel creeping through my body. I had been on edge for too long—the conversation at the docks, the flight from the footpads, the dread of discovery in the Roscovi. I reflexively bit at the inside of my cheek, the motion rooted in the same angry spite as it was when Per'Secosa did it. I chided myself—*child, foolish child*—the words forming themselves into the mask's angry, contemptuous growl within my head.

I drew closer to the light and the open door, stilling myself to listen so as to unpick the knot of voices. One stood out from the hubbub—Perro, a little loud and a little drunk, laughing at his own remarks. I staggered back against the wall, hugging the corridor's shadows in the silent world beyond the warm bright room where my Perro laughed.

Perro, not Antonos. He was unmasked and in company.

"I swear it's true. No, really." He paused, sighing to himself with amusement. His voice was animated, giddy—cruel and childish. I had never heard him speak that way.

"Every day and every night she is either masked or kept under lock and key like a songbird." A laugh, harsh and giddy at the same time. My blood curdled, and the chill in my stomach threatened to creep up my throat and spill out of me. "She has learned nothing from her family's example. She has not learned to simply bow her head and accept the wisdom of her

Elders." I edged near the door and peered through. Perro was standing by the window, dressed in Verocci Claimant's finery. He held a glass of wine in one hand, inspecting it against the light between sips. He was red-cheeked, and stumbled slightly as he counted points off on his fingers.

"She has not learned," he said, slopping wine over the edge of the glass, "what is important. She thinks some dalliance—some affair of the heart—is worth more than the Claim."

Behind him stood two Cousins, silent and awkward. They shared none of Perro's amusement. Other than his retainers, the room held several young Verocci men, their hair as dark as Perro's. Most of them were dressed in high-collared dark tunics that they wore buttoned up to the neck, decorating them only with a spray of intricate lace around the collar, and wore their hair slicked back in the Calderan fashion. I did not need to see their masked faces to know them—Verocci *Stregali*, young men who threw their lot in with the Verocci Crones to buy influence for themselves in the family's business.

"Loyalty," said Perro, savouring the word with his lips tugged up in a playful half-smile, "is well rewarded."

Heaving, I reeled back. Perro among these terrible petty men, revealing my life to them. I had been betrayed. I had always been betrayed—it had been nothing.

I wanted only to run—to break through the doors of the Roscovi and tear along well-lit streets and over stout bridges until I was back in my own bed—but I knew I could not. I had to hear what he would say. I had to hear, and I had to remember.

My family would need to know.

Perro talked at length about what he had planned, of how

he had noticed my interest in him and approached Antonos himself with the opportunity of ending the stalemate and finally taking the Duchy for the Verocci Name—of settling the Claim on Antonos' line. I watched him carefully, studying how his eyes blazed when he spoke—how eager he was for the approval of the bland masked faces that surrounded him. My hand was tight on the door frame, the white-knuckled grip of my fingers all that held me steady as Perro spoke of his plans for the Truce Dance—of burning Per'Secosa's mask in the kitchens beneath the King's Palace and making it look like my work, as if I had gone mad with jealousy or desire and attacked him before ripping off and destroying my mask.

My vision buckling as tears swam in my eyes, I looked away. There was only one way that it could look as if I had destroyed Per'Secosa. The mask was bonded, it was family. My blood was bound to that dirgewood, witch-cursed to prevent its family from rising up against it. Perro—my love, the only soul I had ever felt a true and honest connection with—planned to kill me.

It was then, as I blinked away hot angry tears, that I saw his price.

Perro turned and laid down his glass on the table. Slowly, with reverential delicacy that looked for all the world like love, he picked up a small clay pot. I could already see the sapling that rose up from the grave-earth inside—a grey twig, twisted and warped even though it was no bigger than Perro's hand, topped by a halo of sleek black leaves. My jaw set, and my heart sounded like the roar of the sea in my ears.

He held a dirgewood sapling. Perro had sold me for immortality. Worse, he had sold me to inflict on others the servitude that we had both lived with for our whole lives. He saw me as nothing more than coin, after all.

I spun away from the masked faces and honey-warm light and headed for the stairs, walking with silent steps learned lifetimes ago along the edge of the neat and polished hallway. I had seen and heard enough. Eyes burning and struggling to breathe, I descended in foggy darkness to the lowest parts of the building and worked my way to the Roscovi's enormous kitchens. In less than half an hour they had been transformed from a warm and welcoming place, a cosy respite from the night outside, into some sort of vision of the World Below. I stormed through them, hardly knowing where I went. Trays caught on my cloak and were dragged along in my wake, spilling their contents onto the floor. Angry shouts were raised in my pursuit. I didn't care. I simply walked dead-eyed and silent like one who wore a mask unbonded, teeth gritted and seething with rage. I lashed out, striking over stacks of dirty plates and pounding fruitlessly at steaming joints of spitted meat. Nothing meant anything.

The shouts grew to a crescendo before a hand grabbed at my sleeve and yanked me away into darkness. I blinked, insensible of where I was and barely aware of who I was.

"Hey!" A woman's voice whispered sharply in my ear. Arms shook me roughly. "Are you drunk? Have you been helping yourself to the wine?" A sniff. "The Allarac?"

It was Serra, the kitchen maid who had let me in. I shook my head. My wig had come unattached and dragged down one side of my head, hot and heavy and itchy. I slumped against the wall and tore the damn thing off, shaking my hair loose as I hurled it into the darkness beyond.

"No," I muttered. I looked up at Serra. My clothes were

dishevelled and I had picked up more than a few stains as I stumbled around the kitchens. If she didn't want to believe that I was sober, I would never convince her. "I'm not drunk," I added, my voice thick nonetheless, glowering tight-lipped past her. The streets beckoned. I needed to be home, to think. I needed clean air and silence. "I haven't been drinking."

The kitchen-girl looked at me in shock. Exposed as I was, I was still no one to her. If Per'Secosa's mask had framed my eyes, she would have known. She would have run, or screamed, or fallen on the floor. I—and the many Untrusted before me— have seen all of these reactions over the years. I raised my chin, lips tight, eyes burning with rage and pain. The woman laid a hand on my shoulder, lowering her voice as she looked at me with pity. I winced, looking away. Pity is a reaction we rarely see.

"You've had a bad night," she said, her voice gentle.

I barked out a bitter laugh. "My worst." It didn't feel like an exaggeration.

Her eyes were kind, her expression helpless. "Here." She reached over to a table, one hand raised to keep the others of the staff back, to shield me from any more embarrassment. Cooks and servers alike drew back at her sign, and the rolling-pins and ladles they grasped dropped slowly to their sides.

Serra held up a pie, steam curling up from the vent neatly cut into the crust. "Take this. There's not much else I can do for you."

I nodded. "I know." I held the pie, numb and stupid, hardly knowing what to do. My stomach lurched—I was hungry, but could not stand the thought of eating, of anything. I had been betrayed, and could not comprehend it. Not then, not there.

"Let me do something for you. Let me tell you something."
I swallowed, steadying myself against the great stone table.
"Find work elsewhere. This place will be torn down by winter's
end."

My eyes met hers, and I was overcome by a tranquil hardness.
"Find work elsewhere," I said again. "Perhaps you should
present yourself at the gates of the Vetruvi Estate. Something
new will stand here next year, Serra." With that, I took her
by the shoulder and pushed her aside while her mouth framed
clumsy, silent questions. My stride lengthened, and I felt my
future, long and heavy and cold, gathering in front of me as I
left the shining lights of the Roscovi behind me.

On the way home I looked to the sky. The night was dark,
and the city's lights hid the stars from my view. Only the fat,
heavy Moon lay low in the sky, turning the canals to silver.
Pulling off my gloves and casting them away, I laid a hand over
my heart and swore an oath before the grim bulk of the Moon.

I swore to any gods that would listen—gods of the living
and the dead, gods who favour our people and gods of our
enemies—that I would never be hurt again. Let it be a promise,
let it be a warning. Hurt would find me no more.

Chapter Five

"Idiot." My own lips curled in a sneer as I stalked across the courtyard, collar pulled high against the rain. "Young stupid lovesick fool."

Per'Secosa had been spitting insults at me with my own tongue ever since I had returned home and donned the mask. I had let him in—let him see my whole night. I held none of it back, kept no secrets for myself. After what I had seen, what I had heard in the Roscovi's halls, I doubted that I had the strength to hold him back.

I had wept as he dug through my betrayal, his scrutiny scraping against the raw aching of my new, sickening pain. When he examined my unmasked meeting earlier that day, it took all I had to keep my agreement in Perro's scheme from him—I would never be myself again if he thought for even a moment that I had wanted to see his empty dark-lacquered eyes cast into the flames. If he feared even the hint of such fatal insubordination, he would wear me until I died, allowing me to draw only my last breath as myself before he passed himself over to his chosen heir.

Per'Secosa had plotted through the night until morning in absolute secrecy, pacing back and forth in my bedroom as he cursed and spat at me. My body was numb with exhaustion, and hidden deep inside myself I was beyond fatigued. Per'Secosa saw none of that, choosing to pass on the pain to me along with his bitter, terrible anger. Too suspicious of the Verocci to call an attendant, summon a relative, or rouse a guard, he schemed in silence until sunrise brought an ugly wash of grey rain creeping through the city's streets.

As thick raindrops spattered against the window, he settled on a method of dealing with his enemies that best pleased him, donning a heavy oiled cloak to make the journey through the grounds to the family vault. Still in silk slippers I was dragged exhausted over the quiet dawn-grey lawns and through orchards that whispered with the tap of rain on leaves until, masked and scowling, Per'Secosa reached the thick iron-shod doors of the family's shrine to our undeparted ancestors. The building sat unassuming and grand all at once, a heavy and severe mausoleum of dark stone that held within it the most revered and priceless treasures of the Vetruvi—the heart of our wealth—that nevertheless stood unguarded among our gardens. It was always there, the vault, yet always at the edge of our vision. I knew of none of the family—none of my playmates as a child—who cared to walk in the rose garden that grew near to the vault, or to tarry too long in its shadow.

Still muttering curses, Per'Secosa fumbled a key from my pocket with cold, wet fingers and slowly began to unbind the locks. A misapplication of pressure and I would be poisoned by the darts that hid deep inside the heavy door. I could feel the temptation to rush the opening of the door—to kill me—coil around Per'Secosa's spirit for a moment, thick with malice and amusement, before it passed.

Rainwater gathered in the collar of the cloak, seeping down my back as he worked. His fury burned close beside me, sickly-sweet and hot. I stood, aching and tired, as my hands moved with bored precision over the locks and catches of the vault doors. With a click the last catch was released, and the door swung slowly back to admit the Vetruvi Claimant to the resting place of his family's greatest treasures. He swept on into the musty dark of the cramped passage beyond, dragging me along with him in morose, numb silence.

"I should at least thank you," he growled in my voice. "You have brought matters to a head, and I no longer need to think in terms of this worthless bloodless truce. Too long a woman—too long itching to feel Verocci blood on my hands. Now at least I can contest the Claim as I was meant to—with steel and fire and poison as well as coin and writ." My shoulders tensed, muscles bunching as Per'Secosa anticipated the long bloody days to come. "So much blood will flow." He sounded thrilled, giddy as a child in the chapel on their Naming Day. With my shaking hands he struck a spark from a flint, igniting a torch. The resin and tar took up the spark hungrily, and light bathed the narrow staircase that wound its way down into the heart of the vault.

Per'Secosa moved swiftly and with purpose, striding past alcoves that led to galleries of masterpieces and jewels beyond price without so much as glancing to the side. He knew these treasures. He had placed many deep inside the vault himself; others he had inherited from masks too far gone to bear the Claim, or those who had been destroyed by their enemies, their bearers, or their impatient heirs.

Flickering light danced across the exquisitely shaped facets of perfect emeralds and lustrous chains and bands of gold as he marched me with cold purpose deep into the most secret chambers of the vault. Muttering curses against me and my name through clenched teeth, Per'Secosa fitted the torch into a wall sconce before dragging a heavy chest to one side. Polished wood groaned as iron bracings scraped along the stone floor. A gold ewer spilled from the open chest, bouncing and clattering noisily out of the ring of light. Dimly, at the edge of my consciousness, I felt a sharp, sickening pain tear at my shoulder as the ghost doggedly hauled the chest out of his way.

"Your father was stronger," Per'Secosa hissed as my fingernails dug into the cold, dirty stone of the wall behind the chest.

My father. I had barely known him, save as the Claimant's vessel. Even as my hands cleared the dust from a hidden recess in the wall, my wandering memory could not recall his eyes. I struggled to see more than his death, his body lying at the fire's edge in our home at Villa Anora. Behind that sight lay the memories my Grandfather-Looking-Out enjoyed using to punish me—the last memories of the man who had worn him, of pain and fear and regret.

Stone rumbled as Per'Secosa pulled at the wall. Slowly the hidden counterweights took over, drawing the neatly laid stone aside to reveal a still, silent chamber beyond. No light caught on any surface, and a cold older than dirgewood radiated from the depths beyond. My steps faltered for a moment as some animal part of my soul pushed back against Per'Secosa's will to take up the torch and step into the darkness.

The mask growled a curse in my voice and clumsily snatched

at the torch, pushing forward into the passage beyond. He squeezed down the narrow confines, unconsciously hunching over even though my narrow, slight frame could pass through the vault's path without discomfort.

Dusty and undisturbed since its construction, the secret passage swiftly became so narrow that even I would have had to duck down and bring in my shoulders to navigate it. We had twisted and turned, slipping down galleries and descending and climbing stairs so often beneath the earth that I had no idea where we were—or even if we were still under the ground beneath the Vetruvi estate. The corridor plunged on endlessly into shadow, none of its neat, firmly set slabs of stone any different to the others, when I became aware that Per'Secosa was silently counting paces. Abruptly he stopped and, turning to one side, he felt again at the wall. I could see my fingers by the flickering light of the torch, dirty, bloodied, and bruising. Per'Secosa wiped them absently on my dress before resuming his search.

Finding the stone that satisfied him, the mask pushed down on it. A clasp gave way behind the hinged stone with an audible click, and then the wall receded silently before swinging away. Beyond lay a wide alcove set with a number of recesses. Each held a carved marble bust—the likenesses, I knew and recognised, of prominent Vetruvi from centuries ago. They looked uncannily as they had in life, sculpted with the greatest care by masters of their craft who would have known better than to question why their work had never been displayed. Perched in mute tribute upon its face, each bust held an exact replica of its own mask. My eyes travelled at once to the stern, scowling face of Secosa Vetruvi—fifth in line to the Claim at the time the vault was constructed and filled, and so nowhere near as prominent as the now-pointless masks of Gianno and Carlottiana Vetruvi at the apex of the alcove. My own mask—his mask—stared back at me, Per'Secosa's empty, smooth eyes regarding me blankly above his distinctive sneer. Per'Secosa curled my lip in triumph, mirroring the expression on his own silent marble face. It took all my focus to keep my cool in that moment. I had never seen the substitutes before. Nobody had.

Among the Untrusted, the existence of a small trove of replicas was only ever hinted at, and never accounted with any real credibility. Luciana, lost to us and living in seclusion with the Elders who had been too long bound to dirgewood, had once said that she remembered carving her own mask in a dream, long ago. Nobody believed her—Luciana had many dreams, and the Elders didn't care whether she spun them all out for the rest of the Untrusted. Yet after she had spoken to us of the carving of her own mask, the Crones had come, robed in black, and taken her away in a high-sided carriage to the Convent. Most of us had thought little of the connection between Luciana's rambling and the Crones' arrival—indeed, how could she have carved her own mask? How could she remember such a thing? A few of the Vetruvi children had grasped the significance of her dream, but had known better than to ever speak of it. They had kept it far from their thoughts, where their masks would never see it.

Yet there they were, all of them—the mask of every Elder in our entire clan, all neatly laid out in case one of them ever needed to fake their death. If I could have smiled in that moment, I would. Luciana was right—all of them were right, even those who only held onto the idea of the substitutes out of some sort of ragged hope that the masks they wore were not the true souls of their family's honoured ancestors.

Per'Secosa reached in and delicately lifted the copy of his mask, trying not to look for too long into that chiselled remembrance of his own long-gone features, before turning around and storming back down the winding passageway. His discomfort seeped through the grain of the wood, curdling into a pounding ache in my temples which Per'Secosa duly ignored.

"Now, girl," he hissed, the false mask gripped tight in my grimy hand, "when the time comes for the dance, we give the Verocci what they want. We let them have their moment of victory, their sweet breath of spring air. Then, when blood is spilled, and the King's word cast aside by those thrice-cursed wretches, then... the Claim is mine." I felt the hairs bristle at the nape of my neck as he thrilled, daring to speak those words aloud.

Mine. Not the family's, not the clan's. So much death over so many years in the name of our family, of our Claim, and he exulted in casting them aside to take what he viewed as his own.

Chapter Six

SPRING PASSED SLOWLY. I spent most of my days masked, shackled to Per'Secosa's business and family concerns as he prepared for the coming fulfilment of his centuries-old grudge against the Verocci. My hands had not healed well from scrabbling about in the dirt and stone, so he had taken to wearing gloves regularly to conceal the marks. The burn on my right arm had always disquieted him, and he had taken the excuse of the bruising and cuts on both hands to be fitted for a new pair of gloves—long assassin's gloves in dark leather, with the Vetruvi crest stitched in minuscule detail on the cuffs. They pleased him, and hid what he saw as imperfections from those who called on him.

I was only really allowed to be myself when I was asleep. The release of night came rarely, and I had little enough reserve in body or mind to do anything but collapse in an exhausted heap whenever his presence was removed from me. Day and night, at all other times he was there, chiding and cursing me while he worked quietly on his plan to bring the entire Verocci line low, and to see Antonos dead once and for all.

It was a simple plan. Per'Secosa Vetruvi had little patience for unnecessary complexity, and saw to it that as little as possible could go wrong. Centuries of control had left him with little faith in anything that did not depend directly on his action, and centuries of frustration had left him greedy and impatient for power and respect.

I would go along with Perro's request and appear to betray my family, substituting the false mask for Per'Secosa to be burnt. When the mask was destroyed I was to cry out, letting our own assassins among the kitchen staff strike. I would then be reunited with the Claimant, who would take the attempt on our lives—on his life, truly, for that was what outraged him—to the King, and have the Verocci censured. It was a simple plan, old and brutal and steeped in blood. All it required me to do was to betray the man I had loved, and who had betrayed me in his turn, to the ghost that had stolen my life.

I spent the months leading to the dance in silence, trapped within the numb quiet of my own body as Per'Secosa drank and joked with the ghoulish council of masks that made up the inner circle of our family. I saw them—my cousins and nephews, my brother Vellis and little Sameri—hands meekly folded while the dusty old masks made their own calm and terrible plans to slay generation after generation of their enemies, to pack them away in boxes of pine and see them planted where no dirgewood would grow over their bones.

All this death meant nothing to them. Elders and Crones would carry on as always in a different body. If an arrow or knife or poison took Demetria or Vellis or even Sameri, then it was no more an inconvenience to the old masks than losing a good suit to hungry moths. They would bond again, and it did not matter if they lost one bearer. The ledger was so heavily weighted, as they saw it, to their enemies' detriment that the price they paid by losing a bearer was a true bargain.

One by one the masks slunk away over the weeks, trusted lieutenants and old drinking comrades of the Claimant, to plan assassinations or draw up the necessary legal papers to formulate their new challenge. One by one his brothers and sisters, the dead who laughed and joked in the bodies of the living, faded into the city's shadows to make their plans for bloodshed and to set the stage for the last summer of the Truce.

In my dreams I saw them—the masks, bone-fingered on the skeletons of their original selves, as they stalked through fields of tombs. Their steps were meticulous, each set in time to music centuries old and dressed in ancient and dusty finery, all faded and pale and caked in the earth of the grave. Thin pale roots wound around the bones, driving into empty eyes and binding the sickly wooden masks to their polished skulls.

In time, Perro would be one of them. Even were he to die at the dance as Per'Secosa planned, the tree would twine with his tomb and the wood would take on his spirit. He would live on with the masks and plot with them in the long years to come—years after I was dead and gone.

I continued to sleep little in the weeks leading up to the dance. I prayed often, and to whatever gods would listen. I don't think any did.

The day of the last Truce Dance came in the blistering heat of high summer. The retreat to the valleys alone was a relief—away from the stifling air and choking, rank fug of Terazzio and its canals, rattling down wide leafy lanes in a carriage with the windows thrown open to allow a breeze to pass through.

Per'Secosa cared little for overland travel, so I made the long trip to the Palace bare-faced. When I could I leaned out of the window, feeling the fresh air on my skin and listening to the horses puff and whinny as they pulled the carriage along. The endless rolling green fields, shimmering under the summer's heat, seemed changeless and untouched by our families' feud. Vineyards were arranged in neat rows, prizes greater than jewels in our feud, parting respectfully for domed temples and hunched, red-roofed farms. As I sped through the lanes that led me on to the Palace, to the ballroom and the kitchens and what had been ordained for me in those places, I wished I could just call out to the coachman and bring it all to a stop. If I could, I would unbolt the door and run away into the fields and never be seen in Terazzio again.

I blinked away a hot tear and looked out at the distant silver ribbon of a stream. The coachman would know better than to listen to me—I was just Untrusted, just Carra and nothing more. My wishes would never be heeded. To listen to and obey an Untrusted was more than his life was worth.

Soured even to the simple pleasure of travelling on a bright summer's day, I slumped back into the shade of the carriage and waited for the narrow spires of the Summer Palace to come into view, pinning down the swollen filigreed dome of the Grand Ballroom that dominated the East Wing. It would already be thronged with family members—those who had arrived early, politely but diligently working to make sure that no misfortune befell their kin during the days of the Truce. I knew a second contingent of our own were already deep within the Palace, having taken on their roles years ago and working silently in our service ever since.

Eventually I caught sight of the Palace: bone-white towers like needles reaching out into the endless blue vault of the sky, its immaculate walls of smooth Tiresian stone almost monastic in their cold precision. Within, I knew, the King would be waiting to receive us, head bowed under the weight of his own heavy golden mask, hands folded neatly in his lap. It was said he could barely move on his own, and that soon it would be up to the dukes to choose a worthy successor to the Throne. The Duke of Terazzio, of course, was the most senior of those titles by precedence, and his word would bear a heavy weight in deciding the future of the King's line.

More blood then, I thought wearily to myself as the carriage deposited me in the Courtyard. The coachman and guard stood patiently at my side as I stepped down from the carriage, clutching a lacquered box with gilded scrollwork in my dark-gloved hands. I flipped open the catch and tied Per'Secosa's face in place with clumsy fingers. His spirit rushed into me, pushing me aside as he swept into the Greeting Hall and presented himself to the Chamberlain before I had the chance to smooth the creases out of my dress. I felt my heart race with his excitement as we were swept into the formal pageantry of the Truce Dance, dragged along behind the Chamberlain to our quarters for a few light refreshments before we would make obeisance to the King that Per'Secosa hoped one distant day to replace.

He could wait—after all, he had waited over three hundred years just to rid himself of Antonos Verocci. My palms were sweating. Per'Secosa ground my teeth together, baring them in a fierce animal smile that held more threat than it ever had charm.

Evening came slow to the valleys in high summer. The light bled from the sky, turning it the colour of dark honey. A chill soaked through the world as the Sun dipped below the horizon and the cloudless night crept slowly up, pushing its way over the hills beyond. In my chambers I stood by the window, my unsteady hand pouring another glass of dark wine. Per'Secosa cursed as a drop splashed over the rim, darkening the cream silk of my glove.

I stood on the balcony of my—of his—suite, sipping wine I could barely taste. I could feel the presence of the travelling case behind me, sitting heavy on the table. The false bottom beneath the cushions shaped to the contours of the mask was there, and within it the counterfeit mask. That replica, I had been schooled, would be my weapon, a weapon precious beyond any other in the Vetruvi arsenal. Everything in the Claimant's plan depended on my ability to convince Perro that the counterfeit was the real thing.

It was close enough in every aspect. It had been made at the same time, carved by the same hands and stained with the same lacquers. It had even been treated to ensure it would smell like dirgewood, look like dirgewood, and burn like dirgewood. In the early days, much would have been gained from convincing an enemy that a mask had been destroyed. It would give them the luxury of time to plot their revenge, and the eye-watering expense of creating a duplicate was nothing when weighed against the advantage of surprise against an enemy who thought you long ago defeated.

It only differed in a few key aspects—it had never been worn by a Vetruvi, so it did not bear the marks of generations of wear on its brow and temples. It was not soaked in the sweat of my ancestors, but the ghost had weighed and then dismissed that concern. In the low light of the kitchen on that night, it was hoped that such faults would go unnoticed—that our deception would be aided by urgency and darkness.

"My Lord?" The servant girl's voice annoyed Per'Secosa. He despised provincial accents. I felt my shoulders stiffen at her words, and in my spirit I was cold. I am not devout—I have never felt a strong connection to the gods, neither those of my own land, or those of others. On that night as Per'Secosa stood, my cheeks flushed with wine and a masked eye on the setting Sun, I prayed. I prayed for the life I had never known, for the family I had lost, and for the man I had been foolish enough to love. I prayed to any god that would listen as the servants laid out my dress for the Claimant's approval. Soon I would set him aside and take up my place at the ball. I would stay, it was agreed, for five dances. I had tried to plead fewer, but Racalla, our house's Mistress of Etiquette, had insisted in her disjointed sibilant tone that being seen to be in a rush to leave would be both suspicious, and greatly insulting to the King.

"Good." Per'Secosa marched down the line of hanging dresses like a general inspecting his troops. "The cream one," he said in my voice as he rapped a knuckle on the pale, delicate fabric. "It is bright and cheerful. Innocent." He gritted my teeth, chuckling quietly. "Unlike her." A sniff. *It will more fully display their infamy.* Those words were silent, unspoken. They rattled around inside me, sickening and bitter. Out loud, he spoke to the servants. "Did you not hear me? The cream one. Make it ready and leave me." He looked down at my hand, at the spot of wine that had seeped, faint and pink, into the silk of my glove. "And fresh gloves to match," he shouted after them as they walked, bowing, out of the door.

"It is time." He reached up and undid the ribbons that held the mask in place. I felt the tendrils of his old spirit pulled up from my heart. I could now taste the wine on my tongue. The fading light was almost too bright as I tucked the mask away inside its case and slumped back against my dressing-table. Taking a deep breath I walked over to the case once again, flipping it open to check on the mask. Running a finger over a lacquered cheek, I could feel Per'Secosa's muted bloodlust whispering through the stained silk of my glove. I arranged the mask a little, fussing over it inside the box. Satisfied, I allowed myself a smile before stepping back and stripping off my gloves. I looked at my hands, still bruised and calloused and scarred. The nails were healing, and the bruises were starting to fade. By autumn, they would be whole again—whole, save for the burn that twisted the skin of my right hand.

One last prayer, and I called in the chamber-servants again. It was time to dress for the ball.

An hour later and I was ready—stiff and formal in a dress I could barely move in, laden with jewellery that had more meaning for men and women centuries dead than it did for me. I could feel the pull of the mask where it lay hidden in the concealed pocket woven into my skirts. A deep, shuddering breath nearly choked me. I closed my eyes and nodded to my cousins, Larya and Ceria, who opened the doors to my chamber and swept out before me into the hall.

The Chamberlain's rod sounded like thunder on the tiles of the Palace floor. I could feel them cool and smooth beneath my slippers, even though the Palace itself was uncomfortably hot and the darkening evening was stifling. "Make way!" His voice echoed through the halls as Larya and Ceria strode before me like an honour guard, fans fluttering. "Make way for Carra Vetruvi, bearer of the Vetruvi Claimant to the Ducal Signet!"

At the sides of the hall, lesser nobles stepped back and tilted their heads in polite deference. Larya regarded them icily, the disdain and irritability of Damma Casala etched in the lines of her young face. Beside her Ceria walked with a subdued grace—the mask she wore was that of her own mother, a bully who saw her children as nothing more than the next step in her ages-long life. Ceria had submitted meekly to the mask when it was brought to her, but I could hear her weeping at nights when she thought herself alone.

My escorts swept aside to join the pack of masked nobles in their finery. Only the Claimants went bare-faced for the first day of the celebration—it had been suggested as a mark of trust in each other and respect for the King, though I suspected it had been part of Antonos' design all along to woo an impressionable bearer and so undermine his enemy.

I shivered and looked around the hall, hairs raised on my forearms. Four of the King's honour guard stood to attention by me, their officer bowing stiffly from the waist. Ornate, heavy box-bows were slung glinting over their shoulders, ceremonial in their adornment but no less lethal for it. I smiled thinly and curtsied to the guards, holding out my hand to indicate that they could escort me to the podium where Perro and I would sit while the King declared the first dance of the summer.

Perro had arrived before me and stood patiently next to his chair. He smiled as I approached, his warm honest face lighting up with delight to see me in my finery. This was the man I had fallen in love with, and even as I took his hand and bobbed, holding his gaze as we adjourned to our seats, I refused to believe that it could all have been a lie. He held my hand up for a kiss, brushing my knuckles gently against his lips. I felt heat and pressure through the silk of my glove, and it sent a single needle of cold sweat creeping down the back of my dress. I held my smile.

"Are you ready?" he said, eyebrow arched mischievously.

"Always," I responded in a whisper that was little more than a breath. My heart still stirred at the sight of him, so strong and tall and confident.

"Shall we begin?" he said, his voice as soft and gentle as the memories I held deep inside. I nodded in happy agreement as I ran through the positions of our retainers and assassins, our waiting and bloody hands, in my head.

"I want nothing more," I said. My cheeks flushed as I smiled. Perro beckoned me forward, and we gripped each other's hand tightly as we bowed before the King.

Perro was shaking, as was I.

The night passed swiftly, with the gold-masked King declaring the dances in a thin, tired voice that echoed dimly around the hall. The chamber musicians played beautifully well, their artistry inspiring wonderful movement and colour and life in our two families as they spun and whirled around the room before us, grins fixed and strained as they tried to prove to their enemies that they did not hate every moment of their time in this place.

Perro and I danced twice. For our second dance I remember resting my arm on his shoulder and wondering if I would ever be happy again. He caught my eye.

"What's wrong?" I felt him stiffen in my arms.

"Nothing." I looked away, to where a pair of Perro's maiden

aunts were watching us from behind their fans, eyes glinting from deep within the hollow sockets of their expressionless masks. "Nothing's wrong. It's just—it's such a big change."

"It's for everyone's good. Without us—without the masks— the Claim falls apart. The Crown will have to decree a new Duke, and we can live as we wanted to. Together, Carra. Peace for the land, peace for us. Imagine." He whispered the word into my neck. I held his hand tightly as we spun, the room's heat and flickering amber-gold light making my head swim.

After our dance I made my excuses. Pale and sweating, I retreated to the cooler reaches of the Palace for some air and a glass of wine.

HE FOUND ME in one of the arterial colonnades, wrapping his arms around my waist and nuzzling into my back.

"Is it with you?" His voice was giddy.

"Yes," I said, laying down my long-stemmed glass on the stones beside a heavy pot of strong-smelling roses and turning to face him. "Do you know where we're going?" If I closed my eyes, I could still see the routes from the Lesser Courts to the kitchens. I knew, give or take five paces, exactly how far I was from the furnaces.

He laid his hand on his chest and looked hurt. "Carra, it's me. Of course I know where we're going." He took my hand. "Now, come on. We'll be missed before too long. We must hurry."

I held back. A little reluctance made sense, of course. "Perro. Is your carriage ready?"

He faltered. Amateur. "Yes. Yes, of course. Of course it is."

In a second his smile was back in place—but I had seen his true face for a moment. I was disappointed at how easy it was to make him show it.

"Tell me again," I said, smiling up at him. "Tell me of how we will live in the mountains and raise sheep and fat children together." I laid my hand on his chest. He took it and gently pushed me back. He looked sick.

"Later." I could still see the black-leafed dirgewood sapling clutched in his hand. I had dreamed all spring of its roots twining around his skull. Later.

I could not afford to push him—to make him think better of his actions, to make him afraid. I nodded my assent.

"Let's be away, then. I'll look forward to it."

Our feet rang on the cold moonlit flagstones as we dashed across the courtyard and vanished into the shadows.

The kitchens were dark, lit by cookfires and furnaces to resemble an unimaginative artist's conception of the Torment that awaited the Vicious Dead. Hand in hand we crept silently through them, past sweating cooks and servants laden with heavy trays and carafes of wine. Where I could I directed Perro through subtle means—I would hang back at the wrong moment, or make it appear that I had caught sight of someone in our path. Bit by bit we drifted slowly to the edge of the kitchens, to where a great furnace burned all night to heat the Royal chambers far above. The banked fire flickered through the grate, casting ruddy orange bars of light broken by soot-black shadow onto the floor. High above us, the gears in the palace clock ground away the moments—the muffled toll of the First Bell of night reached us through plaster, brick, wood, and stone.

I could feel unseen eyes on me; the masks reaching out from above, their spirits straining to see beyond their grey wooden prisons, as well as our loyal killers in the near shadows. Cold sweat trickled between my shoulder blades as Perro and I stood in silence before the furnace, watching it blaze like the mouth of an angry god ready to accept our dishonest sacrifices.

"Is he with you?" My mouth was dry. Perro reached into his doublet and slipped out the slim, blank mask of Antonos Verocci.

"Here," he said, holding it out to me. I took the smooth, lifeless thing in my hands and looked down at it. After all the centuries Per'Secosa had fought the Verocci, I couldn't recall him ever having been so close to one of their masks. He had never cradled a lifeless, inert enemy in his hands.

Antonos Verocci felt like a seashell, light and smooth and brittle.

"Are you sure?" I ran my thumb over the empty eye-socket, marvelling at the smoothness of the enamel. I held it in my hands, judging the weight. To me, it felt far too light. More likely than not it was made of ash, rather than inert wild dirgewood. Perro, loyal to his masters. Was I any different to him?

He squeezed my hand, pressing it tight around the mask—his bare hand eclipsing my small gloved fingers. "It's the only way we can ever be free."

"We can leave them here." I looked up, eyes blazing. My remorse had to seem genuine. "We can leave them here and escape. They'll never find us."

"You know they will. You know they won't let this slight on their honour lie—they won't let it be seen that they can be helpless for even a moment. They'll hunt us, Carra." He bit his lip and held me by my shoulders. His voice was warm and soft and sweet as honey. "This is the only way."

I nodded. Perro took up a heavy cloth and undid the latch on the furnace, hauling it open. The grille swung back with the haunted screech of metal against metal, and the fire blazed brightly inside. Heat washed over me, settling like a stole on my shoulders.

The flames danced in reflection on the mask's surface. There were no cracks in the enamel, no artistry of deceit to make it seem worn and aged. It wasn't even a good counterfeit. It hurt to see how little Perro thought of me. Biting back a flash of anger, I closed my eyes and tossed the crude facsimile into the fire. It crackled and spat and flared up. In seconds, it was gone, its last sound the whispered crack of enamel shattering in the furnace's heat.

Perro was trembling. "It worked," he said, his voice thick with relief. His palms were slick with sweat. He hadn't even thought to wear gloves. Perhaps he didn't know.

"Turn away," I said, eyes averted as I reached beneath my skirts. False shame, only natural in reaction to committing a crime considered beyond contemplation by our families. The rustling of my underskirts harmonised with the dim crackle of the shattered enamel on the remnants of Antonos Verocci's false mask.

"Here." I held out the narrow, dark-lacquered face of Per'Secosa Vetruvi. The furious brows glared up at me as Perro's hand circled it, gripping it by one of its eyes. He turned it over in his hands, examining it, running his fingers over the black silk cords that dangled from its edges.

"So old," he whispered. "To hold this…"

Perro fell into a reverent silence as he looked down at the mask. "You must hurry," I said. "We will not be alone here for long."

"Yes," he said, a strange smile on his lips. "We won't, will we?" With a casual motion he flicked the mask away into the furnace. I tried not to watch it dance over coals and ashes before it settled, silk already gone and lacquer bubbling as dirgewood split and charred.

When I turned back to face Perro the dagger was already in his hand, its blade glinting fire-red.

"Perro?" I stepped back, hesitant. "What are you doing?"

"I am being rewarded for my loyalty, Carra." He advanced a step, knife held casually in his grip.

"Perro?" My voice cracked, laced through with notes of panic. "What about us? What about me? Perro—what have you done?"

"In truth I regret this, Carra. You were assigned to me, years ago, but I have come to care for you." He cast a forlorn gaze at me. "I don't know if you'll believe that or not."

"Strangely enough," I said as I slipped around the corner of a table, "I don't. Perhaps it is the knife that undermines your sincerity, Perro."

His trickster grin flickered back into life. "Perhaps. I'll miss your tongue, Carra—I'll miss your bold speech. There will be others, but none of them will be you. Take heart, though—I will always remember you, and treasure your memory forever." He placed his hand over his heart. "A part of you will always live, always be treasured."

I spat at him. "Filth!" I cried. He cursed and sprang forward. I darted to the side—not quick enough—and screamed as he caught me by a fistful of hair and hauled me bodily over the table towards him. His face was contorted with rage. "That was a new tunic, whore!" he yelled, face flushed and mouth twisted into an ugly snarl.

I reached up and snatched at his wrist, trying to push the dagger away as he bore down on me with all his weight. I could feel his breath against my face, hot and sour as he swore again, leaning down on the dagger to try and drive it into my heart. I pushed back, weary muscles working with a fury and desperation I had never before known, eyes welling with tears as they locked with those of the man I had loved.

Like a man inhabited by a creature from the Torment, he bore down, holding me firmly in place as I struggled and kicked on the table. The world around me shook, the point of the dagger all but scoring my skin, and then everything stopped.

I felt, rather than heard, the box-bolt strike home—wet, firm, and insistent. Perro jolted forward as if kicked, stumbling against the table, and then went slack.

A second impact and his grip lost its power, the knife tumbling from numb fingers to land clattering on the wood of the table by my ear. He looked down at me, glassy-eyed, his face as pale and glistening as a Verocci enamelled mask. A thin trickle of blood painted his lips crimson.

I pushed away and slid off the table, leaning on it to force myself upright on quivering legs. Perro still stood, feebly trying to reach out to me—though whether to hold me or kill me or beg my forgiveness I could no longer tell. The heavy barbed heads of two box-bolts, glistening and dark, jutted from his chest. His clothes were soaked in blood. As I stared he fell backwards, landing hard on the kitchen floor.

I ran around the table and knelt by him. "I'm sorry, Perro," I whispered and squeezed his hand. He fixed me with a pale, quizzical look before coughing violently, once, and then falling back senseless against the stone floor. "I will finish this," I promised, as I folded his lifeless hand over his chest.

I stood, my dress hanging awkwardly where the hem had soaked in Perro's blood. Two shapes detached themselves from the shadows—Vetruvi men, in the garb of Palace Guards. "Are you hurt, my lady?" I dabbed at my neck, feeling a sliver of loose skin where Perro's blade had brushed against me.

"No," I said, absently regarding my gloved hands. They were filthy with soot and blood. "I think most of this blood… um … I think it's, I think it's his."

Slowly, methodically, I peeled off my gloves and tossed them into the furnace.

"What should we do?" The guard's voice was muffled, as if he spoke through heavy furs.

I looked down at Perro. His face was contorted in confusion and agony. His eyes, glassy and unfocused, stared up into the shadowed rafters. Dark blood shone on the floor, orange and black in the flickering light. The pool spread slowly, inching towards my slippers. "Do you have him with you?"

One of the guards bowed and produced a slim wooden box. He held it out to me, and I placed it on the table. With shaking hands I opened the lock and brought out my mask. I held it in my hands for a moment before tying it in place.

"There," I said, in his voice. I kept my words steady, fearful that I would be discovered. "The deed is done—the child has no doubt learned her lesson." I dabbed at the blood that covered my shoulders and the front of my dress, and barked out one of his cruel laughs. "And I have won my Claim. You have done well." I waved my hand airily at the guards. "Come with me. We must alert the Royal House to this attempt on my life."

So it was that night, as the last dances were called in the Palace, that Carra Vetruvi swept into the hall in her white dress covered in blood, and brought the peace that had lasted a generation crashing down. I spoke with the voice of Per'Secosa, demanding an audience with the King to tell him of Perro and Antonos Verocci's plan, years in the making, of using the Truce to lure Carra from her family with the intent of murdering both her and the Vetruvi Claimant, Honoured Secosa Vetruvi, all the while professing to love her. Tears stung my eyes. I fought them away, feeling my throat rasp as I spoke in his voice before the King, standing tall and proud and furious as he would. The mask pinched—it felt heavy, inert, unreal, and it sat awkwardly at the bridge of my nose.

Behind me as I spoke, I heard the Verocci wail as Perro's body was dragged into the hall, a trail of spattered blood in his wake. I told how he had wrestled me to the ground, how he had forced the mask from me, how I would have died had an off-duty guard not heard my distant cries on his way to the kitchens for a bite of supper and... I held out my hand, indicating Perro's corpse.

The King stood, weak joints creaking as he gripped the arm of the Summer Throne. "What would you have of the Crown, then? Per'Secosa Vetruvi, you have been wronged to the blood, and under banner of truce. What will you have?"

I ached. Beyond the smell of old lacquer I could sense nothing but the reek of blood in the air. "I would have justice, Your Majesty."

A chill dropped on the room, sudden and heavy. A masked Judge shifted in the shadows behind the Throne, face white as bone. Several of the Verocci men reached reflexively for their belts, though no swords hung from them that night.

"What more justice do you need, Per'Secosa? Your assailant is dead."

"My assailant," I hissed through gritted teeth, "was nothing more than a pawn—a playing piece crafted to lure a young and impressionable host into a place where she could be removed, ending the Vetruvi Claim at a stroke." I raised a finger and jabbed it, white-knuckled, at a tight knot of defensively-gathered Verocci. "This was not the work of one man, but of a family. I will have retribution."

The King nodded ponderously, hands barely moving as he beckoned his Judge forward. Outside, hooves could be heard on the courtyard's flagstones as the more astute members of the Verocci clan slipped away from the Palace in haste.

"I will have Antonos Verocci outlawed." I raised my voice, letting it fill the chamber and beat back the gasps of the outraged family.

"It is done." The King waved a hand. "Antonos Verocci is outlaw. If he, or his bearer, are discovered within the borders of Calrisia, they and their lives are forfeit to the Crown."

With that simple statement, I had won. The trembling, the nervous energy, all of it bled out of me. I wanted nothing more than to slump down on the floor right there, but I couldn't. He wouldn't do that.

A cold smile on my lips, I turned to face the whispering huddle of Verocci attendants. Hands behind my back, I stalked forward as he would have, conscious of the blood drying on my gown. I stopped and leaned in, fixing the dead-eyed mask of Torellos Verocci with a gaze of cold, cruel delight.

"Run," I whispered, baring my teeth in a smile. "Run while you can."

I closed my eyes. The air filled with the sounds of slippers scuffing rapidly across the wooden floor. In a moment the quiet storm had passed, and the room was cleared. Behind me the King wheezed audibly.

With a gesture I dismissed my own family members, save for two distant cousins I would need to watch over me while I returned to my rooms. It was over. I had made the trade—burned the petulant, vindictive ghost who had bullied and dominated generations of my family, and set myself free.

I tried not to think about what it had cost me.

As I turned to take my leave, I looked down at Perro lying in a heap in the middle of the floor. I had never noticed before how vast the dancing-hall was, nor how small we all were. Alone amid its vast space, always loud and festive and busy, I could feel it pressing in on every side. Clearing my throat, I bowed one last time to the King.

"Goodnight, Duke," the old mask said.

"Your Majesty," I responded, bowing low so he would not see my smile.

When I got back to my room I poured water enough to wash in and discarded my blood-spattered dress. Taking off the mask, I looked long and hard in the mirror at a face that was—for the first time—truly my own. I was covered in blood. Taking up a cloth I wiped at my hands, my shoulders, my neck and face. As I worked, my arms heavy and aching and the cut on my neck stinging, the water clouded a pale rose-blush red in the bowl. In time I was clean, and it did not seem so very much work in the end.

I sighed, wearier than I had ever been before. I had done it. I had tricked Perro, tricked Per'Secosa, fooled my family and my enemies and my King. I had killed and lied and cheated, and I was too exhausted to feel much of anything about that.

The night was warm, but I shivered anyway. I picked up the mask, still expecting the pull of Per'Secosa's brutal spirit to flow into me and still surprised that it did not. It had taken so much from me to drive him in the direction I needed—to play on his anger so that my hands were badly scratched from our journey beneath the family vault. Over the long years I had given a little of myself over to drip poisoned whispers to his vanity, stoking it so that my hands would always be covered in public. Covered, so my skin would not touch his dirgewood husk if I were to hold it. It seemed so little, the nudges and whispers, but it had meant opening a part of myself to his bitter soul, and I wondered if it had left any scars—scars that no other would ever see, and that would never heal.

I slipped under the covers of my bed and lay still, staring up at the ceiling. Exhausted but restless, I waited for my ghosts to come as I knew they would—the tight knot of guilt was already starting to push back against the numbing shock that still held me.

My ghosts would come. For the first time in my whole life, they would be my own.

I am Carra Vetruvi, my face bare, and these are my words.

Martin Hall

Martin Hall is a Scottish writer who has worked on the *7th Sea*, *Savage Worlds*, and *Edge of Midnight* roleplaying games. An archivist, historian, and qualified inquisitor, Martin finds his inspiration in the past. He writes fantasy stories, and loves using magic or technology to bend history out of shape.

Figuratively speaking.

Martin lives in Aberdeenshire with his wife and three children.

MAGISTRA TREVELYAN

By Ali Nouraei

Chapter One

JOHN STARED DOWN from Preston College's clock tower as a sliver of sun crested the treetops around him, steeping the Massachusetts oak canopy in a golden light. The rustle of leaves, swaying in the brisk morning wind, lulled his mind as he watched them ripple from the clock tower's rooftop.

He leaned over the stone wall at the edge and looked down to scan the forest again, searching for the source of the sharp ache in his heart. Despite his efforts, he still couldn't shake the feeling that he was being watched; and though he knew it was folly, he tried to stare back into the gloom of the forest floor, scouring it for a glimpse of an unknown threat.

He wrapped his coat tighter around himself, stretched out the ache in his neck and shoulders from a sleepless night hunched over his work, turned, and leaned back on the stone wall that edged the clock tower's roof. The roof's shingles shook slightly as gears whirred beneath him. The clock's mechanism clicked for a moment and the great bell, right below his feet, rang once to alert the college to the start of a brand new day. His heart leapt for a moment at the joy of hearing that familiar call to arms, and he drank in the excitement he had felt all those years ago at what awaited him in the day ahead as a student, rising from his dormitory on the East Wing. He turned to look for his old room's window—but the memory was fleeting, and in a merciless moment he was back on the rooftop, looking for some phantom threat, trying to keep the reason he was here from overwhelming him yet again.

He shuddered as he took in a sharp breath, breaking it into three small gasps, and suppressed another shudder as the chill of the morning air started to yield to the summer sun. He forced his eyes away from the swaying treetops and turned back to the small wooden door leading back into the clock tower. He fished Dean Walter's note out of his coat pocket again and scanned it for the hundredth time, looking for some hidden message, before giving up.

> *Meet me where I caught you rascals smoking the first time. Sunrise, this Sunday.*
> *The Wardens found Kate Hart.*
>
> —*Dean W*

He turned back to the old oaks and breathed in, trying to calm his heart with deep breaths of forest air, but the ache in his chest would not abate.

Unoiled hinges creaked as the door swung open and slammed against the wall as the wind caught it. Dean Walters half stumbled out of the narrow stairwell as he hunched to get through the small door. His waxed, polished Oxfords clacked on the slate shingles as he steadied his footing on the gently sloping tower roof. He wore a simple grey suit, a white shirt with a red tie, and his hair, painted a solid black, stood at odds with the signs of age on his clean-shaven face. He had the kind yet formal smile that he always wore, and turned to offer his hand to a young woman who had followed him up the stairs as they stepped out onto the cramped rooftop. She thanked the dean as she steadied herself on the rooftop and brushed the blonde hair from her face as the wind whipped it up. She wore a lapis-blue uniform suit, with the college's golden Pegasus on both lapels, and shivered in the morning chill. She had tried to look presentable, but her neat, well-ironed uniform contrasted with her pale face and the deep shades under her eyes.

"Mr. Trevelyan," the young woman said with a tired smile.

He recognised the woman as young Anna Hart, and resolved to suppress his own troubles for a moment to focus on her.

"Hello," he answered as calmly as he could manage, "you must be young Anna." He stopped and tried to think of anything at all he could say. As she stared back at him, he recognised the same fresh wound in her heart, the same pain written on her face as his own. "I'm so sorry, Anna. We"—he paused again to steady his voice—"my wife and I were both very fond of your sister. She would have been a brilliant Magistra."

Anna nodded and took in a deep breath as she looked down to her feet.

"Ah," she started, "Kate always loved working with Magistra Trish—"

"That's Magister Trevelyan, Anna," Dean Walters interrupted by her side.

She paused and caught herself, her face falling. "Oh, I'm sorry, Magister Trevelyan."

John smiled and shook his head. She was in mourning, and Dean Walters was standing on the bloody formalities. He suppressed a scoff. "If you called her Magistra Trish, then she's Magistra Trish to me. I don't remember any formalities between her and Kate."

Anna's face rose a touch, and John's heart eased at the first sign of a genuine smile in her tired eyes.

"Oh, no," he continued, "quite the opposite. Kate was more of a friend than a student to Trish. They were always around the house working on some project or another."

Anna nodded, smiled wider, and pulled something from her jacket's inner pocket that sobered the mood in an instant. It was wrapped in white silk, but he could make out the rough outline of a blood vial. His heart sank. Anna stepped past Dean Walters, clutching the silk bundle with care in both hands as she found her footing on the sloped roof and made it the five or six steps over to him. He held out his hand to steady her, but she wouldn't release the bundle and came to lean next to him against the wall lining the tower's edge.

"My dad," she said in a dull, rehearsed tone, "wants you to take Anna's blood vial today. He needs to know for certain that the remains they've found are his daughter's, and her blood vial is the only way you can be sure. He also said if Kate's gone, you don't have any reason to help us now, and he would like to thank you for all you've done to support us."

Money? She held her sister's blood vial in her hands, and her dad was worried about money? John sighed and had to stop himself from giving Anna a hug.

"Don't be daft," he said. "If I even think about not helping you, Trish would kill me."

Anna looked up confused. "But—"

"Oh, don't be fooled." John looked down at Anna and plastered on the warmest smile he could. "My dad used to say that, alive or dead, a Trevelyan must never stop fearing his wife." He placed a hand on her shoulder. "And he's right. Besides, Trish and I paid your tuition in full when we paid for Kate's. She loved you very much." John paused to let Anna steady herself as her knee buckled for a moment. "And," he continued, "there's an internship waiting for you, when you're ready, at The Grove, if you're still a Botanist, or anywhere else you'd like."

For the first time, Anna's exterior started to fray, and tears started to form at the corners of her eyes.

"Kate wasn't only her first student. She was family to us. My Lizzie called her Auntie Kate, and one of her favourite things to do was go to the soft-play centre with her. Please tell your father that. We loved Kate. You're family to us." He took his hand from her shoulder and gave her a few moments to recover. Dean Walters stared on from the door, his face still calm and professional, and indicated the vial.

John put his hand out, and Anna put the silk wrapped vial in his hand and nodded. Its warmth immediately shot up his arm; he shuddered as Kate Hart's life essence filled his mind. She was so warm, so kind; she didn't deserve to—

"Alright," John said, steadying himself. "I've got the image of her." He put the vial back into Anna's hands and turned to Dean Walters. "You'll lend her use of the college apparture? She should take the blood vial home where it belongs."

Dean Walters paused for a moment but nodded. It was a waste of power to teleport one student home and back again, but if anything happened to that blood vial, filled with Kate's essence at birth, her parents would lose the only link left to her.

"Alright, Anna. Thank you," Dean Walters said. "Run along to the sheriff's office, and she'll start the apparture for you."

Anna nodded, turned to give John one last smile, and walked back to the tower, where she stopped, said, "Thank you," and ducked through the door. As she descended out of sight, he was filled with the inescapable thought that she and her family didn't deserve this. No one did.

For the hundredth time that day, he had to fight down the urge to abandon every law he knew and chase down vengeance himself, Wardens and prison be damned. The only thing that stopped him was the thought of Lizzie growing up with a bunch of hags as he spent his life locked in a prison.

He had hardly finished the thought as his mother-in-law, Chief Warden Agatha, swooped down onto the tower, hopped off her broom like a woman a third her age and sauntered over to him, her sardonic smile barely veiled. She wore long flowing purple and rose robes, had her hair pinned up in an oval swirl, and enough brightly coloured makeup plastered on her wrinkles to paint a dozen regular faces. His stomach lurched.

"I tried to refuse this," she said in her elegant tone, her accent closer to an Oxford-trained witch than to the Mississippi river hag she was. She hid it so well. "But Mr. Hart would only give a sample of his daughter's umbilical blood to *you*. I trust you have a picture of her essence, now?"

John glanced over to Dean Walters, who shrugged and gestured to the emblem of the Wardens, a white willow tree symbolising the Star Mother, painted on Agatha's broomstick. He turned away and took a moment to study the treetops again, watching the leaves as they swayed back and forth in the wind as he thought back to the phantom threat he'd felt in those trees. He wanted to leave, but couldn't. Besides, this fear was folly.

"Why did her parents refuse to come themselves?" John asked.

"They didn't," Agatha answered. "I advised them not to. There, ah," she paused and stared up at the sky, holding her chin with an extended index finger, her nails painted a bright red. "There isn't much of her to identify. I thought it best to spare them that. I didn't know they'd ask for *you*."

John sighed hard, stretched out the ache in his neck and shoulders, and held out his arm, gesturing for Agatha to lead the way. She curled her lips into the barest smile, swirled her dress as she swung her leg over the broomstick, and led the way out over the trees.

John hesitated for a moment. Surely the distance would be too great by feather or broomstick, but she seemed sure of the direction. He shrugged, pulled a small dove feather from his inner pocket, and took up his wand, which hung by his side from a leather thong. He consumed the feather into his wand and floated out over the tower wall. Dean Walters joined him a moment later, and the three of them rode in silence over the college and towards the edge of the surrounding forest.

Again, John failed to keep the gravity of what he was here to do from his mind, and when he saw where Agatha was leading, he lost concentration and nearly fell out of the air. There were specks of blood at the treeline.

"What in Nafarin's name is that?" John asked, unable to keep the shock from his voice.

Almost as he finished the sentence, a speck of red—barely the size of a fingernail—rang out at his mind, its pattern echoing in Kate Hart's essence. It was her blood.

"There's more splatter like it for twenty-five miles coming from the southwest," Agatha said, her tone level and calm.

This made no sense at all. Why would Kate have been corporeal at the time of death? There should be no evidence of her in the physical world at all. No witch, however young, would die without trying to escape into an ether wind.

They were at the outer edge of the forest, looking down at a clearing through which a deep stream trickled softly. Some unattuned were already in the distance, setting up fishing lines and unpacking what seemed to be a small camp, placing crates of beer into an ice cooler at six in the morning. John reinforced the wards keeping him hidden and turned back to Kate's blood splattered onto an oak leaf at the edge of college grounds. What was she doing *here?*

"We're investigating why her blood is here, in corporeal form," Agatha said, "but we need you to confirm that—"

"It's her," John said, "that's Kate Hart's blood." He turned to Agatha and Dean Walters, but neither had any answers for him. None of this made any sense.

"Alright," Agatha said. She gestured to Dean Walters. "Get him back to the college."

She paused and turned to him, and John sighed as he realised she was about to try to be sensitive again. It stood so far against her nature that the effort seemed farcical, as though she was trying to mock him rather than comfort him. To his relief, she turned away and closed her eyes.

"I'll see you tonight, John," she said as she turned, nodded to them both, and flew up and away.

*　　*　　*

JOHN HURRIED UP the stairs to his front doors, his shoes clacking on the marble as he climbed three steps at a time. He had promised Lizzie that he wouldn't miss another school shuttle, and he intended to keep that promise. He tapped his wand against the lock, swung in the heavy oak double doors, and ran towards the aviary tower where Lizzie would be landing in a few moments on her school broom. *Damn it, Trish, why'd you make me build the house so big?*

He dashed through the family room, passed the kitchen, skirted around his workshops, and ran as fast as he could up the stone spiral steps to the aviary's peak. Their pet griffon squawked and snapped her beak for food as he passed, but he wanted Lizzie to feed her. He felt guilty for not having been there to see her off, as he'd promised, but Dean Walter's note took priority.

He swung the door open a few moments too late, and felt a pang of guilt as he saw Lizzie looking around the room for him, a stoic look on her face. He needn't have worried. The moment they locked eyes, and for the first time since her mother's passing, her face lit up. John couldn't understand why there was this sudden shift in her, but her amber eyes shone, her heart-shaped face smiled in its entirety, and her gap-toothed grin filled him with warmth from head to toe. He hadn't seen her like this in over a month. Not since Trisha was last home.

Her chestnut hair was tied in a ponytail as Trisha used to tie it, and she wore her pink polka-dot dress; the last dress Trisha had bought her. He had to remember to thank Claire, his secretary, for coming to his house so early to send his daughter off to school. He felt uncomfortable having to rely on so many other people to look after his daughter, but he couldn't avoid being away this morning.

"Daddy!" she screamed. "You're here! Can we go feed baby Daria?"

John had bought Daria as a freshly weaned cub to try and distract Lizzie from her mourning. It hadn't worked, even though she had asked for a baby griffon for almost two years. Why the sudden interest?

Mrs. Murphy, her class witch, turned to check on the restraining spell keeping her broom steady as it floated above the aviary's landing, and descended to the floor. She brushed her hand over Lizzie's hair and gestured for her to go and bring a feed sack for the griffon. There was clearly something on her mind. She wore the black and gold robes of a school-witch, her blonde hair was tied in a bun, and everything from her warm eyes to her smile spoke to her profession, kind and nurturing.

He let her lead him to the side of the oval room and leaned in close to her as she gestured with a concerned look and shook her head. John looked back to her broom and had to look again as he saw it empty. There would normally be seven other girls there as Mrs. Murphy made her rounds, taking her charges home. Where were the other children?

"Mr. Trevelyan," she said softly, "I'm so sorry to burden you with this, but it's starting to be a problem."

His heart skipped a beat. What? What was wrong?

"Lizzie keeps speaking of her mother." Mrs. Murphy's glance dropped to the ground, and she sighed as she shook her head again. "I'm so sorry for you both, but it's not healthy to let her have her mother as an imaginary friend. I know she's been happy again for the past two days, but these repeated mentions of seeing her mother through windows—"

"Wh—" John tried to say but found his voice wasn't coming. Fire and bile rose from his gut and swamped his chest. He leaned on the aviary's plastered stone wall to keep from falling backward. "What?"

Mrs. Murphy furrowed her brows and paused for a moment. She leaned in even closer. "Since yesterday, we've heard her speak to the other children about seeing her mother. It's all in her imagination, we're sure, but she's talking about very little else."

"Her mother's dead, Mrs. Murphy." His gut churned; he nearly heaved his half-eaten lunch out over Mrs. Murphy's robes.

"It's nothing like that, Mr. Trevelyan." She clasped his shoulder and squeezed it, and despite himself, he felt a touch of calm. "Our schools are the safest in the world. There is no malice, no evil intent anywhere near her, I can promise you that. We've asked the Wardens to search the school in full. Only the Star Mother's power exists there."

He wanted to believe her, but a warning in his mind would not abate.

"Anyway," Mrs. Murphy continued as she looked back at her broom. She smiled as Lizzie brought Daria's feed sack over, struggling to haul the thing—it was almost half again as large as she was—with a determined look on her face. "I have to go, but please speak to her? She isn't haunted, but we are very concerned."

John shuddered for a moment but nodded. "Thank you," he breathed out in a hushed tone. Mrs. Murphy turned back to her broom, but Lizzie placed the feed sack down and ran over to pull at her robes.

"Please, will you come, Mrs. Murphy?" Lizzie asked as she stared up at her teacher.

Mrs. Murphy smiled and sighed out.

"Alright," she said, nodding her head. "But only for a moment. I have to get back to the school now, Lizzie."

John thought that he should apologise to the teacher, and stop Lizzie from taking any more of her time, but he stood there as he tried to absorb what he had heard.

He let Mrs. Murphy lead him down the spiral steps to Daria's roost and swung in the steel grate door. He picked up Lizzie, let Mrs. Murphy walk in ahead of them, took one step in, and froze.

"Hi," Trisha said, standing by the griffon's head, stroking it. "John? John, why am I here?" Her voice brimmed with fear and confusion. "What's going on?"

"Mummy!" Lizzie shouted. She struggled free and ran to the spirit.

Chapter Two

JOHN FOUGHT DOWN bile again, trying not to retch. He rubbed his temples to stop his head spinning and tried to focus on calming his short breaths as his wand, raised over his right shoulder, shackled the corporeal spirit to the sofa.

A fresh chill crawled up his arms and down his spine, and this time he nearly lost control of his binding spell as his stomach, no longer under his control, heaved up his lunch onto his living room carpet. *Where in Nafarin's warded ass is Agatha?* He couldn't hold on for much longer.

He threw three more bindings around the spirit, pinning it down harder onto the sofa, wiped the bile from his mouth and tried to stand, but found his legs wouldn't acquiesce. He sighed, and despite himself, looked up.

Trish stared back at him, trembling, her lips locked in a firm line and her amber eyes awash in terror and confusion. John knew that the spirit had taken his wife's form to throw him off and make it past his defenses, and it had nearly worked. He breathed a prayer of thanks to the Sky Mother that Mrs.

Murphy had been there with him.

The school-witch stood firm, with her knees slightly bent and her right arm outstretched as she kept her ward in place. Trish had picked her well: she knew her work. The forward guards of her ward didn't so much as flicker as she held them outstretched, the power emanating from her fingertips. Her left hand, held over her shoulder, hovered gingerly above Lizzie's hair as she kept her asleep, bound to her back. School-witches didn't hold much by way of power, but in protecting children, they were second to none.

It had taken John the space between the aviary tower and their living room to finally lock the spirit in a shackle spell, and he wasn't sure how much longer he could hold it. His stomach lurched and seemed to spin inside him, nearly sending him to the floor in vertigo.

He cursed his body. Where had this weakness come from, all of a sudden? He tried to suppress his mind as it half shouted the answer back at him. He'd replaced sleep with scholin weed extract for nearly a month. His shoulders resumed their familiar ache, and his temples started to throb.

He stood, paused a moment to let his mind stop spinning, and made his way across the living room to his drinks cabinet and took out a fresh bottle of scholin extract, his wand trailing behind his head as it pointed directly at the spirit and kept it trapped in place. He cracked the wax seal and downed the whole bottle in three gulps. He caught the warning label from the corner of his eyes as he put the bottle down.

Don't exceed two 500ml bottles per one calendar month.

How many did this make it since Trish died? Two a day for twenty-seven days? Fifty-five bottles this calendar month. His mind steadied, and fresh currents of power rushed through his whole frame as the scholin's core hit his gut. He drew in a deep breath, held it for a moment, and let the aches and pain melt away from him.

"Alright," he whispered.

He turned back to the spirit. The resemblance was incredible. With the strength the scholin weed had given him, he pushed down the wave of nausea he got from looking at her, but wasn't able to check the fresh shudder that ran up his back. Whatever demon had sent this spirit was a master of imitation. Trish's jet black hair sat unkempt over her shoulders, the ends split and the waves curling into frizzled locks. Stray strands of grey weaved their way through, framing her haggard face. It looked like she hadn't slept any more than he had since she'd left. The bags under her eyes were black chasms, and the lines along her forehead and the corners of her mouth had deepened into trenches.

Every inch of his being wanted to run over, grab her into an embrace and squeeze her against him till he could go back with her to whatever hell this imitation had crawled from, but with a fresh breath, he tried again to calm himself and study the situation.

As he was about to check on Mrs. Murphy, something fresh caught his eye. The scratch on her cheek was there. A week or so before she'd left on her expedition, Lizzie had accidentally scratched her cheek as they play wrestled. The scar was there now. A demon knew to imitate that? How?

He shook his head as he walked over to Mrs. Murphy. Her

face was serene, standing at odds with the immense measure of power pouring from her every second. He didn't know what he'd have done without her here.

"Thank you," he said, before turning back to the spirit.

"Are the Wardens coming?" she asked, but a slight quaver in her voice seemed off.

"My mother-in-law is," he answered, turning back to look at her more closely. "How much power do you have left?"

"Ten minutes," she said, letting out a long, drawn breath between gritted teeth.

That didn't make any sense. "What?"

"Budget cuts," she answered before he'd finished the word. "We only hold half an hour's warding."

John shook his head. Half an hour? What incompetent, heartless parasite would cut funding for children's warding? Half an hour per school-witch was dangerously close; in the farthest communities from the Warden's Tower, it may not even be enough to keep a child safe until the Wardens arrived. Damn.

He skirted behind Mrs. Murphy and touched his hand to a white tile panel beside his drinks cabinet. He turned to tap his wand against the lock without thinking and remembered with a start that he still had the spirit lashed to his sofa. *By the Sky Mother's love, Agatha, where* are *you?*

He turned and manually entered his code into the lock mechanism, then stood back as it clicked, whirred, and swung open. The lockbox held a single canister of distilled mana from the main New England Ley Line. He carried it over to Mrs. Murphy and placed it down by her feet. She glanced down and double-taked, eyes widening. Her ward quavered for a moment.

"This isn't mass-market," he said, "it's distilled. Take small strips, let it absorb, and take in another."

"I—" Mrs. Murphy hesitated. "It's too much, you can't." She paused again. "It's more than I make in ten years."

John walked back to his recliner and tried to ignore the pool of vomit next to him as he eased back into it.

"It's for your ward, Mrs. Murphy. You're keeping my daughter safe."

He relaxed a touch as he heard Mrs. Murphy draw slivers of the power into her wand, and looked back to the spirit. Her white buttoned shirt and beige khakis were marked with red clay, and her white boots were also covered in the stuff. He tried to ignore the form of his wife, following her familiar contours up, then screwed his eyes shut as he forced himself to meet her gaze again.

Its eyes were quivering, as if it were about to cry. He tried to put himself in its shoes. Even as the thought formed, he heard the woosh and snap of someone materialising in his private apparture.

"Listen," Agatha shouted, stomping down the stairs behind them, "I need you to understand normal people don't simply walk around with the power to travel by apparture, prick." She brimmed with anger, but all he had to do was sit and wait for her to come down. "I had to borrow from the Tower," she added, and John could feel the shame in her voice.

"I'll pay it," he shouted back.

"Oh, will you? Now, what was so important that you couldn't wait for me to fly here, you selfish piece of—"

Before he could turn to see her, he felt her release each of his bindings one by one and replace them with her own stronger

Warden's bonds. She tapped Mrs. Murphy's shoulder as she passed, her eyes focused on the spirit, seeming to glide over the carpets in her long, flowing robes as she approached.

The spirit's back straightened and arched as Agatha's bonds tightened around her, and it was all John could do to keep himself composed as he saw the form of his wife writhe under the pressure. It wasn't right. What hell-spawned demon would do this to them?

"Did you take a reading?" Agatha asked in a calm, level voice.

"No," John answered as he struggled up to his feet. "All I could do was lash her down as Mrs. Murphy raised her ward and put Lizzie to sleep."

Agatha nodded.

"Approach from its right, recall your wand and hold it two feet above her head. Tell me what's reverberating there."

John stood, sighed out hard as he stretched out his neck, and tried to keep his step steady as he approached the form of his wife. The imitation was perfect. He did as Agatha asked, but couldn't feel anything.

"Only its heartbeat," he said. "It's a reverberation of its heartbeat. Your bonds are hurting it."

Agatha shook her head. "Look deeper. It's not a fel, and it's not a succubus; what is it, John?"

"I don't know," he half muttered as he tried to peer deeper into the spell that spawned the spirit. "It doesn't feel enslaved or even summoned."

Agatha hissed in frustration. "What *does* it feel like, then?" Her calm tone started to fray.

"It feels like Trish." John closed his eyes and let his heart shudder as his wife's life force filled him. From the first moment he'd seen the spirit, something hadn't felt right. Now that he was this close and peering into it, he couldn't shake the feeling that this was his wife.

But that was impossible.

"Don't be daft," Agatha snapped.

"Look." He turned and beckoned. "It's even got the mark on her cheek from when Lizzie scratched her by accident. I *know* it's an imitation, but I can feel her now. Something's wrong."

"Oh, listen to yourself," Agatha said as she approached.

In two hundred millennia under the Star Mother, there hadn't been a single recorded event of Her bringing someone back. Sure, there had been accounts, rumours, but nothing proven, nothing recorded as fact. As he stared down into the life essence of the being bound to his sofa, he couldn't think of a single explanation.

He tried again, attuning his wand to the demonic channels that course through this world, to the winds of magic on which the djinn surf around the world's skies, looking for prey. He even tried to feel for the resonance of an extra-terrestrial power-well, manifesting here, looking for a victim, but all he could feel was the warmth and strength of the Sky Mother's power and his wife's life force.

Was this the scholin weed clouding his mind? He shook his head to clear it and looked again, and a sharp spike seemed to ram through his heart as his mind started to settle on the idea that maybe—as he had begged since her death—the Star Mother had brought her home to him.

He turned to look at Agatha, and his heart skipped a beat. Fire and terror rose from his gut in waves. Agatha held a blood vial in her left hand, and as the spirit's life force reverberated above her in tune to the beat of its heart, the blood vial responded in flashes of light.

"Is"—John hesitated and swallowed hard—"is that Trish's?"

Agatha nodded, and John's world turned upside down. Trish's blood vial flashed in time with the spirit's heartbeat. That couldn't be. He took half a step back and looked closer as Agatha loosened the tightest of her bonds.

"Ah," he half muttered as his thoughts scattered, "Trish?"

THE SECONDS CLICKED on the grandfather clock outside in the hallway, seeming to hammer John's nerves with every strike. He sat on a stool across the kitchen table from Agatha and Trish. Mrs. Murphy kept Lizzie asleep and paced back and forth near the window overlooking the estate grounds, keeping her bound to her chest with a mild charm and covering her with her black robes. She stroked her hair as Trish stared on.

"Only for a minute. I need to hold her," Trish said. Her voice was hers. Her eyes were hers. This was Trish, materialising in her own flesh and blood, but it was still too much to ask to let her near his child.

"No," Trish said to herself before John could answer. She dropped her head into her hands, her voice edged in a desperate tone. "I don't know what's happening."

She crossed her arms across the table and leaned forward to bury her head in them. Her hair stood up, frayed and jagged, and Agatha put her hand over her head, stroking it, even as she kept the last of her Warden's bonds in place at Trish's waist.

"You *are* a spirit," Agatha said, her voice devoid of any of its natural flair and confidence. She was sure that this was her daughter, but even she couldn't bring herself to let a spirit close to Lizzie.

"What're you going to tell her?" Trish asked, her voice muffled as her head remained buried in her arms.

"It was all a dream," Mrs. Murphy answered. She stopped pacing and looked back at them. "I can tell that only the Star Mother's power lives here, same as you all, but a child—even one like Lizzie—wouldn't understand what's happening." She paused and scoffed. "I mean, none of *us* do."

They sat in silence for a moment as John's head swayed, and his nerves screamed with every tick of the clock outside. He sighed out hard and rested his left temple on his fist as he leaned forward on the table. He idly sipped from his ginger tea, but it did nothing to settle him. He pushed the cup away and leaned back on the stool.

"Can you remember anything before here?" he asked.

Trish looked up. Agatha moved her hand from her head down to her shoulder and pulled her closer. Trish leaned into her mother and shook her head.

"Only a feeling," Trish said.

Agatha looked down at her, silently urging her to go on.

"Like"—she hesitated—"a billion voices speaking together, but one voice speaking out. It—" She paused again and squeezed her temples. "The feeling was inhuman."

Agatha nodded. "And the clay on your clothes. We sensed your life force ending, but nothing else. Do you know where you are?" She shook her head. "Where your corporeal remains are?"

Trish was lost for a moment; she looked over to John and

shook her head. His heart fell. He didn't know why she had been brought back, but he had hoped it had something to do with bringing her killers to justice.

"Nothing at all?" John asked, unable to keep the desperation from his voice.

"No."

Agatha nodded again, trying to get some of her exterior composure back in place. John had to stifle a scoff.

"What was the last thing you recall?" Agatha asked, her voice a touch calmer.

"Preston College, the woods, packing some crate, and"— she paused and screwed her eyes shut, tilting her head to the side—"and nothing. I remember my life, what we had for dinner the night before I left, putting Lizzie to bed, my last night with John, and that's it. I don't remember waking up the next morning."

John found he couldn't sit anymore. He stood and walked over to the fridge, opened it, closed it again, and walked over to the kitchen's central island and leaned over the marble worktop. He shuddered as he tried to force the memory of his last night with Trish from his mind. The memory of her embrace shot straight from his chest to every last inch of him, and he fought with everything he had to keep his eyes dry.

"Trish," he said, trying to keep his voice steady, "the Wardens found nothing in your e-mails, diary, phone. It looked like your expedition simply didn't exist. You don't know why?"

Trish shook her head.

"You don't remember Kate or the professor?" he asked

She shook her head again but paused midway.

"I do remember them, in the days before leaving, but nothing of the expedition itself. It's—" She started slapping the palm of her hand against her head, till Agatha stopped her. "I know I'm here for something, some—it's all a blank."

John opened his mouth to speak, but stopped as Trish stood from her stool and walked over to him. He didn't know whether to reach for his wand or to back away, so he stood there, frozen, as she took his hand, sending his heart racing and a shiver through his whole frame. She felt so real. He held her hand back.

"I think I'm bound to *you*," Trish said, and her soft voice washed over his battered mind like smooth milk and honey. "I materialise to you." She dropped her head in thought. "And Lizzie, too."

It took every shred of his strength, but he kept himself from pulling her into an embrace. He knew he couldn't ever let go.

Agatha hummed, turned to him and furrowed her brows. "Her e-mails were wiped, as were Kate's," she said, taking control of the room as she gestured to Trish.

John nodded in agreement and waited for her to go on. Trish let go of his hand and walked back to her mother.

"Margaret Goodland refused to speak to us, and Professor Goodland's notes were destroyed, same as all the e-mails. She still hasn't said a word to us."

John nodded as he started to follow her idea.

"She was always so fond of Trish," he said. "If we show her the blood vial—"

"Yes," Agatha said, turning to Mrs. Murphy. "Can you stay here at all? With Lizzie? Maybe for a day while John and I investigate this?"

Mrs. Murphy looked back from the window, hesitated, but

nodded. "We are all but servants of the Sky Mother," she said.

Trish sat back next to Agatha, and the two of them turned to him. He felt as though his mind ought to be going numb by now, but every time he looked at her, a fresh spike seemed to ram straight through his heart. He shuddered for a moment and collected what remnants remained of his wits. He took in a long breath, stretched out the ache in his shoulders, and looked at his watch.

"It's one in the morning here, should be past six in the morning in Scotland." He sighed and dropped his head as the gravity of the situation dawned on him yet again. "We can apparture to Fort William and fly the rest of the way into the Highlands." His mind swam in a hundred different currents, but going to Professor Goodland's widow seemed to offer the best chance at an answer. He was with Trish when they died. He'd never kept notes electronically. Maybe whoever had murdered them missed something. Maybe his widow would help them, assuming she could accept that Trish wasn't a demon's apparition. "We can be with her by eight or so."

He looked up, breathed out a prayer to the Sky Mother, begging for strength, and finally released his clutch on his wand. He let the power it held dissipate, and unclenched himself. He'd need another bottle of scholin weed before leaving. Margaret Goodland was not a woman to suffer dull minds.

Chapter Three

JOHN DREW ANOTHER dove feather from his breast pocket and fed it into his wand to maintain altitude. He suppressed a yawn and poured more power into the wards protecting him from the surging air as they raced towards Loch Carron, flying below a rain cloud the size of the sky that seemed to be in some monstrous hurry to empty its bowels onto the land below.

The ground below was awash in lush green canopies, beige hills—some snow-capped—and golden fields of rapeseed breaking the otherwise wild landscape here and there. He weakened his wards against the air for a moment and breathed in the rich scent of life all around him, letting it settle into his core as the air inside his ward started to swirl and rush about. In a few moments, the few slivers of rain poking through his wards drenched him, and John relaxed a touch as the cool highland rain washed away the ache from his weary frame.

He turned to check on Agatha. She barely seemed to be feeding any power into her broomstick at all, and her charm against the air even kept her lilac robes from flapping as they raced across the Scottish sky. He wondered at how little power her flight seemed to take and patted his breast pocket again to make sure he held enough feathers for the flight back.

"Offer's still open," Agatha said, focusing her voice into a tight spell that shot straight through his ward and into his left ear.

John suppressed a shudder. *Not this again.* "There isn't enough room on your broom for the both of us," he answered through the same spell.

Agatha shook her head and stared down towards the ground, as though to study some building miles below to their right.

"You know she's only trying to be nice," Trish said in his mind. He wasn't sure he could ever get used to that, the voice of his wife playing in his mind. He wondered for the hundredth time that morning how the life essence of one departed could attach itself to his. From what he knew of the Sky Mother, it wasn't possible.

Trish materialised behind her mother on the broom, looked over at him with a mild glower, and shook her head. Alive or dead, he wasn't about to let Trish talk him into sharing a broom with her mother. Exhausted, unshaven, and still wearing his suit and underwear from yesterday, he nonetheless had his dignity to protect.

"It was here, wasn't it?" Agatha asked, pointing to a village ahead of them in the distance.

John stared at her in confusion for a moment, but her meaning dawned on him in a rush. He remembered where he was. He swallowed hard and let a little more rain drench his face. The mound of grief that he locked in the core of his heart was calm for the moment, but he didn't want to look down. He kept his head raised and nodded.

"You knew?" he asked.

Trish had a smile on her lips as she sat behind her mother, facing towards him and swinging her legs underneath her. Somewhere between the house and here, she'd fixed her hair into a ponytail, the deep wells under her eyes had been replaced with her usual rich amber hue, and the light in her eyes had returned. He suppressed a shudder down his back, but found he couldn't look away from her. He couldn't help the smile that parted his lips.

"You think I'd let my nineteen-year-old daughter out of my sight? Especially with a Trevelyan?"

John's heart lurched for a moment.

"You watched us?" he asked, not able to keep the shock from his voice.

"No, imbecile," Agatha said as she tutted at him. "I knew where you were taking her and chose not to stop you."

This was it. They were right above it, the hotel he and Trish had run off to twenty years ago. *We were so young.* He looked down to find the hotel still there, still the same. Twenty years and the building hadn't changed a bit. He turned to Trish, and their eyes met. His smile seemed to widen itself.

"I told her she could do better than you, but she seemed set, despite my efforts," Agatha said.

John frowned and turned to defend himself, but found Agatha smiling back at him. He wasn't sure, but as she turned away, he thought her lower lip trembled.

"Best nights of my—" He had to catch himself as a wave of grief threatened to break the banks of his heart. He tightened his lips and stretched out his back. They didn't have time for this; they were almost at Laird Bellard's exclusion wards. He shook his head, trying to push the memory of escaping to the highlands with Trish from overwhelming him, and steadied himself.

He raised his wand higher in greeting as they approached the mild shimmer in the air that marked the outer boundary of the exclusion ward, but found himself met with a solid rejection. He furrowed his brows and turned to find Agatha slowing to a halt too. She raised her Warden emblem to open the exclusion ward, but it refused her and stayed shut.

He shook his head, but before he had found Laird Bellard's number in his phone, the ward rippled and shifted and two clansmen floated out to them, each cradling a yew branch brimming with force under their right arms and wearing the black and red Bellard warrior robes.

He turned to find Agatha alone on her broom, Trish having dematerialised, and raised an eyebrow at her. She turned her hand and gestured for him to stay back as she nudged her broom forward and flew straight up to the clansmen.

"What the hell kind of greeting is this?" she asked in her imperious Warden's tone.

"Ah," the lead clansman said as he surveyed the two of them. "We weren't expecting visitors." He turned and exchanged a look with his colleague. "The Laird has locked our lands," he said, bowing his head slightly in apology.

Agatha turned to look at him. John floated over to the clansmen and tried to remain patient. They were only doing as they were ordered, and they each held a branch of power long enough to vaporise them both.

"I've yet to find anything but a warm greeting from the Laird," he said in as formal a tone as he could manage, "despite the cold outside." He gestured to the air around them.

The lead clansman bowed his head but still shook it. "I do apologise, sir, but our orders come from the Laird himself."

John decided that the two men weren't going to budge, and so he dialled the Laird on his phone, waited for a few moments, and smiled as a raspy voice coughed twice, muttered something, and talked to itself.

"Ah, what's this? A call. Oh, it's John. How do I answer this damned thing? Phi," he called, "Phiona, come here. How do I answer this poxed trinket?" His voice had grown a touch more hoarse, and John wondered if he'd quit smoking pipes like he'd promised the last time they'd met.

"What?" the Laird continued. "What do you mean it's already connected? John?"

"I'm here," he answered.

"John, you grey-haired bastard, where the hell have you been?" Laird Bellard shouted. John put the phone on speaker and turned it so the clansmen could see the screen. "Times like these you need your *real* family, boy, not the fat-arsed Warden bitch you call a—"

"I'm here too, my Laird," Agatha said, doing nothing to hide her contempt. "Have you grown out of another reclining chair yet, you manatee?"

"Hah!" the Laird shouted down the phone. "Almost."

"We're being held at your outer wards by a couple of burly-looking men," Agatha said. "They're packing some serious firepower. Expecting trouble?"

"Always," the Laird answered. "Alan, Calum, that you?"

"Ah"—the lead clansman lurched forward a touch—"yes, my Laird."

"Let 'em through. Where're you going, John?"

"We'd like to see Margaret Goodland, if you'd permit."

"Me?" the Laird laughed down the phone. "I can't permit a damned fart with that woman. But you can see her, if she'll see you. I'll meet you there in five. Bye."

"Bye." John hung up the phone and gestured to the clansmen. They bowed, turned, and led the way through the ward.

JOHN SMILED AS he watched Laird Bellard hunch over a basket outside Goodland Cottage's heavy oak front doors. He stood a head and shoulder shorter than the clansmen flanking him, but even in his old age the raw power of the man hummed from his every nerve and sinew. John couldn't help but smile as he walked the stone-paved lane, lined with waist-high hedgerows on either side.

The Laird kept glancing back to a list in his left hand as he poked through the basket with his right. "Two loaves, two dozen eggs," the Laird said as he rummaged, oblivious to their arrival. "Three bunch of sausage. Cheese, pickles, grapes, and—" He paused and grimaced. "Shite. I forgot the fruit," he added, turning to the clansman on his right, a tall, thin young man wearing the familiar black and red of the Laird's guard.

John's heart rose a little as the Laird spotted him, flashed a wide grin and walked over in his relaxed gait, extending his hand.

"It's been far too long," John said as he took his hand. The Laird's handshake was characteristically subtle, barely registering. In their world, where others tried to infuse their handshakes with etheric force to seem more powerful, Laird Bellard barely even twitched his hand muscles. He reminded him of John's father in that way, his power being self-evident and always understated.

His grey beard was cut short and pointed at the chin, and his short hair, still shot through with a few black strands, was combed back, sitting drenched against his head as the rain clouds kept up their deluge. He dressed in his usual oiled long coat, deep green except for patches of black grease stains here and there, and a pair of worn jeans.

"It has," he said, his deep highland burr sounding even raspier in person than on the phone. He turned and walked up to Agatha. "Well, I could've gone a bit longer before seeing her again." He turned back to John with a grin and gestured over to Agatha, towering at least two feet above him. She smiled and inclined her head.

He gestured for them to follow him and led the way over to the cottage's front door. He raised his hand to knock, but Claire Goodland, the professor's daughter, opened the door and stepped out. She wore a white blouse that was immediately specked with rain, tight-fitting blue jeans, and a pair of pink slippers. Her blonde hair framed her face as it sat across her shoulders and her green eyes, usually bright and warm, seemed etched with a heavy weight—like she too hadn't slept in weeks.

She held a steaming cup in her hands and took a sip as she raised her eyebrows and looked at the Laird with an exhausted smile on her lips.

"Hi, Claire," Laird Bellard said as he extended an arm and patted her on the shoulder. "I know what you'd said, about the spell and all and visitors, but I thought she'd make an exception for two friends? Phiona also gave me this for you." He turned and gestured for the tall clansman to place the basket down by the front door. "I forgot the apricots and peaches."

Claire reached out and hugged him. "Thank you," she said, her voice dripping with fatigue. The sound took John by surprise. She had always been so sprightly. Grief affects everyone in its own way, he supposed.

John stepped forward. "Hello, Claire," he said. For the first time, she looked past the Laird and over to him. Her face lifted a touch, and she returned his smile, then turned to greet Agatha.

"Yes, please do come in out of the rain," she said, turning back to open the front door. "Sorry," she half sighed as they all stepped into a dimly lit hallway with ornate wallpaper and a low ceiling, "the house is in a bit of a state."

"Oh, don't fret your arse over that," Laird Bellard said. He sent the clansmen out to stand guard outside the front door with a gesture of his hand. "Want me to send Mimi over to you again, refill your freezer with cooked meals?"

Claire smiled but shook her head. "Thank you, but we're still going through the last batch. Neither of us is eating much nowadays."

The Laird shook his head and sighed as he took off his coat, revealing a green woolly jumper over a white-collared shirt. He shook off the rain and hung the coat up.

"I understand. I'll go see to the ward stones while you all talk, if it's alright," he said. He gestured back to John and Agatha. "Think our friends want to see your mother. Let me know if you need anything."

Claire smiled again but shook her head. "The wards are fine, Laird, thank you. If it's all the same to you, I think my mother would like to speak to them in private."

He paused and stared at her for a moment, but nodded and

walked back to the coat rack, put on his coat, and clasped John's right arm. "It's good to see you again, lad. Come see us, once in a while, will you? We miss you."

John smiled and nodded as he shook his hand again. "As soon as I can, I promise."

The Laird smiled, bowed his head slightly to Agatha, and walked out, the clansmen at the door falling in behind him. In half a moment, they were up in the sky, heading back to Bellard Castle.

"Welcome," Claire said, as she placed her cup down on a side table in the hallway and closed the front door, "to Scotland. It's been a while."

Agatha stepped forward and took her hand. John glanced over to her, and had to look again as he saw a genuine look of concern on her face. It seemed so out of place.

Claire squeezed Agatha's hand back and led them both to a small study through a door along the corridor's left. The study was filled with mahogany furniture, empty bookshelves lined every wall, a waist-high globe stood by the tall window, a large circular table sat in its middle on a round rug, and seven or eight small chairs were dotted around.

Margaret Goodland sat on a chair at the table, mouthing silent words as she held a slip of paper against an oil lantern and read it over and over. She was frail at the best of times, but she'd aged a decade since he'd seen her last year.

She looked up and seemed to stare past them for a moment, distracted and unfocused as she kept muttering to herself. Then she turned to Agatha, and it was as though she'd flicked a switch. All of a sudden, her eyes, the same green as her daughter's, focused, her frown disappeared, and she sat up straighter. She ran a hand through her wispy grey hair and tied it behind her in a ponytail, smoothed her red, floral blouse and grimaced for a moment as she pushed her chair back and stood.

"Agatha, John," she said, her voice filled with warmth and love, as he always remembered her to be, "welcome. Oh, Sky Mother's love, it's good to see you both. What are you doing here?"

John stood by the door and leaned against the side of a bookshelf as he watched Agatha walk over and take the seat next to Margaret. She had furrowed her brows and looked over to the note Margaret had been reading.

"Oh," Agatha said, her voice suddenly strained with pain, "oh, Margaret, I'm so sorry." The two women looked at each other for a moment and embraced. Tears formed at the corners of Margaret's eyes, though she screwed them shut.

"If I'd known, I'd have come—" Agatha tried to say.

"I know," Margaret cut her off. "He was never registered in your Warden Tower; you couldn't have known."

John stared, lost. He went to ask about the note, but Claire took his hand and led him out of the room. She pulled him across the corridor and into a kitchen, out of the back door and into a small, well-kept garden. They stood under a short awning over a patio as the rain hammered down around them.

"What's going on?" John asked once Claire had closed the patio door. "What was that note?"

"A letter from Raghav's mother in Sindhustan."

John gestured for her to go on, but she turned away. Raghav was a post-doctoral student at Preston College with Claire. They studied medicine together and were the best of friends. As her face started to glow red and a solitary tear formed in her left eye, ice clutched at his heart.

"Is he alright?"

"No," Claire said. Her lips began to tremble, and she turned away to wipe fresh tears from her eyes.

"What?"

"He was with Trish, Kate, and my father," she whimpered.

Though he wasn't sure how, John found his heart sank lower yet, and his shoulders hunched down as he breathed out hard. He hadn't known anyone else was with them, but Raghav and Professor Goodland were nearly inseparable. He should have known to check in on him after the incident.

"I'm so sorry, Claire. He was like a brother to you."

She nodded, still with her back turned to him as she wiped her eyes.

Raghav would have been registered at birth in Sindhustan, but should have been visible to the Warden Tower in America. Why hadn't he registered with them when he arrived? Petty politics and jurisdictions, he supposed.

"After Damavand," she started to say; she paused to catch a sob. "Damavand, and through the eighties, there were symposiums and conferences around the world, every year, trying to talk through all of our differences." She took in a deep breath, held it for a moment, and let it out in a long, drawn-out sigh. "People like my father, and yours, identified the cost of war on our Sky Mother. It was beyond anything we could imagine, and beyond even the most selfish will to take from Her. But they had to learn that the hard way." She turned and looked up, and a fresh pain shone out from her eyes. She shuddered and dropped her head.

John slowly nodded and stared on, waiting for her to go on, but she didn't.

"Yes," he said as he stared at the back of her head. "The symposiums are still meeting every winter equinox."

What did any of that have to do with Rhagav? He reached a hand out and placed it on her shoulder. Her body shook at his touch, and she turned further away.

"Raghav and I were born on the same day," she said as she drew in a long, halting breath and tried to compose herself. "We were meant to be born a week apart. My dad had budgeted to stay with my mum for a week, then apparture over to Sindhustan and see his second child born."

That didn't make any sense. "What?"

"At one of those symposiums in 1985, my mum and dad met a Maji from Sindhustan in the hotel bar." She started to cry again and shook her head as she suppressed it. "That night, my brother, Raghav, and I came to be."

By Nafarin's warded ass. What?

"It was a different time," Claire continued. "They both grew up in the sixties."

John sighed out hard. "So Margaret grieves for her husband and his son too, and you for your father *and* a brother." John shook his head and thought of anything he could say. "I'm so sorry, Claire. If I'd known I'd—"

"It was a bit of a secret. The Laird knew. He had to lend my dad use of his apparture in the town to let him go back and forth between the two women bearing his children. Your dad knew. He funded it. I thought you knew."

John shook his head as it dropped. "I'm sorry, Claire. I thought we shared our grief, but now I can't even imagine what you two are going through."

She twitched her lips as she tried to smile at him. "So now

you know," she said as she exhaled a long breath and wiped her eyes clear one more time. "We didn't know he'd taken Raghav, but he was with my father when they died."

John was reeling. Why wouldn't Trish have mentioned Raghav coming with them? She'd have normally taken a mana canister over for him on any expedition, but she hadn't. He thought about asking her and started as he felt her materialise in the next room.

"What was that?" Claire asked as her face shot towards the house.

John turned and walked back into the kitchen, crossed the corridor, and entered the study to find Margaret standing by Agatha at the room's far end. He looked around, but Trish was nowhere to be found.

Agatha had a hand on Margaret's shoulder, who was visibly shaking and leaning on the back of one of the chairs. Margaret gave John a look and shook her head slightly before glancing over to Claire as she entered the room behind him.

"Mum, what's wrong?" Claire asked.

Margaret did her best to smile as she lowered herself into the seat she was leaning on. She sighed, tried to compose herself, and turned to her daughter.

"I'm alright, dear. Nothing to worry about. Chief Warden Agatha has asked about your father's latest work."

Claire looked on, confused.

"I've told her that no one has broken in here. Your father and Trish themselves burned and wiped every vestige of their work before leaving." She looked up around the bookshelves and grimaced for a moment before recomposing herself. "The reason there's nothing to be found is that they didn't want anything to be found."

So, whoever had murdered them didn't wipe the records of the expedition, as the Wardens had thought. But that raised a hundred fresh questions, and he felt the familiar ache at the base of his skull as he tried to focus his mind. He stretched out his neck and shoulders, took a seat by the door, rested his chin on his fist as he sat forward and yawned. He'd need more scholin extract soon.

"Do you know why they destroyed the records?" he asked.

He looked up to find Claire staring at him. She exchanged a look with her mother and seemed to hesitate for a moment until her mother nodded, and pulled up a chair near him. She reached a hand into her blouse. John turned away in embarrassment until he felt something leathery tap against his leg. He turned back to find Claire proffering him a sheet of suede.

He took it, though his cheeks flushed in embarrassment at the warmth of the leather, unwrapped a piece of paper from it, and handed the cover back. He looked up to find Agatha staring intently at the paper and Margaret urging him to read.

He unfolded the small square of paper; it looked like a page torn from a journal. He read Professor Goodland's hand.

7th of April, 1993
Oxford

What makes Shangri-La, Shangri-La? A hermit found a world engine in the mountains and tapped it. What makes the Desert Spring flow endlessly into the world's ley lines? A nomad found a world engine in the dunes and tapped it. Why does Damavand flow mana into the world? Because a miner found a world engine there and unsealed it. Until those exact moments in our species' evolution, our knowledge and capacity to absorb the strength of our Sky Mother was limited.

Since then, with the now seven world engines flowing as they are, we as a species are taking unprecedented flows of mana from Her whom we revere, and not caring one iota for the pain it may cause Her. We are children, suckling at the teats of our Mother, believing Her milk to be endless, unaware—or unwilling to accept—that we are killing Her.

The engines that feed us, our Sky Mother's teats, may be the organs through which She draws breath. If my friend Antony Trevelyan is right—

John paused at the mention of his father. Though that wound had long since scabbed over, he lacked the mental strength to think about it now. His father had lived a long and full life, but now, more than ever, he wished that he would swoop in and fight away his worries like he had done so many times before.

"I'm sorry," he said. He continued reading.

—the world engines may exist to feed our Mother, not us. Like Shangri-La, our objective lays hidden, waiting to be found. If our research is blessed with success, and we can find and unseal an American world engine, bringing it into the partnership between the American Tribal Circles and the Trevelyan network of colonial ley mines, for the first time since humanity tapped her power, our Sky Mother may be able to draw a breath.

We don't know what celestial forces enable our Sky

Mother to live, but we are now sure from studying the pattern of yields from ley mines across the world, that if we don't find and activate a world engine, under the control of Antony and the Grand Shaman, humanity will suffocate its own Sky Mother as it draws from Her unceasingly.

John stood from his seat as Trish's mind flared in his. Something familiar rang out to her, but she couldn't remember what. *Sky Mother grant me strength.*

The quest for an American world engine had driven his father's life for more than two decades, and then, a few months before his death, had come to an abrupt halt. He wasn't aware that his father's madness was shared by another.

For the last months of his life, all his father would talk about was 'them.' The others, watching him, listening to his thoughts. His father had driven himself mad in a deluded quest of self-sacrifice, trying to lead his phantom pursuers away from a truth that only he could see. John had never believed him.

He sat there, stunned. Talk of the Sky Mother's weakened strength was near heresy, and though he couldn't deny the hard data his father had collected about the weakening of the ley network, especially after the battle at Damavand, this talk of the Sky Mother 'drawing breath' through the world engines was madness. Even so, he couldn't help but think back to Preston College's clock tower, to the phantom threat he had felt as he stood there—was it just yesterday morning?—and the unshakable instinct that he was being watched from the treeline. His heart shuddered.

"My father," he said, though his voice croaked and he burst

into a fit of coughs. "My father," he tried again, swallowing hard. He dropped his head into his hands and tried to calm his nerves by drawing long breaths.

"I think," Margaret said, the strength in her voice at odds with the grief she had shown moments before. "I think my husband had found what your father and he sought, all those years ago. That's why he wiped his steps. You remember nothing of what Trish was doing in the days before they left?"

John looked up and shook his head, ashamed. He had been so buried in his work that he hardly ever had any idea what Trish was doing. All those nights, locked away in his study, protecting his father's company. He'd give it all away to have her back now. He dropped his head and shook it again as his mind drew itself back to Preston College's clock tower.

John felt as though his heart should tremble, that he should worry. He wanted to be afraid, as his father had been of the phantoms chasing him. He had thought his father mad, all those years ago, imagining an unseen pursuer. But at this moment, now, he welcomed them. He wanted them to chase him. He wanted to be found, to confront the bastards and bring every ounce of his wealth to bear on them, to blast them to oblivion and back, and kill them again. He found his face shook in his rage and calmed himself.

"And you?" he asked. "Do either of you remember anything about his work before the expedition?"

Claire shook her head, but Margaret lurched forward again and stood from her chair with force that took John by surprise. She shuffled over to the globe by the window, lifted the top half open, pulled a cork from a glass decanter there, and took three deep gulps of what smelled like fine whiskey.

She coughed, cleared her throat, and shook her head.

"After," Margaret said as she turned to Agatha, "what you've shown me, am I safe in assuming that you're not linked to your Warden Tower?"

Agatha didn't respond for a moment, but nodded as Margaret handed her the whiskey. She took a gulp and leaned forward on her chair, rested her elbows above her knees, and breathed out hard.

"I cut the link yesterday," Agatha croaked. She took another gulp of whiskey.

Margaret paused for a moment, exchanged a look with Claire, and reached into a pocket at the side of her skirt. She pulled out an official looking letter with the emblem of the Hungarian Tower of Magi and threw it onto the middle of the table as she stared at it with distain.

"He destroyed everything," Margaret said, her face screwing into a deep frown, "every last shred of paper but the one you hold. He bound the two of us into secrecy. But, there's nothing in what we swore about his posthumous mail."

John looked forward and studied the glyphs on the letter. The last one, from Laird Bellard's mailroom, was dated the week after Trish had left on her expedition.

"And Trish?" Claire asked.

He turned to meet her eyes. "Hmm?"

"My father," Claire said, "destroyed every shred of paper he owned, but left me that." She gestured to his hand and shrugged. He gave it back to her. "Did Trish not bind you to secrecy?"

John couldn't help but scoff at himself. "She didn't need to."

Claire slowly nodded and gestured over to the letter. "The

truth," she said as she kept her eyes locked on the letter, "is that even if we weren't bound to secrecy by his power, there wouldn't be much we could tell you beyond what that letter contains." She grimaced with pain for a moment as a restraining spell flared in blue arcs of energy at her neck, but she still nodded over to the letter. "It came a week after the Wardens came and told us that his life force had been snuffed out somewhere in America."

John stepped to the table and took it, his hands suddenly unsteady as he hurried to open the letter, bile flaring in his gut as he unfolded the first real piece of information he'd seen about what Trish and the professor had pursued. There were two sheets. The first was a covering note from the Hungarian Mining Network, asking the professor to pay a bill.

"What?" he whispered under his breath.

Clipped behind the note, an official state treasury invoice was signed by Maurius Duma, Force Commander of the Hungarian Interior Militia, for the provision of seven sets of military GPS trackers tagged with the reference, 'Goblins.' John looked over to Agatha, his head swimming. *What did any of this have to do with goblins?*

"Did the professor ever mention goblins?" he asked, but no one answered.

He glanced over to Agatha who shook her head, looking about as confused as he was, but something familiar rang from Trish in his mind. He felt her start to say something, but the thought scattered.

He looked down and sighed. Hungary. He'd need more power for the apparture.

Chapter Four

JOHN AND AGATHA floated a mile above the main Hungarian ley line, following the Danube's path through Budapest. The city lights lit the night beneath them, the Danube a solid black amidst the blazing suns of bridges and palaces. People moved about in the pools of light, little more than specs at this distance, and a tourist boat, nearly a hundred feet long, lazed through the water with the occasional camera light flashing from its upper deck.

He tapped his wand against his thigh impatiently as the Hungarian Tower slowly started to materialise above them, seeping into the corporeal world in a sea of mist and sparks, as though a thundercloud flashed with a million tendrils all at once above them and pushed the crystal tip of a grand obelisk out of itself. He wondered at the power it took to hide all of this from unattuned eyes. He floated a hundred meters below the cloud, but even this close the warding around it prevented all but the faintest hiss from reaching his ears.

The tower emerged upside down and turned on its axis as it

slithered out of the cloud of mist. It was made of a solid black stone, the seams between the colossal bricks almost invisible in the night, making the tower a solid mass of shadow. It was a four-cornered obelisk, capped with a crystal pyramid that would normally hum with power; now it seemed dim, almost dead to his eye. Something was wrong.

He glanced over to Agatha, who craned her neck up to the tower's apex, now several hundred meters above them and climbing up into the night sky as it twisted. She shook her head and looked back down to the river.

Above them, the tower's base began to emerge from the mist. The tower proper hovered above the base, suspended on a cushion of azure-blue haze. The tower's base was made of seven interlocking disks, spinning around one another, together forming a giant circle—almost two thousand meters in diameter—that clicked and whirred as the circles turned.

The circles were flat, less than a meter thick, but made of intricate filigree meshing, as though knitted from steel wires, and filled with the same azure-blue haze of power that supported the tower. He looked back down to the Danube and saw the film of mana snaking its way up from the base of the river and binding to the wheels spinning around the tower's base. The lines of power filled the sky above him as far as he could see.

He floated over to Agatha, tapped her on the shoulder, and gestured for them to go up and around, but she didn't move. She shook her head and kept her eyes locked on the river.

"Pride of Hungary," she said, an unfamiliar, grim look to her face. She kept her head bowed, raised her wand arm up, and held her fist out in salute. John started as Trish reminded him with a whisper in his mind that Agatha was there at Damavand, forty-three years ago. She was there at the mountain's peak, where the fighting was at its thickest. He looked up again with fresh eyes, trying to imagine what Agatha had seen, forty-three years ago. He imagined a tower, exactly like this, materialising out of the mist and loosing all its batteries down on her enemy.

The Pride of Hungary, the sister tower to the one above them, had rushed into the fray and saved her allies from total massacre by the Ashabaltari, sacrificing herself to blast their enemy back from the cusp of victory. It now rested somewhere at the bottom of the Caspian Sea, lost to the Hungarian Magi who had built it.

Agatha never breathed a word about it: it was so easy for him to ignore her past, but Trish had mentioned some details about her mother's life during the great wars.

"Fort Endurance Militia, weren't you?" he asked.

She didn't answer for a moment, but then tried to smile and nodded to him. "Still am," she said.

He inclined his head and gestured for her to follow, but paused as he caught a glimpse of an emblem pinned above her heart. The wind shifted the folds of her robe, revealing her Gold Order of Damavand. That was strange. She never wore any outward sign of her wartime past. The usual air of superiority that she exuded while flying was missing, and in its place, a grim stoicism had descended upon her.

They crested the spinning discs of the tower's base and almost immediately the first of the Hungarian tower guards approached them, but instead of a challenge, he saluted. John looked around to find almost every guard there, uniformed in a deep navy blue with maroon leather shoulder pads and golden buttons, giving them a strange look as they passed. They were unusually well armed, holding long branches shimmering with azure power, though some of their branches looked drained. Several guards flying above had stopped on their broomsticks to stare at them, and at the opposite end of the tower, John thought he could see the white plumes of a Polish Hussar, though he couldn't be sure at this distance. What would they be doing here?

They reached the tower's portal without challenge, and the guards didn't hesitate before swinging the colossal stone doors inward for them. Though Anton, John's best friend from Preston College, was now Arch Magus of the Tower, even he hadn't ever been welcomed inside the tower without identifying himself. He conjured his name-bracelet and looked around for someone to present it to, but the man who'd opened the door ignored it as he ushered them inside with a curt gesture. This felt wrong. He hesitated, but walked in.

They passed through the entrance into a small atrium, lined on both sides with guards, and descended to the floor. John put his wand away, and Agatha dismissed her broomstick into a haze of mist and light. But when they walked through a doorway and stepped into the heart of the tower, the calm silence of the tower's exterior was shattered in a moment as movement surged passed them in all directions.

The central shaft of the tower was an oval, extending high above them to the tower's apex without interruption. Rooms and levels lined the tower on all sides, and lights shone from countless windows into the tower's central cavity.

A thousand conversations buffeted their ears as officers dashed this way and that, all of them in some inexplicable hurry. The looks on their faces seemed panicked, and no one looked quite sure of what was going on. He tried to catch anyone's attention, but everyone around them was locked in their own turmoil. No one even noticed them as they walked into the tower's central cavity.

Halfway up the tower, the industrial levels hissed vapored mana into the air, filling it with a metallic tang that struck his nostrils, and the various mechanical arms and wheels operating this way and that drew in the power in thin tendrils of azure-blue power through the air. The sight always took John's breath away, but something seemed wrong this time. He remembered the crystal at the tower's apex, dim and drained, and started as he saw tendrils of mana float to power banks normally reserved for weapons of war. He peered closer, and a chill ran down his back as he saw even the tower's interior Arkannon batteries empty of power. Someone had loosed every ounce of energy in the tower, and judging from the hiss and shimmer still escaping from the heat banks beneath the tower's main arsenal, they'd done so mere minutes ago.

"I don't agree with this," Agatha mused as they walked on towards the central desk, a circular table with three officers around it behind computers. "If someone knocks this out, all of Hungary is vulnerable."

"If," John answered. "That's a very big 'if.' Do you think they've been running drills?" He looked back up at the depleted mana-cells and overheated power banks, struggling to find an explanation as to why their weapons had been pushed so heavily, or used at all.

Agatha nodded but went on as she pointed up to the tower's central weapons systems. "Look, the central emitters are empty, and even the interior Arkannons are spent. Stacking all of a nation's power into one structure, it makes them vulnerable."

"They didn't, though," John said, raising an eyebrow. "They built two."

Agatha's face fell. She sighed and nodded as they picked up their pace toward the central desk, but were beaten there by a crowd of young soldiers. By the time they arrived, all three clerks were occupied with at least a dozen soldiers of varying ranks querying the whereabouts of their commanders.

John recognised a few of the names they sought as Anton's deputies. From the frenzied conversations, John caught snippets of some great upheaval out east, but with his basic understanding of Hungarian, and the urgency of the competing conversations, he wasn't able to make out any details.

His mind turned back to the crystal at the tower's apex. The weapons couldn't possibly have been used in anger, could they?

"John?" Trish asked in his mind. "John, look."

He let her turn his head up towards a window to his right, roughly a third of the way up the tower. It looked like a cafeteria, and a massive television screen took up an entire wall. Even at this distance, John could make out the shape of the Hungarian Tower, tilted on its side, the crystal at its apex flashing tendril after tendril of power down onto a target on the ground.

"By the Sky Mother," Agatha said as she walked up beside him and looked at the footage. "What is that?"

"Arkannon Class HL-7," John answered, his mind numb. The footage was recent. In all likelihood, the tower had only just rematerialized here from whatever fight was being shown on the news screen. He had to find Anton.

"What?" Agatha asked, still staring at the screen in the distance.

John looked over to her. "Like our Mark 33 Trebuchet," his mind answered as though unbidden. He shook his head, tried to focus, and fished another scholin weed bottle from his jacket. He cracked the wax seal and down the whole thing in three gulps, ignoring the glance Agatha shot at him. "War," he said, as the gears of his mind shook off their rust and whirred back into action.

All around them, soldiers still dashed this way and that, but he knew from some unknown instinct that they were being watched. He wanted to go to the front desk and ask for Anton, but nothing he'd seen since they'd arrived had made any sense. Why were they ushered in without challenge on arrival, especially if the tower had been in a fight?

"Trish," he whispered. "Can you get a closer look, maybe hear what the news is saying?" He peered but couldn't make out any text running along the bottom of the screen from this distance, only the emblem of the Oxford Broadcasting Wisdom's World Service. The anchor, who John didn't recognise, seemed shaken, her skin almost as pale as her ivory blouse and jacket.

"Hold on," Trish answered as he felt her drift out of his mind. Within the space of a breath, the anchor's voice rang loud in his head.

"These images, again," the anchor said, "from some minutes ago outside the Khanate's perimeter wards, where former Arch Magus Anton Virga still resists the mutineers with what remains of his forces and the support of his Cossack allies." The anchor paused, straightened her jacket, turned in her chair, and looked straight at a new camera. "We now move live to the Hungarian Tower, where our correspondent Sofia is ready to report from the press conference being held by the leader of the mutineers, former commander, and now self-appointed Arch Magus, Maurius Duma."

"We need to leave," John said, but he felt Agatha's hand on his arm.

"Shh," she answered, "don't move a muscle now. Don't even turn your head."

What in the Sky Mother's love was happening? Where was Anton? Who was this Maurius, and what was he doing bearing Hungary's might down on the Cossacks? How could anyone succeed in a mutiny here?

"I need to find Anton," he said.

"For now, they're closing in around us. Hold for my signal."

John's heart skipped another beat. Who was coming for them? Was that why they'd been ushered inside—straight into a trap? But why wouldn't they use an internal turret to kill them, if that's what they wanted? "But, if they wanted us dead they'd—"

"Whatever idiot was in command must have ordered the internal turrets drained to power the attack on the Cossack perimeter wards on the news screen. They're empty, and I think the same idiot ordered the big weapon recharged first."

John tried to keep his head still as he turned his eyes to follow the drifts of mana moving through the tower's industrial levels. Agatha was right. The internal weapons structure seemed completely drained. As the reality of their situation began to dawn on him, he found his mind wouldn't be still anymore. He needed to act, but for the moment, patience was the best path forward.

"Here," Trish said, drawing his attention back to the screen. A tall, burly man, dressed in the same deep blue uniform as the others around but with the golden chevrons of the Arch Magus on his brown leather lapels, stood at a microphoned podium. The black falcon seal of the office of the Hungarian Arch Magus adorned the podium and hung on the curtained wall behind him. He was flanked on each side by Knight-Magus Etienne Louis of the Frankish Confederacy in the azure robe and chestnut staff of his full battle regalia, and Commander Leon Grupa of the Polish Hussars, with a similar staff and the ceremonial plumed armour of his order.

This was wrong. A hot pain gnawed at his chest, and he had to grip his wand handle tight to try and keep himself composed as the imposter on the TV screen started to address the room.

"Magi, sorcerers," he said in a rich baritone, "warlocks and witches, ladies"—he paused and inclined his balding head—"and gentlemen." He gestured to the men on either side of him. "The Hungarian Tower of Magi, the Frankish Confederacy, and the Holy Order of the Polish Hussars welcome you to Budapest, where the first action of this new holy crusade has begun in earnest."

John's legs struggled to keep him upright. What in the Sky Mother's name was happening?

"I am not one for lofty speeches, so I shall be brief. The honour of our great nation shall be restored as we begin construction on the recommissioning of the Pride of Hungary. Long have our people suffered abuse at the hands of the very peoples that destroyed the great sister tower to the one in which you all sit. Well, we say now, 'No longer!' As Arch Magus of our illustrious tower, and commander of this crusade, I issue three declarations."

John tried to glance around without moving and found the

soldiers watching the press briefing on their phones or the various computers that were dotted around. He cursed himself for having come here. When he'd set off from Goodland Cottage, Anton was the Arch Magus of the tower, and in the space of an hour the world had turned itself upside down and he'd walked right into a lion's den. Still, if Anton was alive and fighting alongside the Khanate as the news report said, he had to find a way to tell him that the tower's interior turrets were drained. He didn't know why'd they'd been let inside—any trap they'd been led to would have been sprung by now—but he still thanked the Sky Mother that she'd let him learn this much at least.

"My first decree," Marius continued on the TV, "as Arch Magus of the Hungarian Tower of Magi is to secede from the Treaty of Damavand. We will no longer be restrained by its callous terms, or a party to the corrupt, bureaucratic Oxford Forum that governs it."

Agatha grabbed John's arm. He glanced over at her. The serenity of her countenance was brutal. Ever sinew and muscle in her frame was taut, and her jaw clenched. She was a flat sky, coiled in power, about to burst into a storm.

"My second decree," Marius continued, "is the declaration of war on the powers of Sindhustan and Ashbal. In the Sky Mother's name, we shall exact justice for what was taken from us."

The appartures leading out of the tower were pressed up against its outer walls; they were all blocked shut by strong wards, but they were their best hope of escape.

"We need to get to the appartures," he whispered.

Agatha scoffed. "They're blocked. Are you blind?"

"My third decree," Maurius continued in his briefing, "is

to demand reparations from all major world powers to begin the reconstruction of the Pride of Hungary. Thank you all for coming. There will be no questions. Good day to you all."

John turned back to see Maurius stomp away from the podium as the room erupted in a furore, but he paused as a young reporter pushed her way through his guards and shouted her question out almost at his face.

"Maurius Duma, by what thought process do you believe the Sky Mother would sanction such an act of pure greed and barbarity?" the reporter asked, her glasses on her head and a notepad in her hand.

Maurius paused a moment, and the room erupted into open violence as the guards pinned her to the floor and he ordered her thrown from the tower's apex.

Time was up. John glanced around, trying not to move his head, as he counted at least three dozen guards coming in to encircle them.

"Do you know how appartures work, Agatha?" he asked.

"No," she hissed.

"I do, and I know we can't fight our way out of here, so please listen to me. On my count, we'll dash to the leftmost apparture on the east wall of the tower."

John took in a long breath, held it. He ran a hand along his long coat's inner pockets, feeling for his mana stores.

"I have three canisters. You?"

"Again, John, you need to understand normal people don't walk around with condensed mana."

He shook his head. Nowhere near enough to fight off so many. He took one canister out, placed it in Agatha's hand, and tried to steady his galloping heart.

"Don't take it yet. I'm going to blast open a ward at the appartures."

"And then what, genius? They've blocked all access, and unless you've gone blind, I'm sure you've seen the guards."

John nodded. "Blocked to every other apparture in the world, yes."

"And so what's the point—"

"No one ever blocks access to the same apparture, though. It's never even considered. Who in their right mind would waste so much power, given you couldn't go more than a few meters?"

"What?"

"If we can make it to the outside, we can blast a hole in the tower's base and dive down to safety."

For the first time, Agatha tore her gaze from the TV screen, on which the young reporter was now being carried to the tower's apex for execution. She looked over at him.

"Wait," he said.

Though every nerve in his body screamed at him for the delay, he paused to see where they were throwing the reporter from.

"West appartures," he said as he gestured over to the TV screen. "We need to come out at the northwest edge of the tower."

Agatha stared at him for a moment and slowly nodded.

"Brace your neck. Ready?"

She took in a breath and nodded again.

In an instant, John drained the first of his two remaining canisters into his wand, shook away the sudden rush, and summoned a monstrous gust of air behind them. He braced his neck as he was wrenched forward, crossing almost the entire width of the tower to the appartures against its outer wall in less than a second. He didn't have time to recover, but flowed from the spell straight into a warding disc that he cut loose and let float behind them.

His heart caught for a moment as he saw the interior turrets of the tower turn towards them, their automated wand arrays whirring into action, but they had no power left to loose. He thanked the Sky Mother for the idiocy of whoever commanded them to be drained. He had to get that information to Anton. A few moments later, the first of the soldiers opened up, leveling a small chestnut branch at them and crashing three sharp bursts of power against his ward. John poured the last of his power into it and turned to the apparture.

He cracked the last canister open, drew its power, shuddered for a moment, and shaped it into a sharp point that he drove straight into the apparture's warding. It held for a moment, but as further blasts crackled and snapped off his ward, he felt Trish's mind lend strength to his spell and together they managed to tear the warding away from the apparture.

"You first," he shouted over the cacophony of blasts as his ward started to fray at the edges.

"How do I do this?" Agatha asked, but John only took her by the arm and shoved her into the apparture.

"Hold on." As he'd predicted, the apparture's control screen flashed red for every destination on Earth; but he read the serial number above the entry portal and punched that into the destination field, and it flashed green. In a moment, Agatha snapped out of existence, and he heard the woosh and snap of her materialising on the outside. He glanced back as his ward started to bulge inward and tear under sustained attack, then punched in the same destination—shifted two meters to the right—and darted into the portal.

His insides twisted and lurched as he snapped into existence above the metal walkways that criss-crossed the tower's base and fell onto it, managing to maintain his balance as he bent his knees. He glanced back to see that he was mere inches from the cushion of mana that supported the tower, and breathed a prayer of thanks that he didn't miscalculate. Agatha stood holding her head to his left, but they didn't have time to recover.

"Hurry," he said, fighting down the nausea. "Empty the canister and shape it into a cone."

She looked over at him, breathing hard, and did as he asked. He led her over to the intersection of two revolving discs beneath them, visible under the tightly woven mesh they stood on, and pointed at where the power flashed when the discs beneath them aligned.

"We only get one cast, so make it count. Blow through that exact intersection," he said, pointing down.

"Well, get back then," she half shouted back.

He stood up and scanned the air around them. A few soldiers had spotted them and were turning their brooms to intercept, but he found what he was looking for as a gut-wrenching screech started to sound from above him. He summoned the last of his reserves into his wand, formed a net, and caught the young reporter as she plummeted. He'd been sure from the image shown on the TV screen that this was the right side, but still breathed a prayer of thanks as he found her.

He eased her down to the ground as she shook from head to toe, her green suit splattered with blood, urine trickling down her leg.

"Is it aligned?" Agatha asked.

He turned back to find her holding a conical spell of destruction above the intersection. He was about to ask her to turn her spell the right way around, but realised she would know exactly what she was doing.

"Yes." He took the shaking reporter by the hand and shielded her as Agatha thrust her spell down, inverted it mid stream, and crashed it straight into the tower's base. Nothing seemed to happen for a moment, but as the spell's outer edge crashed into the tower's warding, driving all of its power into a concentrated point thinner than a human hair, neon blue sparks of North American mana shot out in all directions, and Agatha's spell started to burn like molten metal through a sheet of ice.

At first, the warding kept every sound contained so that all John could hear was the wind buffeting them, as the acrid taste of burning mana clawed at his sinuses. But soon the ground shook beneath them, the solid metal below their feet rippled like flesh, and the entire tower shook on its azure-blue cushion of mana.

As he turned to shield the cowering reporter, the spell burned through the outer warding shielding the intersection and a soul-crushing crash blasted his ears and knocked him off his feet.

Before he could stand, the first of the soldiers' attacks smashed into the ground in front of him. Agatha spun, raised her wand and lanced the attacker through the heart. He lurched back and fell from his broom, his corpse splattering and falling through the mesh a hundred meters away.

"Now!" he shouted as he picked up the reporter, tried his best to shield her from the flames still gushing from the hole Agatha had blasted into the tower's base, and jumped through it.

* * *

"'STAND ALONE, DIE alone. Death knows no border,'" John whispered. Those were the opening words of the Treaty of Damavand. The last time a war of this magnitude raged, death had come to every corner of the world. Every power had sworn never to let the blood of innocents sate the thirst of war again. Yet here they were. A few short hours ago, the world was at peace: and now, war.

He shifted his weight as the train carriage rattled and moved, and sighed heavily. They'd waited only long enough to see the reporter picked up by the unattuned ambulance they'd called. Her injuries were physical, and no one would think to look for her in an unattuned hospital.

He shuddered again as he recalled leaving her, but he'd done all he could for her. They'd moved through every dark alley they could for the first few minutes, eventually coming to a main road busy with bars and restaurants, all packed with unattuned people reveling through the night. It hadn't taken him long to find a station for the Budapest Metro lines.

He took the invoice Margaret Goodland had given him out of his pocket, and read it again. "Maurius Duma," he whispered to himself, "Force Commander of the Hungarian Interior Militia." Now, he was Arch Magus, and according to that Oxford Broadcasting Wisdom anchor, Anton sheltered with the Cossacks. This couldn't be allowed to stand, not if he could help it.

Trish had started to remember snippets here and there: she was sure that whatever was happening had started with those GPS trackers. But how? He needed answers, and he needed power. He and Agatha were both unmarked by the battle they'd survived, but completely drained of power, and their nerves were frayed to the point of exhaustion. John had given his last scholin weed bottle to Agatha.

"John," Agatha hissed as a man's backpack jostled her and almost knocked her off of her feet. "What is this accursed place?" She grabbed the handrail tighter with both hands as the carriage lurched, shook for a moment, and rolled to a halt at a station.

"It's an underground railroad, one of Europe's first electrically powered ones. Made in the 1890s."

She scoffed and shot a glare at another man who had tried to hold the same handrail as her.

"Have they upgraded it since then?"

John smiled and nodded. "It's one of the nicer ones."

Agatha shook her head, "And what in Nafarin's tits are *we* doing here?"

"Budapest's skies are tightly controlled, the flight paths are watched, apparatures are shut. We have to get to the old city unseen."

She scoffed again and gestured all around them. "In broad light, surrounded by people?" she asked, her voice near exasperation.

John nodded. "If you'd dressed a touch more—normal—we'd be near invisible in the crowd, but, even as we are, no one watches these unattuned transit lines. They're full of pain and misery."

John took another swig of the water bottle they'd bought from a machine to wash out the acrid taste of unattuned commutes, and shuddered as he swallowed, the water sitting uneasily in his gut. Few places in the world caused more pain to a servant of the Sky Mother than mass transit systems. Even during quiet hours, they dripped with the agony of tens of thousands.

They stood in silence for another three stops, rode the electrical stairway up, and paused at the exit from the station to see if they could gather enough power from anywhere to throw up a basic ward: but they were completely depleted. John tried to act natural as he scanned the skies above them, then stepped out into the glow of a street light and led the way towards Bohdan's Emporium.

Agatha kept pace, though he could see she was uncomfortable. After leaving the main road, they walked ever deeper into Budapest's hidden underbelly, streets scattered with pools of urine, garbage, dog waste, and—here and there—brief flashes of alchemical lights heavily warded and hidden from unattuned eyes shining above doorways.

John tried to remember exactly which door marked Bohdan's shop, but stopped short as he caught sight of a Hungarian uniform standing guard outside of it. He instinctively dropped his hand to his wand, but even as he remembered that he was completely powerless, three violet sparks flashed from the shop's windows, and the guard at the door dropped to the ground, followed by two other similar thuds from the inside.

John approached slowly to find Bohdan and his son, Pavlo, dragging two more uniformed bodies out from inside the shop.

"John," Bohdan called, his voice cracked and raspy from decades of tobacco abuse. John had offered to pay for the corrective surgery many times, but Bohdan liked it, claiming it gave him an air of danger. Like the Cossack needed it: the man's bald head, scarred right eye socket, glowing blue eyes, and gold-toothed grin dripped lethality from his every movement. His muscles were gnarled and knotted, and his ears cauliflowered from decades of boxing.

"Bohdan," he answered as he approached, but Bohdan was looking past him.

"You bring a Warden here?" he asked, shooting him a questioning look.

John nodded. "Needs must, my friend. I need your help."

Bohdan finished chewing on something, turned away for a moment, nodded, swallowed, and turned back.

"These new guys, John, they want to make me an offer."

John gestured down to the three bodies outside his door. "And that's your answer?"

Bohdan rolled something with his tongue, turned away, and spat it out onto the road. "Da." He turned back and stared directly at Agatha. "I don't like her here."

"I don't like *being* here," she answered, unperturbed.

Pavlo stood leaning up against the door, holding a minor oak branch in his hand, humming with the violet hues of pure Khanate mana.

"The Khan?" John asked.

"At the front line, where you can always find him," Bohdan answered, and John could taste the pride in his words. Whatever else this man was, he was loyal to his Khan.

"You know why I came to you?" John asked.

"The apparture network is shut. I can guess what you want."

John nodded.

"Alright, one trip, where do you want to go?"

John drew in a deep breath and released it in a long, drawn-out sigh. "I need to speak to the Khan and Anton."

Bohdan paused for a moment and looked him up and down with a deep frown. He rested his hands on his hips, and Pavlo stopped leaning on the doorframe to stand up straight.

"Bohdan," John continued, "time is not on our side, and the opportunity is passing farther by the moment. I had to take the Metro lines to get here unseen, and we're now out of time. Will you trust me?"

Bohdan didn't answer for an age, and John found that he was holding his breath: but the Cossack shook his head, stepped back for a moment and growled, staring at the floor.

"You know what we'll do to you if you are with *them?*"

"I'm not," John answered, never losing sight of Bohdan's wand arm—not that he could do anything if attacked.

Bohdan coughed, nodded, and stood up straight. "Da," he walked over and placed his hand on John's shoulder and gestured for young Pavlo to make way at the door. He led them inside and walked over to a drinks cabinet to pour vodka.

The inside of the shop was as squalid as it was breathtaking. It looked unchanged from Soviet days, the outdated utilitarian decor standing at odds with the ridiculous array of weapons systems hanging along its walls, branches of all shapes and sizes, from a dozen different varieties of trees, shining with the hum and glow of power from all corners of the world. Above an old, cracked mirror behind the wooden counter, Bohdan's pride hung on two chains from the ceiling: a whole limb of a Persian Ironwood tree, still charged with power from the now sealed world engine at Damavand.

Agatha had paused at the door; John had never seen her so visibly uncomfortable. Pavlo, a tall sixteen-year-old with jet black hair, bright brown eyes and a thin frame invited her inside, covered the three bodies with a ward to conceal them, and closed the door. Then he raised a wand and asked her permission to cut her link to the Warden tower.

John started as he realised Bohdan had allowed her inside, thinking she was still linked. To help him, he was willing to give up his entire shop.

"She's already cut her link," John said, placing a hand on Bohdan's solid shoulder. "But thank you for the show of trust."

Bohdan visibly relaxed, blew out his cheeks, and nodded.

"Pohzahlstah," he said, stooping to pull a threadbare Persian rug from the floor, uncovering a hidden trapdoor. He coughed as he opened the trapdoor, releasing a plume of dust, and pulled a lever on the underside of the floor to lower a staircase into the space below.

He tapped the wall with his wand as he stepped down, lighting a number of alchemical globes that bobbed along the cellar's ceiling. They all joined him downstairs and Bohdan called to Pavlo to uncover the hidden apparture. The 'dark network', as it was called, a series of secret appartures used by smugglers and thieves, was something the Wardens had been trying to infiltrate for decades. It would take a lot for Agatha to forget what she had seen here today.

Bohdan drew a power canister, glowing a rich emerald green and bearing the state stamps of the ley mines of Sindhustan, and fed it into the apparture to awaken it.

"Address?" he called as he hunched down by the apparture controls above the floor.

"Air, alum, cinnabar, amalgam, and copper," John answered.

Bohdan typed in the symbols and waited as nothing happened.

"Hello?" called an ephemeral voice from beyond the apparture's portal. "Who's that? We can't see where you're calling from. Who is this?"

"This is John," he answered, stepping closer to the apparture.

"What the—" The voice paused. "John what—what are you doing on this line, where in Nafarin's accursed breast even are you?"

"A cellar under Bohdan's Emporium. Anton, listen, when we skipped class in year seven, and my dad caught us on our adventures, where were we?"

The voice laughed, and though he couldn't recognise the voice through the distortion of the apparture, the laugh was unmistakable. "Lady Ethel's Dance Parlour."

John smiled for a moment despite himself, drinking in the memory before it slipped his mind.

"Oh, really?" Trish asked in his mind, and John smiled wider. "Even in year seven, huh?"

"Anton," John said, "Agatha and I blew the main conduit on the west edge of the tower. Whoever commands it had drained every last bit of energy from the tower itself. Half an hour ago, the interior turrets were still empty, and they were recharging the main Arkannons first."

There was silence for a moment, but before John could start wondering what was happening, Anton's form materialised through the apparture, followed by three guards.

His friend seemed to have aged a decade in the months since they'd last met. His chestnut hair had greyed a touch, but even worse was the half-grey stubble that now adorned his normally clean-shaven face. His blue eyes were haggard, and an arc burn forked along his left cheek. His deep blue uniform, bearing the Arch Magus' gold chevrons on the brown leather lapels, was speckled with blood, burnt in places, and torn at the right knee. His friend had been through hell.

The three guards—two men and a woman—seemed even

worse off. Before he could step forward to embrace him, a brutish hulk of a man with a dyed black moustache stepped through behind them. His face was calm, but authority came off him in waves. He wore a thick circular hat in black fur and a red coat with gold buttons bound by a white sash at his waist, with a curved birch branch hanging from it. The signet ring of the Khanate glinted on his right index finger. Bohdan and Pavlo immediately dropped to their knees.

John paused, halfway over to Anton, locked eyes with the Khan, and bowed his head.

"Great Khan," he said, trying to think of anything appropriate to say. Even a family as powerful as his had never been invited to the courts of the Khanate. He'd never met the man in person. "I wish our first meeting had been in better circumstances."

The Khan snorted, walked over, and placed a hefty hand on John's shoulder.

"The interior Arkannons," he said with a grin, "are drained?"

John nodded.

The Khan turned back and raised an eyebrow at another Cossack, dressed similarly to his Khan, who had walked through the apparture with three giant canisters of pure violet Khanate mana. The man nodded.

"We wondered," the man said in a young, assured voice, "at how they could sustain their attack so long. At the least, father, it's worth a try now."

John bowed to the young man, who turned to feed the apparture with enough power to portal through half an army. The Khan and Anton eyed each other.

"Your men hold here," the Khan said, but Anton immediately stiffened and shook his head.

"It's our tower; we have to be there."

"Your men are spent, man; you can't ask them for more if—"

"They will fight for their tower." Anton's face had taken on a desperation that John had never seen before. He didn't like it. The Khan nodded and started issuing orders to the men arriving, one at a time, through the apparture.

"How long before this criminal's wards fail and we are spotted?"

"Great Khan," Bohdan said as he bowed even lower, still on his knees, "seven minutes."

"Khan," John said. He locked eyes with the man as he turned towards him. "Bohdan and his son Pavlo—not to mention his wife, Natalia—whatever else they are, I know them to have always been fiercely loyal to their Khan."

The Khan paused for a moment, studied him, then nodded and turned back to study Bohdan. He walked over, placed a hand on his shoulder, which sent Bohdan to prostrate himself on the floor beneath his feet, and nodded.

"No good deed goes unpunished," the Khan said, "but whatever else happens, know you will not suffer as a result of siding with me in this crusade." He looked back over to John. "Is he an honourable thief?"

John nodded. "Wouldn't have come here if he wasn't. I trust him with the bulk of my trade from this region."

The Khan, seeming to have made up his mind, ordered mana canisters to reinforce Bohdan's wards, and slowly started to assemble a strike force in the shop.

John took Anton aside in the commotion, despite his protests that he had to organise the remaining Hungarian forces, and pulled him up the stairs to Bohdan's computer behind the shop counter. He handed Anton the invoice slip that Margaret Goodland had given him and breathed a prayer to the Sky Mother than Anton would be able to help him.

"Please tell me you still have a burner login or two on you," John said.

Anton looked confused for a moment, but nodded.

"What's this, John?" he asked.

"Everything started with these trackers. I went to the tower to try and find the transponder codes attached to the invoice, but you weren't there, obviously. Can you find them from here?"

Anton stared at him with uneasy eyes for a moment, glanced back to where his men were assembling, and sighed.

"It's important to you?" he asked.

"Critical," John answered as Agatha climbed the stairs and walked over to them.

Anton nodded, logged into the Hungarian militia's intranet, gestured to the computer, and stood up.

"Log out when you're done," he said as he turned and walked back down to the cellar to see to his men.

It took John a few minutes to find the transponder numbers attached to the order on the invoice, write them down, and borrow a tracker from Bohdan's near endless supply of military hardware. He programmed the unit and looked at the weapons around him. Despite John's best efforts, Bodhan wouldn't take a single credit note, but much to his Khan's delight was beggaring himself by outfitting every soldier around. He refilled John's supply of scholin weed without asking any uncomfortable questions, and pointed him to a small back room where he kept what he called "the good shit."

John and Agatha stooped their heads to walk through the

low black door, and entered the armoury. They each took a fresh wand, packed two yew branches filled with the emerald green power of Sindhustan on their backs, picked out seven canisters of condensed mana from a crate marked with his own Boston factory's emblem, and picked out a main battle branch of pure North American mana, produced in Mississippi by the Choctaw Circle of Shaman. *The good shit indeed,* John thought as he turned on the GPS tracker.

As the Cossacks and the remaining Hungarians started to form ranks outside in the alley and prepare for their assault, all John wanted to do was join them, but Trish insisted that the answer lay with the GPS trackers. He returned to the computer terminal and pulled up the notes on the order.

Order 672B202AK
25th of May 2019

Request received for a non-lethal response to goblin infestation at Danube mine in Budapest. Prf. Goodland to lead the effort in the coercion of goblin nest to disperse. Per request for study, goblins to be shot by GPS transponders supplied by Hungarian Interior Militia. Approved 25/05/2019 Maurius Duma.

"Trish?" John asked in his mind. Something had been gnawing at the back of his mind for days.

"Yes?"

"Professor Goodland specialized in Egyptian power down through the dynasties. What would he want with goblins?" But the answer came to mind even as he finished the question.

"Damavand," he whispered. He looked over to Agatha. "There are goblins in Damavand."

Agatha nodded, and Trish started to struggle to remember something in his mind. Her efforts seemed to drain his energy as well, and he downed a fresh bottle of scholin extract.

"He wanted to track where they'd go."

"Goblin colonies exist nearly everywhere in the world," Agatha answered, furrowing her brows.

"Managed colonies," John said, scoffing. "Camps, prisons. I remember Trish telling me about the goblins at Damavand."

To his surprise, Trish didn't chide him or even joke about his paying attention to her work for once, but urged him to go on, seeming unable to access her own memories.

"Goblins who choose to live in freedom go to Damavand."

"They'll die."

"Most do," he said as he nodded. "The reverberations of the spells cast there will echo on for countless millennia, killing any of us in a matter of days. But for those goblins able to survive, somehow, they find the one place in all of this Earth where they can live free. The only place where we—humans—cannot."

Agatha raised her eyebrows and nodded. "They live there in numbers?"

"Several thousand," Trish said in his mind.

"Several thousand, according to Trish. I think the"—he leaned in closer and hushed his voice—"I think the world engine the professor and Trish sought is another place goblins run to when driven from our ley mines."

He turned to the computer and typed in the transponder codes into the tracker, then clicked on the world map view. As expected, almost all of the goblins tracked were within Mount

Damavand itself, but two, soft little specks on the map, seemed to be in Oregon. John's heart froze, and he swallowed hard. This must have been what the professor found.

Trish screamed in his mind, forcing him to hold the counter for balance as she nearly knocked him off his feet.

"Yes!" she cried again. "There was an apparture there."

"What?" John said out loud. He looked to the floor in confusion, then headed down to the apparture—the soldiers now outside ready to depart on their assault—and punched in the approximate coordinates in Oregon where the goblins had run to.

He tried to keep his mind calm as an apparture portal chimed back at him, opened, and signalled that it was ready to receive. He dashed up the stairs, logged out of the computer, found Anton outside, and—with his heart racing as he realised this might well be the last time he saw his friend alive—embraced him. As Anton led the Cossacks and Hungarians up in force towards the tower, John and Agatha rushed to the apparture.

Chapter Five

John stepped forward as Agatha materialised behind him in a whoosh and a snap. The scent of tombs and incense filled his head as he stepped into a wide sandstone atrium with torches everywhere, sending the golden light dancing off the strange hieroglyphs lining every wall. He levelled his branch and raised a personal ward as he craned his neck up to find the vaulted ceiling lost in shadow high above them.

All around, depictions of what he thought was the Sky Mother, but in a style he had never seen before, loomed over and around every group of hieroglyphs. He felt the Sky Mother's power all around him, but he kept his wards raised, eyes scanning for any hidden threat.

"Professor Goodland," Trish said in his mind as John walked forward to study the room. "This was his life, here, right here. He and countless others spent their careers searching for this very room."

"What?" John asked as he continued searching the room. It was bare except for the apparture, made of stone and filigreed strands of mana resembling the ones in ancient murals and rock paintings he had seen in Australia. As he recalled, the spirit healer there had told him they were depictions of pre-human ascendancy technology. He scoffed.

"Yes, exactly," Trish said.

John froze. "Hold on; you can read my thoughts?" He loved feeling Trish's presence in his mind now, nearly all the time, but he didn't know she could read—

"When we entered this room, yes." She paused for a moment as John felt her attention turn to a particular hieroglyph of a bull's head. "But not before."

He stopped, turned back, and called Agatha.

"Trish says this is what Professor Goodland was seeking."

Agatha nodded slowly, studying every corner of the room. "Esoterological archaeology," Agatha half whispered. She turned and looked at him. "The professor studied Egypt, not for Egypt's sake, but cross-species mimicry."

John stared at her for a moment, trying to make sense of her words, but Trish started to fill his mind with her thoughts. He shuddered for a moment as he was filled with her warmth, her love, her kindness, and before he knew what was happening he was down on the floor with a sharp pain shooting down his hip where he had fallen, his branch behind him. He shook his head, stretched his hand out on the sandy floor to sit upright, grabbed his branch to recast his wards, and tried to concentrate.

In the jungles of Uganda, Trish's thoughts said, *a tribe of primates live near a community of magi who perform their rites and draw power directly from the air in an inefficient process called inverse radeon saturative induction. Unlike most other communities built on the power of the Sky Mother, these sorcerers didn't hide after the Dark Ages but still interacted with both unattuned peoples and animals living near them, providing health care, advice, and on occasion, bringing rain to farms or pasture land.*

A clear image formed in his mind, through Trish's memories, of a giant silverback leading his tribe in imitation of the rites that greet the Sky Mother at dawn. No animal could know what those rites were, but by watching the sorcerers, the primates had learned to mimic the same rites almost exactly. This phenomenon was not unique.

Professor Goodland had posited that Egypt and the Aboriginal tribes of Australia, as the first human civilizations to attune to the Sky Mother's power, had followed a similar path, now lost deep within the dark web that surrounds human knowledge of its ascension to sentience. His theory supposed that humanity had once observed—and been inspired by—an older race, a pre-human civilization.

"Professor Goodland thought we mimicked our way to sentience?"

"No," Trish answered. "He believed we were already mimicking another race before we were sentient, and as we ascended, we held some knowledge of the rites that empower our Sky Mother. Humanity, he posited, *inherited* its attunement to our Sky Mother."

John shook his head. "From whoever built this place?"

"Yes," Trish said aloud as she materialised next to him. She still wore her clay-stained field clothes, white leather boots, and white linen trousers and shirt. She took his hand, and he relished the soft feel of her fingers as she helped him up onto his feet. He stood there, staring at her for a moment, breathed in, and turned his attention back to the room.

An upside-down-kite-shaped door stood ten meters high at the room's far end, a gentle draft pulling them towards it. He followed the building scent of burning incense as he stalked towards the door, his branch levelled. Agatha followed to his right, her own branch held a touch higher than his in the Oxford Manual's style. Trish had walked over to the hieroglyph of the bull's head to peer at it more closely.

"Go ahead," she said. "I'm in no danger here. Neither are you."

John believed her, but couldn't bring himself to let down his guard. He went through the door first, keeping his branch ready to blast anything that came at him, and emerged into a far larger room, like a cave of colossal proportions, but with marks along the bare stone walls that suggested it was excavated, rather than natural.

He looked around to find the source of the light filling every corner of the cave, but couldn't find any. There were no alchemical bulbs, torches, electric lights, and yet the entire chamber was as bright as sunlight.

He looked at his watch. It was coming up on midnight of the day after he had left the East Coast, so here, it should be near nine at night. He instinctively took his phone out of his pocket and breathed a sigh of relief as Mrs. Murphy's hourly text reassuring him that they were safe had arrived. He felt guilty for not having checked, but the message had come while they were in Bohdan's shop and he hadn't noticed.

"There," Trish said, emerging from the door and pointing to the far end of the vast room.

John peered, making out the outlines of a cluster of tents

pitched at the base of a deep, wide bowl, carved into the chamber's floor about five hundred meters away. The walls of the cave were dark stone, but aside from a set of rough stone steps down into the bowl, the floor was sand.

He let Trish lead the way down to the camp, but as they neared and he recognised the tents as Trish's, his steps became heavy, the dormant grief flaring into life in his heart. He had to fight back tears from his eyes. He steadied his heavy breaths, both from the long walk and the shock of seeing Trish's familiar gear strewn all around, and made his way to the large central tent.

Inside, everything was as he remembered it to always be. Her red rug adorned the floor, the two-meter-high walls were decorated with fabrics from Sindhustan and Scotland, and the ceiling peaked high above their heads. The round table in the center was covered in maps, ley line readings marked with pen, and a set of Trish's handwritten notes.

He went to reach for them, but something else caught his eye. Professor Goodland's tea set stood on a side table. The Sindhustani Samavar had long since turned cold in the frigid air, and two ornate glasses sat on the table holding the dregs of tea, a few loose leaves, and what looked to be sugar settled at their bottom. That was odd.

"Wasn't the professor on his third stroke?" John asked.

"Yes," Trish answered as she flicked through her own notes.

"Wasn't he on strict orders not to take any sugar?"

Trish looked up for a moment and screwed her eyes. "Yes."

John nodded. Raghav's short-bread biscuit tin was opened, with only a few crumbs left inside. He looked around and found every canister of power Trish normally took on expeditions present, all drained.

Whatever happened, they had time to prepare. He glanced back to the central table and saw Professor Goodland's leather shoulder bag lying opened, with the ornate wooden wand box he kept his good wand in empty and open on the floor. Raghav's bag was a little farther back, but all he could make out inside was stationery, paper, and an orange drink bottle. He sighed.

"You knew what was coming," he said.

Trish didn't react at first, but slowly raised her head and nodded. She looked over to him. "It was something of Egypt. The professor recognised it and knew his end had come. He took sugar, ate the biscuits; we all did."

Trish's face had gone pale. She shook slightly as she stood, and a fresh terror filled her eyes, setting his gut churning.

"We were trapped here, in its power. It didn't attack, but we had to break free."

John found his legs trembling and tried to force himself to calm his nerves. He could almost taste his vengeance. "Let's go find it," he said as he drew more power into his branch and checked the three wands strapped to his chest, "and make the fucker bleed."

Agatha's hand clasped his shoulder. He spun and despite himself, a small part of his tension fell away.

"Relax, John," she said as she looked into his eyes and raised her eyebrows. "When we find it, we kill it calmly, and carefully. It took down two Oxford-trained warlocks, and two witches of Preston College."

"I didn't," a metallic voice called from outside the tent.

John spun, dropped to his knee, pulled the branch up to his shoulder and loosed one arc after another of violet power towards the voice. Agatha joined him a moment later, and by the time their branches were depleted, and they'd each dropped them to pull a fresh wand, half the tent was disintegrated, the air shimmering in a haze of smoke and the acrid stench of burnt mana. A blue figure was visible through the blasted gap in the tent, his hands outstretched, his empty palms turned towards them.

The figure was human-like, with cobalt-blue skin. He stood roughly eight feet tall, dressed in a skirt made of black and gold metal plates in a strangely Egyptian style, with similar bracelets and anklets, and a tall conical helmet adorned with a golden emblem of the Sky Mother—a wide-branching tree with deep roots in filigree gold—on the front.

John's rage overpowered him. He threw the wand to the ground and pulled the two smaller branches strapped to his back, levelling them at the strange figure, but before he could loose their power, Trish's hand gently stroked the back of his head.

"John," she whispered. "Don't."

The figure still stood there, his palms turned towards them, and seemed to be bowing his head.

"Please," he said in an accent John didn't recognise. His voice was metallic and forceful, yet restrained. His eyes were a solid blue, with narrow, angular pupils.

John swallowed hard, kept his two minor branches trained at the figure as Agatha dropped her drained branch and drew the branches strapped to her back.

"Mum," Trish said, still keeping her hand on John's head, "he's not going to harm you."

John tried to stand, but found his legs were barely keeping him upright on his knees. Still, he forced every bit of strength left in him into them, and with a wobble or two, eased himself upright onto his feet. He stood before the figure, meeting those unsettling eyes, and waited, the two branches still trained at his chest.

"You're the demon?" John asked, cursing himself for the weak crackle in his voice.

The figure shook his head. "I am a Hecarim, called Tamokameses." He inclined his head in a mild bow.

"He's what the professor called a 'demon of Egypt,'" Trish said.

The being winced. "For what I've done to you," it said to Trish, "I can never remedy you." He gestured to her. "But at least I can do this much."

John's mind spun again, and before he knew what was happening, he fell backward and planted himself down ass-first into the sand. His brain tried to gather its wits, but couldn't. He fished another scholin weed bottle, downed it, and paused for the few seconds it now took for the bottle to take effect.

He looked up, and in the naked light, he saw the being anew. Everywhere in and around him, the Sky Mother's power saturated the air, so thick John could almost taste it. How could any being not of the Sky Mother even dare to breathe here? The emblem on the being's helmet was strange, though still vaguely familiar. It wasn't too dissimilar from the Warden's insignia.

"You serve the Sky Mother?" he asked.

The being nodded.

"You brought Trish back?"

He nodded again.

"But you also killed her?" His voice cracked again, and he had to swallow hard.

The being sighed, looked down, but nodded. "I had not meant to."

"And how," Agatha asked as she stepped forward, branches still raised, "may I ask, does one kill four people without *meaning* to?"

The being seemed to swallow, or pause; John couldn't tell, as its throat didn't move, even as it talked, and he realised with a start that it wasn't formed of flesh. The way the light reflected from his skin, it was made of stone.

"The older man and young man attacked me first. I had received warning of servants of Nafarin infiltrating my charge—the world engine here." The creature turned to gesture at a hollow crater at the cave's far end. "I did not believe your Trisha was attempting to flee, but to flank me. I intercepted her, and by the time I realised she was trying to distract me, to draw my attention away so that the young woman could escape, it was too late."

The being dropped his head even lower and shook it.

"I am so sorry," he said.

"And so you chased the young woman down and killed her?" Agatha hissed as she raised her branches even higher.

"No," the being said, his face still unmoving. "Trish's act of self-sacrifice could never have come from a servant of Nafarin. When I confirmed that the young woman served only our Sky Mother, I transported her to her desired point."

"What?" John asked as he stood again.

"She wanted to go to somewhere called 'Preston College.' I sent her there, and watched as she was collected by a man."

John and Agatha stared at each other for a moment, and neither spoke as they turned back to the being.

"I'm sorry, what?" John asked again.

The being cocked his head to the side, and raised his right hand; a stream of light shone from its bracelet, painting an image of Kate Hart in the air. As they watched, Kate materialized above the trees surrounding Preston College, was met by Dean Walters, enveloped in a protective ward, and led back towards the College. The recording stopped there.

"I stopped watching when she seemed safe," the being said.

The implications of the vision nearly tore John's mind apart. He found his hand shook and his heart shook with it.

"I was deceived," the being continued. "And now, my failure is total. Nafarin's servants took the world engine, and as we speak, are trying to awaken their lord."

John took a step back but bumped into Trish. She took his hand and pulled him closer to her.

"For two hundred millennia my servants and I have guarded the world engine from our Sky Mother's enemies. We now disassemble our life here, piece by piece, and join our people in the stars."

Trish pulled him towards her. "John," she said, but paused and seemed to struggle to frame her words. "When my life ended, I didn't see the Sky Mother. I saw darkness. I remember now." She looked straight into his eyes and nodded. "Tamokameses' people left this world eons ago, their consciousness melded into a single being, looking for a world in the stars."

John shook his head as he tried to wrap the remaining shreds of his mind around what Trish was saying.

"Listen," she urged, "we don't have time. That's how—" She paused again. "I *think* that's how our Sky Mother reproduces. By seeding life until it, ah, ascends."

"Yes," the being said. "I am individual, my servants are individual, we are the last of our people outside of our collective consciousness, here to serve the Sky Mother until the time came to join with the minds of all our people, to become one with all. To our shame that time comes at our moment of failure."

John's mind had started to numb, but as heretical as this sounded, he could see it, almost as though the Sky Mother was willing him to. As the enormity of it all started to dawn for him, he felt suddenly calm. His mind grasped for more details, for the answers to a million questions, but he remained still, and listened.

"John." Trish pulled him even closer. "Nafarin and the Sky Mother, they are the same, the same as what I joined out in the stars. Nafarin is the collective consciousness of a deathly people, a single face, a being of evil. They fight for control of our world."

He slowly nodded and looked over to Agatha. For the first time in his life, he saw tears flow freely from her eyes. Thin tendrils of azure-blue mana seemed to be flowing straight into her chest from the air around her. She shuddered as her mouth stiffened into a grim line.

"My father was right?" John asked.

"Yes," Trish answered. "We have suffocated her, and this world engine, large enough to sustain her, the only space She who we revere has to draw breath, is now filled with the cult of Nafarin. She is dying fast."

John's heart tried to reject what he'd heard, but as the Sky Mother's love filled him from head to toe, he knew it was true. He had known when his father had first started to talk of this madness, of galactic beings vying for power across the cosmos.

For the first time since Trish's death, he felt fatigue fall from his shoulders like lead weights. His mind emptied itself of the rushed urgency of scholin weed. He breathed in a lungful of free air, filled with the Sky Mother's love; held it as power radiated to every part of him, and breathed out a plume of neon blue vapour.

"John Trevelyan?" the being called. "I was the last guardian of the Sky Mother left of my people. We share a mother, you and I, and Her life is now in your hands."

His mind whirred into action. He took out his phone, sent a message to Dean Walters to meet for a midnight drink at the twenty-four-hour café by the waterfall outside the college, and picked his depleted branch back up. He held it to the sky to refill, gestured for Agatha to follow, and turned back towards the apparture room.

"And you?" he asked the creature as he turned to look over his shoulder.

"I re-join my people. The power I spent to bring your wife back to you was the last vestige of my people's presence on this world. If the Sky Mother wills it, She will allow the link to continue."

John nodded. He had come here seeking answers and vengeance. He thought back to Preston College, to young Anna Hart, to her sister Kate, enveloped by Dean Walter's ward. He considered for a moment whether the vision the being had shown them was a lie, but Trish seemed convinced, and something—a still, quiet voice in his heart—whispered to him: this was truth. Trish dematerialised into his mind, and with this newfound energy he couldn't explain, he left Tamokameses behind and ran back towards the apparture room.

Chapter Six

JOHN SIPPED HIS black coffee as he sat on a table outside the café. He stared into the early morning sky as a waterfall roared to his right and the odd motor car drove along the near-deserted road. The server was chatting with the chef through a window. He breathed in another lungful of the brisk morning air and studied the humbling immensity of the stars.

Urged by what he had felt of the Sky Mother—what he had felt to *be* the Sky Mother—he had hurried from the world engine at Oregon, but now that he was here, he forced his mind to calm itself, to approach the coming conversation with care. He tried not to glance over to the other side of the river where Agatha lay prone and hidden, covering him.

Despite the Sky Mother flooding the world engine with unfathomable power, so much so that he was able to simply breathe it in from the air, he had still felt the reverberations of spells cast eons ago, echoing through the ages in their gargantuan scale. It had felt as though a celestial giant had torn a chunk out of the Earth, and even after hundreds of millennia, he had walked through the very heart of their workings.

The exclusion zone around Damavand was nothing compared to that. Any magi could survive even a whole week there at a time, using their own wards to keep back the reverberations of the spells cast there forty-three years ago. In that cave, deep in the south sister mountain in Oregon, it felt like the Sky Mother had to bring Her own personal power to bear in keeping the three of them alive. He wondered at how Tamokameses and his servants had lived there for so long, but that was the least of his questions regarding the being he had trusted so easily.

Doubt rose in him again, but Trish's thoughts soothed him. Yes, he had killed her, but in bringing her spirit back, he had allowed Trish to see inside his mind. She was sure that he had been deceived by some unknown person, that he believed her to be an enemy. Trish's real murderers were the cult of Nafarin, and as the vision showed, Kate Hart was alive, somewhere. He needed to focus.

He had barely finished the thought when he heard Dean Walters' shoes clack on the pavement behind him as he landed. He walked around him, took the seat in front of him, and smiled. John had to force every ounce of will to return the bastard's smile.

Dean Walters wore a charcoal grey pinstriped suit, but with his waistcoat unbuttoned, his tie loosened, and his hair dishevelled, which took John by surprise. His eyes were reddened, and he wheezed a little as he caught his breath. He picked up the iced chocolate drink John had ordered for him, downed it in five big gulps, folded his hands across the table, and leaned in.

"John," he said, "what's the emergency?"

"Nafarin," John answered without skipping a breath.

Dean Walters scoffed for a moment but leaned in closer as John composed his face.

"You want a history lesson at one in the morning?" he asked, suddenly furrowing his brows and leaning back in his chair as he locked eyes with John.

Before John could answer, his other guest, the one Agatha had invited, landed next to their table, dismissed her broom, and sauntered over to them, her air of complete superiority deservedly in its customary place.

"Grand Master," John said, turning to greet her. He would normally stand, but he had his wand balanced above his knee and pointed at Dean Walters under the table.

Grand Master Coahopa, commander of the American Warden's Tower and chief of the Choctaw Circle of Shamans, stood indomitable in a dark-blue trouser suit and white blouse, with ornate golden jewellery fashioned after totemic depictions of owls around her neck and wrists. Her face was as calm as it was dangerous, her amber eyes, narrow nose, and pinned up hair resembling the great horned owl that she embodied in life. She blinked and looked down at John with dangerous ease.

She stared at him for a moment, glanced over to Dean Walters, and took a seat next to John without saying a word.

"Thanks for coming," John said, before turning to Dean Walters. "And you, thank you for getting up so late to see me."

Dean Walters nodded, looking between the two, confusion in his eyes.

"It's nothing," he said before reaching over and taking a strawberry from the dish at the centre of the table. "I was awake."

John nodded slowly. "Lots happening at Preston College?"

Dean Walters chewed on the strawberry for a moment, picked up a napkin to wipe his mouth clean, and nodded.

"An expedition went out tonight."

"Yes," Grand Master Caohopa said in her sharp voice, always concise and to the point. "First to Yellowstone, and then to throw off pursuit, an elaborate chain of apparture turns and flights, landing in Mauna Loa, Hawaii, three minutes ago."

Dean Walters looked surprised at that. "Preston College is being watched?" he asked, barely able to hide the incredulity in his voice.

John had to fight down the urge to blast a hole straight through the man, but for the first time, he allowed the hostility in his heart to seep into his face.

"Nafarin likes volcanoes, doesn't He?" John asked. "According to the legends. Been up any mountains lately? With Kate Hart, perhaps?"

Dean Walters bowed his head and stared at the table. His half-grey hair shifted in the wind, and he tapped his index finger against his empty glass for an age before looking up. John's stomach lurched as he expected a burst of anger from him at any moment.

"John," Dean Walters said, locking eyes with him, "it will be a strange new world for you, I'm sure, not being responsible for mining ley lines any more, but think of the future of your country."

John's heart shuddered as a chill ran its icy hand up and down his spine. He sat up straighter, keeping his right hand on his wand. To this point, he'd still been uncertain. How could this man, this righteous man, be a cultist to Nafarin? But, as all doubt scattered, he resolved to fight this darkness with all his might.

"Nafarin is death to all."

Dean Walters scoffed and leaned forward. "You condemn that which has never even had a chance to be born on our world, John." He raised a finger to emphasise his point. "How can you tell that He won't be every bit as benevolent as the Sky Mother? And if not, so what? She feeds every pissant and backwater grass-hut shaman the world over, and look at Her now. Only the strong deserve mana, John."

John smiled. He leaned forward to match Dean Walter's posture, slowly shook his head, and looked over to Grand Master Caohopa. "By our reckoning," John said, turning back to Walters, "the Grand Master is a Mississippi water hag, like my mother-in-law, like my Trish."

Dean Walters stared, silent for a moment, but then curled his lips into a smile. "You married beneath yourself, John."

Trish's mind flared at that, and John had to fight her anger.

"Everyone deserves mana, or no one does," he answered. "Do you know why my ancestors were able to tap every ley mine in North America?"

Dean Walters shook his head, but a sharp look in his eyes betrayed his interest. The origin of the Trevelyan network of ley mines was the most closely guarded secret in all of the Americas. Every major power in the world wanted to know why the elders of all tribes, from Greenland to Antarctica, had allowed an Oxford Colonial family to consolidate and run every ley line in the land.

"It's the same reason why Nafarin is warded and contained. When we came to these shores"—John paused and his hand twitched on his wand as Dean Walters shifted his weight—"the people here were in the grip of a cataclysm the likes of which our minds cannot comprehend. Death on a scale that makes Damavand look like a minor skirmish."

Dean Walters didn't respond.

"The nations of this land battled Nafarin for generations. He *was* manifested here, and *millions* sacrificed their lives to defeat Him."

"Lies," Dean Walters half shouted, drawing the attention of the server. "Every accursed shaman and," he paused to spit on the floor, "pipe smoker across this land yaps on and on about Nafarin's curses on mankind, but I say they lie!"

John couldn't help but to laugh. "The reason," he continued, unperturbed, "that we tap every ley mine in the Americas is that we share it with the people who lived here before us, and run it for the benefit of all mankind. Do you want to know what they do with almost half the power of this continent?" He paused. "They keep Nafarin's wards charged." He watched for a reaction, but the Dean's frown didn't move. "If you serve Nafarin, you've done well. I look at the news, and see the East and West, turmoil roiling across every power, their minds turned to only their own needs. But the Wardens of *this* land, they see all. Are you ready for them?"

Dean Walters didn't even try to hide his disdain. He laughed.

John's clasped his wand handle as Dean Walters reached into his jacket pocket, but all he brought out was a cell phone. He unlocked it, placed it screen up on the table, and grinned as a video feed connected.

"I didn't want to have to do it this way, John," he said with a sneer. "If you're not with us, you're against us."

"Against the cult of Nafarin?" He laughed as he looked over to the Grand Master, her hunter's eyes locked on Dean Walters, every inch of her ready to strike. "Yes, I'm against you."

Dean Walters nodded and gestured down to the screen.

"You think," he said, rising, "a school-witch can contend with the cult of Nafarin? Shame, Lizzie was such a sweet girl."

Everything seemed to happen all at once. Agatha, still wielding the violet power of the Khanate in her branch, shot an arc of violet lightning, perfectly aligned and aimed, that crashed off Dean Walter's outer ward.

A wand slipped from Dean Walter's sleeve into his hands, but before he could raise it, John emptied his own wand in one concentrated point that knocked the Dean back and shattered his forward ward. The Grand Master extended her arms like wings unfurling, and shot two neon blue streaks of light at Dean Walter's chest, but before they could land, he summoned a gust of air and threw himself two meters down the pavement away from them. The Grand Master's spells blasted holes through the concrete pavement.

Agatha's next arc crashed into his side ward again, and this time the ward spat hot mana and fizzled out. In the space it took John to pull his spare wand, a broom materialised underneath Dean Walters and darted up and away to the north. The Grand Master matched the Dean in speed at summoning her broomstick, but paused to point at the cell phone still on the table. She locked eyes with John, snapping him back to reality.

"Go!" she shouted.

She darted away after Dean Walters. Above them, three more Wardens joined her in pursuit, and Agatha dashed towards him, closing the fifty meters between them in less than a second, and John jumped onto her broomstick behind her. They raced towards his mansion, the wards discharging clouds of tiny sparks under the onslaught of the rushing air, and John quickly raised his own ward to reinforce hers.

The image on the cell phone filled his mind: Mrs. Murphy holding her ward as three black robed figures closed in around her. He went to call Trish, but she wasn't there.

"Sky Mother," he begged, "please, no."

THEY DIDN'T WASTE any time, but crashed straight through the high, arched windows of the mansion's living room, shards of reinforced glass exploding into the room in a shower of sparks, molten mana, and neon blue arcs of power. John and Agatha slammed to the ground on their feet and raised their wands in near unison. The room was empty and dark.

The wind swirled the white silk curtains behind them and the remains of the venetian blinds clattered against each other. The sofas, coffee table and fireplace were as he'd left them, and he couldn't sense anything but the Sky Mother's power manifesting here.

His heart leapt into his mouth as he thought the intruders he had seen in this very room had long since departed, their objective achieved.

"Trish!" he shouted. "Trish, where is sh—?"

"John," she called from the next room. He ran to the door, darted through it without caution, and fell to the floor as he saw Trish cradling Lizzie, alive and safe, inside Mrs. Murphy's ward. He tried to draw in a breath, but his lungs shook and his heart pounded as Lizzie met his eye. He thought he should thank someone, thank Mrs. Murphy, thank the Sky Mother, but all he could do was sit there, dumb, staring at his daughter, drinking in the sight of her, listening to the sound of her breathing.

"Look," Agatha said, pointing to the far corner of the room. The bodies of three black-robed cultists lay on the floor, large holes still smoking and glowing through their chests. The one lying face up was Professor Anders, a mana distillation engineer at Preston College. He guessed that another of the dead, lying face down, was Professor Collins, a herbologist and alchemist.

But, how had Mrs. Murphy managed to—?

"I'm sorry," a metallic voice called from behind Mrs. Murphy's ward. John stood, stepped around and saw Tamokameses sitting propped up against the wall, his hand covering a grapefruit-sized hole above his left hip. John walked over and knelt beside him. The wound should have killed him on impact.

"What can we do?" he asked.

Tamokameses tried to raise his head, but couldn't.

"I came, because I saw how you reacted to the image of the young woman. I thought I could try and find where they'd taken the world engine, but instead—"

He shook, rasped what John thought was a cough, and screwed his eyes shut for a moment.

"I"—he paused and turned to Trish—"I saw a chance to repay what I did, my debt to you." He gestured over to Lizzie.

Trish's eyes welled with tears. "Debt paid in full," she said with a sob.

John placed a hand on his shoulder. "What would you have done had you found the world engine?" he asked.

"I don't know," Tamokameses half whispered in his metallic tone. "Interrupt them, do—Nafarin can't be allowed to—" He stopped and shook again, raised his arm up to pull John closer, and even in his blank blue eyes, John sensed a desperate urgency.

"I've—called help, but my people are too far away. Sky Mother is alone with you, and Nafarin. She must not—" He shuddered again. "Please help Her."

He went rigid, shuddered, and his eyelids closed.

"Damn," John said. He wanted more answers, but breathed a prayer to the Sky Mother as he left Tamokameses, the being who had taken his wife and saved his daughter, and turned his mind to the fight ahead. He took out his phone, dialled Laird Bellard, and as quickly as he could, filled him in on events since Budapest. The Laird, sensing actual war, had lost all of his mirth, and was focused purely on facts and John's assessments. He promised to gather aid.

John then remote accessed his apparture and opened a portal to Fort William. Laird Bellard kept a garrison there. "Thank you, Mrs. Murphy," he said, turning to the school-witch. "I can never thank you enough."

She shook her head and stroked Lizzie's hair. "It's my duty, Mr. Trevelyan. I only held a ward."

He nodded to her. "We couldn't possibly ask anything more from you—"

"You don't have to ask for a thing. I don't know what that person was, but I'm not an idiot. I see the news, I feel the weakening of our Sky Mother like everyone else. I will not leave her side," she said, gesturing to Lizzie.

Two of Laird Bellard's men stalked into the room, dressed in the red robes of Bellard warriors, their branches of power held ready ahead of them.

"Mr. Trevelyan?" the lead man called in his thick highland accent.

John thought he should answer, to try and explain what had been going on, but couldn't spare the time. He gestured the clansmen over to Lizzie as he walked through Mrs. Murphy's wards, picked her up into the tightest hug he had ever given her, kissed her forehead, and though it tore his heart apart, forced himself to hand her back to Mrs. Murphy. He couldn't protect her where he was going.

He left the room as Trish said her goodbyes. To his surprise, Lizzie didn't ask many questions, and accepted that her mother was only visiting here, and as Lizzie sent a prayer of thanks to the Sky Mother for allowing her a chance to see her mother again, John's strength finally cracked, and it was all he could do to stand there, outside the door, and keep the tears from breaking the flood barriers in his eyes.

As the Bellard warriors took Lizzie and Mrs. Murphy with them back to the safety of Glasgow, John led Agatha back through the living room, into his study, and down the spiralled stairs at their far corner into his private armoury.

"By Nafarin's warded t—" Agatha said as they entered the basement armoury before catching herself. "Suppose I can't say that any more. John, what in the Sky Mother's love is this place?"

John took in a deep breath as Trish joined them down the steep stairs in the basement armoury.

Solid lengths of wood, from spruce, to chestnut, to oak and more, lined every wall, all glowing in a solid neon blue from the main Mississippi Ley Line, reflecting off the white walls. On shelves lining every wall, hundreds of wands sat ready for action, and thousands of condensed mana canisters sat in crates at the room's centre.

"It's an armoury for the Massachusetts Colonial Coven Militia," he answered as he took down two large chestnut branches from the wall.

"I see," Agatha said, her mouth agape as she looked around. "But what's it doing here?"

John shrugged. "As good a place to hide it as any. My house serves as a fortress in a defensive war."

John looked back and followed Agatha's gaze to the room's far end. At the back, behind a stack of canister crates, a smooth oak tree trunk sat suspended on a bed of glowing mana vapour.

"Is that—" Agatha tried to ask.

"Mark 33 Trebuchet. Weapon of war," he said. "We can't carry it."

Agatha nodded slowly as she made her way over to the opposite wall and started testing out lengths of wood, packing wand after wand and canister after canister into the folds of her robes.

John looked down at his suit. He desperately wanted to change, to wash, to shave: he didn't want to meet what could be his end like this, but they lacked any time. He shrugged and packed himself with as many weapons and canisters as he could carry.

"Ready?" he asked as he turned back to Agatha. Above them, he heard the rumble and thunder of a form materialising.

She nodded and led the way back up into the house. Out of the shattered living room window, they saw Castle Bellard seep out of mist and hover above their front lawn. Eleven hundred years old, and packed to the teeth with the most modern weapons they had yet devised.

"Actually, I'll grab those trebuchets," he said. "They'll look great on Bellard's battlements."

Chapter Seven

Castle Bellard materialised over the summit's tourist vista point; all wards raised threefold. The sudden change in temperature and the stomach lurch from the castle's outdated self-apparture made John almost heave up the handful of strawberries and cherries he'd eaten at the café while waiting for Dean Walters.

As he stood at the castle's crennellations and looked down, his breath caught. It seemed all the peoples of the world were gathered there. He swallowed hard and held onto the stone walls as the castle leaned forward and drifted down to join the formation of the Sky Mother's forces.

Dozens of craft were gathered, forming three interlocking circles over the summit of Mauna Loa. He counted two dozen tribal totems, the stark stone tower of the American Wardens with the Grand Master's colours flying from its top, and several minor towers bearing either totemic emblems or colonial coven markings. He swelled with pride at the forces gathered from the Americas, but trembled at the same time as he scanned the rest of the craft, representing every power he could imagine.

The twelve-spired gothic castle of Knight-Captain Gustav of the Hexé Krieg floated on its mist of mana next to Grand Jenny, a colossal pirate ship on which the Greek Seirenes still lived. Three Egyptian and two Maya pyramids clustered together, and the sandstone citadels of Sindhustan interlocked with the cream-hued stone colleges of Oxford. Around them, thousands of magi floated on brooms, plumes, carpets—even one armchair, next to a Mongolian yurt.

On the ground below, chaos had broken loose. Arcs of power flashed in all directions and different hues. Here and there, spurts of flame shot out as land forces engaged, and even at this distance, the roar of wands and cries of battle were clear.

"Never thought I'd see war like this again," Laird Bellard said as he joined him on the battlements. His men had finished loading the last of the trebuchets alongside his own weapons. John looked over to find the Laird's eyes locked on the fight below, his jaw clenched into a grim vice.

"Are we ready?" he shouted.

The other forces seemed poised, but hesitant, even as magi fought and died beneath them. At the heart of the three circles, Nafarin's ward rose from the summit of the volcano like a half-sphere of blood. John couldn't make out anything happening within it, and no one seemed willing to take the first shot.

"To hell with them," Laird Bellard shouted, scowling. "Break formation, bring us right above the ward."

Behind them, a young officer twisted and pulled on the great bronze levers set into the battlements, and the stone shook under John's feet as the castle deftly skirted a domed Ashbal castle and tilted over Nafarin's ward. John looked around once more to see if Anton and the Hungarians were here, but he couldn't see them. He made out a few blue-robed figures of the Frankish Confederacy, fighting against the Sky Mother's soldiers in the hundred different skirmishes raging around the ward's outer perimeter far below.

"Well?" Bellard shouted, elevating his voice to carry for miles in all directions. "Someone shoot something."

"Shoot what, my Laird?" a warrior asked from the wall below as Agatha flew up to join them.

"The ward, idiot!" Bellard shouted back. "Loose everything we have!"

Castle Bellard loosed the first major spell of the battle. Three of the Mk. 33 Trebuchets opened up, casting a tendril of neon blue power each into a ball and sending them down onto Nafarin's ward in a solid line of power that scratched across its outer face for three seconds. The ward didn't so much as wobble.

The hesitation still held for a moment, but in seconds the air filled with the hum and reverberation of dozens of different spells of war, causing sudden waves of nausea to buffet him, and chaos the likes of which he'd never seen erupted all around him.

Wave after wave of power crashed against Nafarin's wards, and though strands of it broke loose here and there, it held.

"Fuck!" Bellard shouted as he studied the ward. "That bastard's tough, John. We'll not make it through in time."

John glanced over at Agatha, still sat on her broom above the castle's tower. She beckoned him over. He squeezed Laird Bellard's shoulder and leapt up onto Agatha's broom behind her, trying to bind himself as tightly as he could to the broom and avoid smashing his face into the two branches strapped to Agatha's back.

"Hold on," she shouted as she dove headfirst towards the ground, weaving through arcs of power that would vaporise them in an instant. She headed towards a smaller exchange at the edge of the ground skirmish, where he made out the form of Grand Master Caohopa leading an attack on a group of Polish Hussars guarding a depot of crates.

All John could do was hold on and keep his wards raised as Agatha danced her way through withering enemy blasts, and John shook as two of them found their way to crash against his ward.

"Keep it steady," Agatha shouted as she leaned forward and dove faster.

John drained two more canisters into his wards. As they approached, Agatha let go of the broomstick with her right hand, drew a minor wand from her robe, and lanced a Hussar straight through the heart.

He barely had time to marvel at her accuracy before the soldiers below them saw her, spun, and loosed streams of power straight towards them. She spun, dipped and dashed forward towards her fellow wardens, but before she could reach the safety of the Grand Master's wards, a spell glanced off her broom's tail, immediately bursting the thing into flames, and sending them both hurtling to the floor.

John staggered from the impact on the broomstick, tried to shake his head clear, and scrambled to right himself as he fished a feather from his pocket. The ground reared up from the corner of his eyes, but he suddenly felt cushioned and slowed, and he reached the ground to find Trish standing there, controlling his and Agatha's falls.

"What took you so long?" she shouted over the ear-splitting

ruckus of the battle raging around them. She didn't wait for their answer but led the way straight to the ward's outer edge. John looked around for any sign of the soldiers who had shot them down, but they were turned away, still engaging the wardens. He didn't blame them. That fall should have killed them both—and would have, if not for Trish.

She now wore her Magistra war robes, a tight-fitting black and gold robe with platinum metal accents at the wrists and neck. She didn't carry any weapon that he could see, but her hands hummed with power. His mind screamed that this wasn't possible, but he didn't question it. Tamokameses, as he recalled, didn't use a wand either. Agatha ran with the alacrity of a woman a third her age and joined them as they sprinted across bare volcanic rock towards Nafarin's ward.

As they neared, the ground bucked beneath their feet and John stumbled and nearly fell. The power from the gathered forces above them was near constant, and the ward's fibres were breaking one at a time, sending power to ripple along the stone. He struggled forward, trying to keep pace with Trish, but as they neared, he felt eyes on him.

One of his two main branches had snapped, but he drew the other and raised a fresh ward as he ran. He glanced around, but every soldier there was engaged in battle. It seemed no one had seen them land here, but he still couldn't shake the feeling that he was being watched again. He tried to force his mind to focus on the task ahead.

The ward's outer perimeter was a swirling mass of crimson. Power flowed in all directions and set his mind spinning. He steadied himself, turned around to make sure they weren't followed, and as he reached for a bottle of scholin weed, he realised with a start that he hadn't drunk any since leaving the former site of the world engine.

"Mum!" Trish called.

John turned and dropped the bottle to shatter on the ground as he saw a small hole in the ward, with Trish's hands on either side of it.

"John, Mum, come on!" she whispered.

John had a hundred different questions, but he didn't waste any time on them here. He ran forward, bent down, checked to see his wands and canisters were in place and crawled through the chest-high hole Trish had opened. As they both followed him through, he raised an eyebrow at Trish.

"You can open holes?"

Trish nodded but gestured up. John followed her gaze. The ward, hundreds of feet above their heads at its tallest point, periodically rippled under the assault.

"The attack's matching the total power expended at Damavand every few seconds, John. They're going all out up there."

John gasped as he tried to wrap his mind around the numbers.

"I don't know how much power is in me, John. That hole though was about as large as I could make it, and there's no time to call for help."

John didn't question it. He nodded to Agatha as they both drew their main battle branch, reinforced their wards, and strode towards the cultist camp at the volcano's summit. He started to get anxious at the ease with which they were advancing, surrounded by Frankish and Polish soldiers on all sides, with a few Hungarians and Americans scattered here and there, but no one so much as looked towards them.

The camp was a hellscape. They'd drawn magma out of the active volcano, and all around them, it crawled in streams. They'd erected metal bridges and platforms over them, and a central stage hung over a deep precipice from which molten rock continually spat.

"Our Sky Mother is almost suffocated," Trish said as she pointed to the central stage, "but Nafarin has the world engine. He hangs over it like a poison mist, ready to infect and kill Her the moment She can't hold any longer and draws breath."

John's heart shuddered. The idea that the Star Mother was mortal seemed as strange to him as his dead wife standing here before him in all her fierce beauty. He swallowed, scanned around for a place to strike from, and froze as he saw young Kate Hart, stripped naked and bound in chains inside a cage hanging over the rift. Her cage spun slowly, and her face looked devoid of any hope.

"When She draws breath," Trish continued, "they'll throw Kate in as the virgin sacrifice, enact the rites, and bring their vile lord into being."

"Not if I can help it," Agatha said, stalking forward.

John went to follow her, then turned and reinforced his wards by instinct as an arc of power crashed into it. He loosed a return blast from his branch—it splattered off a Frankish soldier's ward—and dove for cover. A storm of magic enveloped them within moments; repeated blasts stripped his ward, and three shackles snaked their way around Trish's feet and bound her to the ground. He looked around to find the source of the shackles, found a Frankish soldier holding them, raised his wand and lanced her through the heart, but even as she fell, three more spirit shackles curled around Trish. How could they know that she was a spirit? He cursed himself for ignoring his instincts that he was being watched.

A soldier tried to lash him, but the binding passed through his living flesh, and he emptied a full wand against the soldier's ward. But before he could draw another wand, three full branches of power were pointed at his head. He glanced over to find Trish bound and Agatha sprawled on the floor, looking up with her hands empty at two charged branches pointed at her head.

John swallowed hard. He wanted to reach for another wand, but he'd be dead before his hand moved half way. He looked to Trish again, to find her shooting him a strange look of urgency and a wry smile. He raised his hands in surrender and didn't resist as they disarmed him, bound his hands, and poked him in the back with their branches as they led him forward to the stage.

For the first time since standing at the bell tower of Preston College, looking out into the trees for some phantom threat, he realised what had been watching him. A group of men huddled on what looked to be a command post in the network of metal bridges and platforms crisscrossing the volcano. He recognised Etienne Louis, Leon Grupa, Maurius Duma, Dean Walters, and a man made of stone. The stone man turned to him. He was of solid black stone, maybe obsidian or basalt, stood seven feet tall, and had black eyes. He had a smooth head and no adornments or accents in colour.

John's steps faltered, and the soldier behind him jabbed his branch into his back, sending him to lurch forward and fall in front of the stone man. John recognised the shape of his face in a moment, but found his heart unable to grieve at yet another betrayal. The world had already turned upside down for him.

"So you found how to use their technology, Professor?"

Trish writhed and struggled so hard that she seemed to actually break one or two of her bindings, but Professor Goodland smiled and waved her away. John felt Trish's pain, her raw struggle, but found he didn't share her anger. He was calm. He looked around and found only lost souls; he pitied them. They sacrificed sanity for meagre scraps of power. He dropped and shook his head. If this was to be his end—indeed, the end of life as this world knew it—he'd be damned if he would meet it in anger.

"She's made of pure power from the Sky Mother," Professor Goodland said in a similar metallic voice to Tamokameses, but with the professor's distinctive highland accent. "Take her to the feeding chamber and bind her to a stack; she'll be a good meal for our Lord when He emerges."

My wife, John thought. He studied her, the scratch from her play fight with Lizzie still on her right cheek, and tried to drink in the sight of her.

Maurius Duma stepped forward, but Professor Goodland raised his stone arm to bar his way.

"Not you," he hissed, "you couldn't even hold a tower for me, imbecile. Etienne?" He turned to return to a flashing computer terminal, and Maurius stepped back chagrined.

Good, John thought. At least Anton had triumphed.

"The other two?" Etienne Louis asked, stepping forward to take Trish's bindings.

"Let them watch, then kill them."

With that, they were dismissed. He knew now that Professor Goodland had watched him, hidden in shadows and darkness. The one thing he couldn't figure out was *why*. The professor had always been a good man, but, as his father had once said, the lure of Nafarin levels humanity, afflicting king and beggar, pious and pagan alike.

Etienne Louis and two of his guards led them into a makeshift building made of empty crates up against the volcano's crevice. As Trish was lashed to a stake up against the edge of a river of magma, ready to be consumed when Nafarin emerged, John and Agatha were roped to two crates on the ground behind her.

Trish hadn't stopped fighting this entire time. She was bound with her back to them, but was still trying to break free through sheer force of will. Etienne posted two guards, an older man and a tall woman to watch them, reinforced the shackles on Trish, checked first Agatha's and then his bonds, and left the 'feeding chamber,' heading back towards the command post.

Agatha looked around her with her customary coiled anger, and Trish continued struggling to break free. John felt that he should struggle too, but found he couldn't.

He drew in a lungful of the acrid, sulphurous air, tried to hold it despite it burning his throat, and released it. He thought back to a poem he'd read when they'd run off to Scotland together. Its title was lost to the shadows of his memory, but that evening, alone with Trish for the first time, a bottle of wine, a book of verse, lobsters, samphire, and boiled potatoes in butter sauce played clear as day in his mind. The warmth of the memory soothed him.

"Trish," he called, "tell me of love. My heart remains forever young within you."

She relaxed in an instant and sagged into her bindings, and John's heart cracked anew as he saw her shoulders shake.

He couldn't help the tears that welled up in his own eyes, but he forced them away. Now was not the time for sadness. He didn't notice at first, but Agatha wasn't to his left any more. He turned to find her holding a wand the size of a toothpick in her right hand and grabbing the female Frankish guard's fully charged branch with her left. Before the other guard could react, she slapped the toothpick into her face; her head shattered in a haze of blood and brains.

The second guard spun, and Agatha slammed her hand against his throat to stifle his warning. He jumped back to make enough space to level his branch, but Agatha followed him, lowered her shoulder and charged, knocking him into the lava. She fell to her knees on the edge of the rift herself. Her left hand had been burnt to a crisp by the first guard's wand.

He tried to lurch to his feet but was still bound to the crate.

"Frankish sack of shit," Agatha growled as she picked herself up. "Elite guard? Well, I'm a motherfucking Warden, bitch."

The magma below had flared, throwing up spumes of fire as the guard hit, but over the din of battle above them, with power crashing like thunder into the ward, John wasn't sure that they'd been heard. Still, he didn't waste any time.

The female guard's body had fallen close to him, and he shifted himself over to try and reach for her wand, but Agatha came over and tightened his bindings with her one good hand.

"What are you doing?" John whispered.

"It's for your own good," she answered. She placed the guard's wand at the outer edge of the wall of crates, and set it to glide towards him slowly.

"This is in case you have delusions of heroism." She gestured down to his bindings. "You'll get the wand in five minutes. Take Trish and go."

"And where in the Sky Mother's love do you think you're going?" he asked as Agatha bound Trish to John, and released her other bindings. She snapped over to him, her body crashing into his and knocking the air out of him.

Agatha paused. "The Wardens," she said, "know a thing or two about Nafarin. His rites better be exact, or else the cultists will incur His wrath. If we can anger Him enough to expose Himself…" She left the rest unsaid and started to walk out, but John called her again.

"What?" she snapped.

"Have you gone *mad*?"

Agatha walked back and bent over by the two of them. Trish seethed at her.

"Look," she continued, "the rite demands the blood of a young virgin. I was young in the sixties, back when love was free. If I dive into the lava, and not Kate Hart, how do you think He'll react?"

John tried to suppress the image of Agatha being young in the sixties, but found her logic sound.

"Alright," he said, "but I'll go. If the spell needs a virgin witch, a married warlock would—"

"No," she snapped at him. "Witch, warlock, piss on your distinctions!" She shook her head. "It's all the same to Him, John. Those are *our* distinctions."

He fell back to the crate and nodded.

"I, ah—" he tried to say.

"Get her out of here, John," she said. "I always liked you." She turned back to the gap in the crates that formed the exit from the makeshift prison, cradling her wand-burnt hand. "You're a good man, like your father. I never said this, but

I knew when Trish married you that I'd never have to worry about her again."

She dropped her head, bent down, kissed her daughter on the forehead, and strode off.

She hadn't been gone for a second when the wand snapped over to them, and Trish, who had been laying against him, gestured down to it. He swallowed, shook his head, and picked up the wand. He blasted the rope around him and released Trish's bindings.

She lay against him breathing for a moment, but rolled onto her side and clambered to her feet.

"Right," she said as he stood to join her.

What in the Sky Mother's love was going on?

"Could you have done that the entire time?"

She shook her head.

"I didn't fetch the wand, the Sky Mother did."

John started and swallowed hard. "What?"

"Nafarin," Trish said as she pointed up to the ward. "He wants this bad, John, so bad. He's invested every bit of Himself into that ward. If He gets the world engine"—she grimaced— "I don't even want to think."

"And your mother's plan will disrupt his attention long enough to weaken the ward, at least."

Trish nodded but then shook her head. "Our Sky Mother is exposed here, John. Yes, we'd expose Nafarin, but She's right here behind him, and other than Professor Goodland and us, no one understands Her link to the world engines. If my mother succeeds, and the ward collapses long enough for our friends overhead to break through, they'd probably kill our Sky Mother with collateral spells as they obliterate Him."

John shuddered at this reminder of the Sky Mother's mortality. He didn't want to imagine that what they did here decided Her future as much as their own.

"John," Trish said, suddenly serious as she took his hand. She looked straight into his eyes, kissed him, and dug her head into his chest.

His mind melted. Without controlling himself, he clasped his arms around her, dropped his head to hers, breathed in the scent of her hair, and sagged as her warmth filled him from head to toe.

"I love you," she said, and John felt her tears against his chest.

He breathed for a moment, relishing the smell of her hair and her breath. He pulled her chin up, kissed her on the lips, and smiled.

"I love you too. What do we have to do?"

"Nothing," she answered. "I'm here, like... like an autoimmune cell in the Sky Mother's body. Nafarin is the virus. My mother is about to do something stupid."

John didn't want to let her go but stepped back to look at her. "And?" he asked.

"When I say, summon that guard's broom from her wand, fly over, grab my mum, grab Kate, and get as much altitude as you possibly can. You'll be heavy, but you have to get clear, as close to Nafarin's ward as possible."

John nodded, trying not to think about what was about to happen.

"And you?" he asked.

"She brought me back for a reason."

"I thought Tamoka—"

"He thought so, too, but it was our Sky Mother, John.

Nafarin has sunk everything He has into this world engine, and the Sky Mother, into me."

She stroked his face and gave him one more kiss.

"It's time. Don't let me down," she said as she dematerialised.

John dashed over to the wand, felt for its contents, summoned the broomstick, and darted up and out of the semicircle of crates. He couldn't see Trish, but in the distance, he saw Agatha had reached the central platform and thrown up a ward around herself and Kate Hart as she released Kate from her cage.

John didn't hesitate. He summoned every bit of speed he could manage and didn't slow as he approached.

"Agatha!" he shouted, and she looked up with a split second to spare. He lashed each of his arms, one to Agatha and one to Kate, keeping his balance on the broom with his thighs, wrenched the broom ninety degrees back with his feet tucked under him, and as he struggled against the extra weight, summoned every last ounce of his strength to ascend.

As the first of the arcs of power crackled near them, a white flash filled his sight. He screwed his eyes shut against it, but it still stabbed at his eyes as he felt his balance waver and the broomstick stall.

Chapter Eight

"Yes, thank you, Simon," a strange man's voice said. "It's taken my colleagues around the world by surprise; we're struggling for an explanation." The voice paused to clear his throat. "If you look closely, you can see that it resembles the great eye of Jupiter, but from what we know of Venus' weather patterns, we can't explain its origin."

John tried to open his eyes, but his eyelids seemed stuck. Panic gripped him and he tried to force his eyes open, and a searing pain spiked through the back of his head. He became aware of a dull thudding, like a rhythmic echo pounding at the burning nerves of his mind, and he tried to sit up despite his head spinning in darkness.

"Oh, what does this bawbag know anyway?" Laird Bellard said. "Turn that shite off."

A man laughed, and John's panic deepened. Where was Trish? He felt for her presence in his mind, but all he found there was the old familiar darkness, the hole she'd left in him when she passed.

"Hey," Anton said from somewhere behind him in his soft-spoken Hungarian lilt. "Turn that back on. I want to see."

"What's to see?" Grand Master Caohopa answered from somewhere behind him, with the sound of sharp footsteps. "Nafarin ran to Venus."

"Hold on," Margaret Goodland said from right above his face. "He's awake." She gently pulled at his right eyelid, and pain surged and flared straight through his head at her touch.

John's panic overwhelmed him, and he lurched up, tried to find something to hold on to, but a kind pair of hands stroked his head as Margaret Goodland hushed him back down.

"It's alright, dear," she said. "My husband's truly dead now. We're safe."

John struggled to stand and fresh agony seared across his head as he tried to tear his eyes open.

"Relax, John," Margaret said, "look here."

She took his hand and placed it on what felt to be her chest. Between the beats of her heart, John felt the power of the Sky Mother pulse in a strange spell. His gut still flared in panic, but as the spell's machinations swirled about him, he sensed that she did not share her husband's treason, she didn't hold a shred of Nafarin's power, and he relaxed as another pair of hands squeezed his shoulders.

"Relax," Anton said, close behind him. "You're safe."

"Margaret," Laird Bellard said from somewhere on his left, "what's happening?"

"Nothing—Oh, stay back, you oaf," she moaned. A loud smack sounded nearby.

"Don't you raise your hand to—"

"You're in my light," Margaret said, exasperation dripping from her voice.

Anton's hands released his shoulders from behind him, urged him to lay back down on what felt to be a sofa with large cushions to his left, and gently held either side of his head.

"Brew's ready," Claire Goodland called from another room.

"Alright, bring it here," Margaret answered.

As footsteps shuffled all around him, Margaret muttered something else about blocking her light, and what sounded to be a bubbling cauldron clanked to the ground near him.

"Draw ten CCs for me," Margaret said.

Waves of agony bounced from the walls of his skull, searing his nerves and making his head spin. He had to fight to keep bile from swelling in his throat.

As Anton firmed his grip to keep his head steady, he felt droplets land on his eyelids. A chilled wave of power spread immediately from his eyes to the back of his head and started to bounce around inside his skull, chasing the waves of pain away and soothing his burning nerves.

"Ten more," Margaret said. She placed rubber-gloved fingers on his eyelids and gently pulled.

More droplets soothed his eyes, and as Margaret pulled a little harder, the first rays of light burst into his eyes, making him screw them shut and wince.

"Try, dear," Margaret urged, "keep opening them a few moments at a time."

His eyes screamed at him, but he forced them open a crack at a time, and as Margaret Goodland's potion took hold, the pain subsided, and his vision, though still blurry, started to clear. The now dull echoes of the pain ringing through his skull still kept him sitting on the sofa, though, gingerly holding his head.

He looked around. He was in a cluster of sofas near the entrance to Castle Bellard's banquet hall. Tapestries and paintings of Bellard's ancestors hung on every wood-panelled wall, metal-disc chandeliers were lit with hundreds of candles, and above the enormous stone fireplace at the end of the hall, a painting of the Sky Mother covered the entire wall.

Over the lingering scent of burnt blood, he picked up hints of nettles, mint, dandelions, and the various other Earth scents that form the core of modern medicine. He looked around. The Khan lay senseless on a fold-out bed close to him with three flasks of glowing white potions in medical drips connected to his arm, and two battle-stained Cossacks stood guard as his son held his hand.

Agatha sat up on a sofa against a wall, looking none the worse for wear except for her hand bound in a linen bandage, which seemed odd given the severity of her burns, and to his immense relief, Kate Hart lay next to her, dressed in a hospital gown and sedated. He went to call Trish, to tell her the good news, but again, only the silence of his mind echoed where she had been.

He wondered where the wounded were, but caught the edge of a conversation one of Laird Bellard's officers was having on the phone, tracking the whereabouts of the Highland Fighting Men. They had been taken to infirmaries in Boston, Isfahan, Oxford, Moscow, Tokyo, even Shangri-La in Tibet. The whole world had joined in defending their Sky Mother.

Margaret Goodland filled his vision again, shining a light from the tip of her wand into his eyes, peering at him until his eyes burned. She nodded, stood, and moved over to Kate Hart.

Around him, Laird Bellard stood in his highland battle tartan, Grand Master Caohopa leaned against the sofa, still wearing the same suit as last night, and Anton sat next to him in his uniform with the Arch Mage's echelons rightly in their place at his lapels. Laird Bellard stepped forward.

"Lizzie's gone to see the whales with Phiona," he said, a strange, uncertain look in his eyes. "You still have her, lad, and you have us. You're staying with us for the summer, and I'm not accepting any arguments."

John's head spun.

"The—" He sputtered, coughed, and took a glass of water that Anton held for him. He drank, cleared his throat, and thanked him. "The world engine."

"We connected it to your ley mines," Grand Master Caohopa said. "Our Sky Mother breathes free."

John looked up. She smiled and nodded at him.

"Shangri-La, the Desert Springs, even the custodians of Damavand, everyone has stopped tapping their wells for now, but, ah—" She paused.

"What?" John asked, unsure as to why his heart still brimmed with panic.

"This world engine, John, it's more powerful than anything we've ever seen."

"It was, we think," Anton said, oblivious to the sharp look the Grand Master shot him for interrupting her, "the orifice that supported our Sky Mother as She filled every other engine in the world."

John turned to the Grand Master.

"The other Chiefs?" he asked.

"We all agree. As for division of power, we treat it the same as every other ley mine in the Americas, but, if you colonials agree, we all only draw from it in dire emergency."

John nodded. As CEO of the Trevelyan Mining Network, he spoke for the Colonial Government in matters of mana, and his word was binding upon his descendants, as his father's words were binding on him. The pact upon which centuries of coexistence had depended seemed more important now than ever.

"Were we all there?" he asked.

"Every tribe, and all colonies of your people. All of us." Grand Master Caohopa smiled.

John smiled back and dropped his head. He wished Trish was here, but before he could start to think how to grieve again, Agatha stood, coughed, and picked up a bulging trash sack that rattled as though filled with dozens of empty glass bottles.

"How are your eyes?" he asked.

"Fine," Agatha said as she walked over. "It wasn't your eyes that were the problem."

John furrowed his brows. "What? The light when Trish dove into the volcano, it—"

"That was the Sky Mother's power. It stung, but no. If I ever hear you're drinking scholin weed again, I'll tear your balls off. You almost killed yourself."

He looked around, confused, and the Grand Master placed a hand on his shoulder.

"We've all been there, lad," Laird Bellard said, kindly.

He wanted to shrink back into himself, embarrassed beyond reason that so many knew he'd been drinking as much scholin weed as he had.

"You did have two life forces to support, though," Agatha

said. "Not sure how you could have done it otherwise, so don't be too hard on yourself."

If anything, her trying to comfort him stung even more. He forced himself to smile, tried to stand, and immediately fell back onto the sofa.

He turned to Anton. "What happened to—?" He paused. He couldn't even bring himself to mention the bastard's name.

"He fled," Anton answered. "The Sky Mother had poured everything She had into Trish. She used her consciousness to slide in-between the Sky Mother and Nafarin, cut Him loose, and when His ward fell, and He saw the power arrayed against Him, He ran; to Venus, we think."

John shook his head, confused.

"The planet's temperature dropped three degrees in a day, and a new storm now rages where we believe He impacted the planet."

John nodded slowly, but he wasn't sure that his battered mind was following. He lay back down, looked around his gathered friends again, and closed his eyes. As he felt himself drift into sleep, the world around him dissolved.

He sat up, but he wasn't on a sofa anymore. He stood on grass as a gust of wind blew into him. His stomach lurched, but then he felt Trish's presence, and all fear drained from him.

"Trish?" he called.

"I'm here," she answered, and her voice sounded sweeter to his ears than milk and honey. He looked around, but he stood alone on top of a grassy hill.

"Am I awake?" he asked.

"No, my love. You're dreaming."

He shook his head, but as far as he could tell, this was real.

He looked around again, and below him, down the hill, he saw the hotel in the highlands of Scotland he and Trish had run off to as students. His heart almost tore apart as a well of joy burst inside of his chest.

"Where are you?" he called.

"Here," she answered from behind him.

He spun. She wore the same floral yellow dress she'd worn those days they'd spent here, decades ago. Her skin was smooth and young, her hair was tied into braids, and she'd woven daisies through it as she had done back then. He went to step forward, to grab her and squeeze her so tightly that she could never let go of him again, but she stepped back.

He followed, but with every step he took, she backed away again, and his heart shattered more and more.

"What's happening?" he asked, unable to keep the desperation from screeching through his voice.

Trish smiled, but the sight only set his heart racing harder.

"John, listen," Trish said, a sudden new joy in her eyes. "She says that She can't speak to you directly."

"What?"

"Our Sky Mother says Her voice would melt your mind to mush in moments. She wants to use my voice."

John's breath caught.

"What?"

"Eons ago," Trish said in her own voice, but with a strange accent that calmed him in seconds, "I brought people back at will, but, to my regret, I cannot reward your service with that." She shook her head, a look of apology in her eyes. "The organ that I used to bring souls back and forth is now"—she paused and seemed to ponder for a moment—"my womb."

"Sky Mother?" John asked. Trish, or rather their Sky Mother, nodded and closed Her eyes.

"John!" Trish shouted in her own voice. "Oh, John, you should see it! My father's here, *your* father's here, in Her womb, all of humanity we"—she nearly jumped in her excitement—"we are all together, John."

She calmed herself, and John could tell that the Star Mother was about to speak again.

"When your people are ready, like that of my servant Tamokameses, you will leave into the cosmos together. Until then, you live in my womb. For this reason, I cannot bring her back. Even bringing her out of my womb again for this conversation is drawing more power from me than Shangri-La takes in a decade. It cannot be done."

John's mind spun, and he had to fight to keep himself up on his feet. In all of humanity's history, he hadn't heard of a single occurrence of the Sky Mother speaking as directly as this. He wanted to record it, to study it, to tell the world. But most of all, he wanted Trish back.

As though reading the look in his eyes, she bowed her head.

"I'm sorry," she said again.

As Trish beamed into a smile, he sensed that their Sky Mother had gone. Trish stepped forward and took his hand.

"This..." she said. "After what She'd spent to bring me back to fight Nafarin, this is really hurting Her, John."

John didn't want to care, but he did. He wanted to stay here, forever, to sit, here on this hill, nowhere else. He wanted to spend the rest of his life with his wife, simply looking at her. But, every moment they shared now was agony to the Sky Mother. It wasn't that She didn't want to spend the power, he knew that now, but after all that had happened, She simply didn't have it. He thought about begging to join them, but what about Lizzie?

Trish sighed, and John found he'd leaned forward to kiss her before he realised it. She kissed him back, and the feel of her warmth shot up and down his body. He shuddered.

"It feels like a lifetime," she paused and smiled, "and for you, it will be, but I'll see you again before I know it."

He couldn't think of anything to say. He didn't want to cry, not here: he wanted Trish to see him happy, and despite the soul-shattering pain in his chest, he forced himself to smile back.

"I love you," he managed to croak.

Trish started to fade. "I love you too," she whispered back.

Ali Nouraei

Ali Nouraei is a Persian-British writer who blends history, philosophical debate, and cultural paradigms from East and West in his writing. He is a qualified Barrister, a practicing Mediator, and has written fiction for fifteen years. His passions include history, literature, and cake. He tweets as @AliNouraei.

FIND US ONLINE!

www.rebellionpublishing.com

/rebellionpub   /rebellionpublishing   /rebellionpub

SIGN UP TO OUR NEWSLETTER!

rebellionpublishing.com/sign-up

YOUR REVIEWS MATTER!

Enjoy this book? Got something to say?

Leave a review on Amazon, GoodReads or with your
favourite bookseller and let the world know!